THE LONGING

Celebrated British actress of stage and screen, Jane Asher is also well known for her many other activities, especially her non-fiction books and journalism and her successful cake making business. *The Longing* is her stunning debut novel, and was published in hardcover to widespread acclaim in 1996. She lives in London, with her husband and three children, and is working on her second novel.

Critical acclaim for *The Longing*:

'Topical, emotion-charged, [*The Longing*] grips from the first page and conveys with extraordinary vividness the terrible anguish experienced by couples who cannot start their longed-for baby.'   VAL HENNESSY, *Daily Mail*

'A writer who does convey real emotional power . . . *The Longing* is a story about infertility: the desperation that overtakes couples who can't conceive and the tragic consequences of that desperation. Like all really good novels, it is true – not in the factual sense, but in the way that its characters seem real and the world in which they move is one we recognise. Even better, its power increases as it goes on, drawing you further into its plot, gripping more tightly with every page . . . if Jane Asher were not already famous, this book would make her so.'   *Daily Express*

'Thought provoking, polished and professional, a modern tale of Gothic horror.'   *The Times*

'Strong dialogue drives the plot along and short, inter-cutting scenes add structure and drama.'   *TLS*

JANE ASHER

THE LONGING

HarperCollins*Publishers*

The characters and events in this book
are entirely fictional. No reference to any person,
living or dead, is intended or should be inferred.

HarperCollins*Publishers*
77–85 Fulham Palace Road,
Hammersmith, London W6 8JB
www.fireandwater.com

This paperback edition 1997
5 7 9 8 6 4 2

First published in Great Britain by
HarperCollins*Publishers* 1996

Copyright © Jane Asher 1996

The Author asserts the moral right to
be identified as the author of this work

ISBN 0 00 649050 6

Set in Spectrum

Printed and bound in Great Britain by
Omnia Books Ltd, Glasgow

ACKNOWLEDGEMENTS

My thanks to Rachel Hore, Liza Reeves, Lucy Ferguson, Jenny Parr and Nick Sayers of HarperCollins and to Carole Blake of Blake Friedmann for their help, support and encouragement.

I am also extremely grateful to PC Geoff Twigger of the Metropolitan Police, Professor Ian Craft, Dr Georg Hogewind and the staff of the London Gynaecology and Fertility Centre, Daniel Brown of the Department of Psychology of the Institute of Psychiatry and Dr Lewis Clein. Many thanks too to the patients who allowed me to witness their treatments and investigations and talked to me so openly.

ACKNOWLEDGEMENTS

To Gerald

Prologue

The effort was exhausting him; instead of getting excited he felt depressed and hopeless. He sighed and stretched his arms out in front of him until his linked fingers cracked at the knuckles, then looked down again at the magazine on his lap, turning the page to be confronted by yet another tight, artificially tanned bottom thrusting uninvitingly up at him, breasts lolling in the background. Instead of making him stiffer, it merely made him despair.

Throwing the magazine back on to the table he stood up, moved over to the line of videos in the small bookcase and scanned the covers in search of inspiration, humming an unidentifiable tune as he turned his head first one way and then another to read the titles. 'Might be worth a try,' he muttered to himself as he pulled one out, then slotted it into the open-mouthed recorder and sat back to watch. After a few moments of fascination at the proportions of the girls gambolling on the beach, he realised he had completely forgotten the purpose of it all and had let his mind wander off into thinking how small the little lines must be to fit in six hundred and twenty-five on the screen. 'Oh, this is ridiculous,' he said out loud, and blew out his lips in exasperation as he got up and switched off the recorder.

Another tack. He sat on the plastic seat of the nearest chair, leant back against the wall, closed his eyes and thought of Julie, picturing her undressing in the slowly casual way she did when she knew he was watching her. He felt a comforting little twitch of response and persevered. Julie arching her back as she undid her bra, leaning forward to pull down her tights, smiling at him from under her hair as if shy of him after ten years of marriage.

Disappointingly, she was suddenly dressed again and putting the Sunday joint in the oven. He managed to force her clothes off again with a huge effort of will but as soon as she was naked they irritatingly snapped back on again.

He opened his eyes, resisted a strong temptation to look at his watch, and picked up another magazine.

Chapter One

At last Harry was sleeping. After a night of walking the baby up and down, rubbing his back as he struggled against her left shoulder in the seemingly unending battle against colic, Anna had spent much of the morning trying to settle him in his cot. Finally she had given up and decided to go out, hoping that a long journey in the old-fashioned pram would work its usual magic and lull him to sleep. He had still been wide awake and grizzling as she reached the row of shops where she usually stopped, so she had kept going for half a mile or so towards another supermarket where she hadn't shopped since before his birth three months earlier. He had drifted off only moments before she turned the corner into Streatham High Road, his eyelids closing in spite of himself, his natural curiosity at the extraordinary business of being alive stifled by the irresistible drowsiness produced by the comforting jolting of the pram wheels over the pavement.

She pushed open the heavy glass door of the shop with one hand and manoeuvred the pram inside by pushing it with her body as she gripped the handle and her bag with the other, then stopped in annoyance. It was immediately clear that there would be no chance of the large second-hand pram fitting comfortably back through the checkouts on her way out, and even the narrow aisles, though they were empty of customers, were littered with dump bins carrying special offers, and looked dauntingly difficult to negotiate. Letting the glass door swing shut behind her, she instinctively reached down to pick up the baby, then hesitated as she looked at Harry's peacefully dreaming face, his brow smooth and untroubled, his eyes gently moving under their pink translucent lids.

'Oh God, I can't wake you up again, I just can't,' she muttered under her breath. She sighed, then parked the pram just inside the entrance where she could keep half an eye on it, pushing her foot down to lock the brake in place. She bent down and kissed Harry very lightly on a flushed, rounded cheek, then pressed her mouth to his unconscious ear and whispered gently, 'It's only a few things. You're out for hours by the look of you. Won't be a moment.'

She picked up her bag, collected a trolley and, making her way into the heart of the store, pushed it quickly but without enthusiasm down the aisle, bored by the very idea of the shopping she had to do, and wearied at the tiresome business of having to keep count of every price as she chose the things she needed. The cardboard boxes balanced on the shelves on either side towered over her in depressing brown walls as she collected tins of baby food and baked beans, and she looked away from them and down into the cabinets, where packets of frozen vegetables were piled in their plastic bags, each covered with a thin white film of frost.

She chucked two solid, icy packets of peas on top of the tins then stopped and pulled a small piece of paper from her pocket. 'Now, what was it I knew I'd forget?' she muttered as she stood in the middle of the aisle, studying the neatly written list, but with her other hand still firmly holding on to her small fake leather knapsack which she had rested on the handle of the trolley.

She instinctively gripped it even more tightly as a grey-haired woman wearing a padded coat like an eider-down came round a corner and pushed past her, tutting a little as she did so. Anna looked up at the large pear-shaped figure as she waddled away towards the gravy powders, and threw a disinterested 'What's your prob-lem, then?' after her.

The woman stopped and turned to look back at Anna, whose small figure with spiky jet-black dyed hair, huge earrings and spindly calves, exaggerated by tight, black leggings and loose white shirt hanging down below a thick black jumper, was dwarfed by the mountains of goods on either side. 'It's people like you that's the problem, love,' she answered. 'Learn some manners.'

Anna looked down at her list again, murmuring quietly, 'Oh go fuck yourself.' But she felt suddenly uneasy and glanced up towards the doorway. Her view was blocked for a moment by a blonde customer in a blue blazer coming through the door, but as the woman moved towards the stacked row of trolleys Anna was reassured by the sight of the pram still sitting where she had left it. She stuffed the list in her pocket and headed for the nappies.

Juliet turned back from the trolleys and moved quickly over to the pram. As she looked down she suddenly knew for certain what she had suspected when she had seen it through the large plate-glass window. The baby looked so sweet lying there in his blue baby-gro, so securely tucked in and peaceful that it seemed a shame to move him, but she knew she must. As she bent over the pram she breathed in his warm, milky, almost edible smell and felt her womb contract in sympathy. She pulled back the blue cotton blanket, gently slipped her hands under his armpits and lifted him up confidently on to her left shoulder, letting his head fall softly against the wool of her jacket as she held him with one hand and picked up the blanket with the other. He lifted his head slightly, making it wobble on its red, pleated neck, gave a little whimper and screwed up his eyes, then made a small sucking movement with wet lips before giving a tiny sigh and settling back into a deep sleep.

Juliet smiled to herself as she rubbed the side of her face against the fuzzy head, then pushed open the glass door and made her way quickly out of the shop. She tucked the cover round the baby with her free hand as she moved away from the supermarket and crossed the road, walking purposefully up the street and away from the shops: a tall, striking woman dressed in expensive-looking but creased blazer and trousers, her streaked blonde hair unkempt and wearing no make-up; the very picture of a harassed middle-class mother carrying her young baby.

Nappies were the last thing on Anna's list, so after picking up a large economy bag of the three-month size, she began to make her way back towards the checkout, but stopped as her eye was caught by a display of chocolate sauces. She stood for a moment or two, adding up once more in her head the prices of the goods already in her trolley and considering half-heartedly whether a squeeze or two of chocolate would cheer up the quarter slab of vanilla ice cream she thought might be left over in the small iced-up freezer compartment of her fridge. In an effort to remember she tried to picture the open fridge but, instead of ice cream, saw the bowl of half-eaten baby cereal she had put there that morning, and started guiltily as it reminded her of Harry. As she turned to move on she glanced over again at the pram by the door and, as she did so, felt a spasm of shock roll up her body in a wave that broke at her throat in a little gasp of fear. She tried to identify what had caused it, and as she stood for a split second still staring at the pram, immobilised by anxiety, suddenly knew. It had moved. Only the smallest amount, but to Anna's eye the change in angle was unmistakable. Unsure why this filled her with such foreboding, and praying that it had simply been knocked a little by a passing shopper, she left the trolley and raced down the aisle, her brain at first refusing to make sense of what her subconscious saw more clearly every second.

The baby's face had changed colour.

It was flatter, creased — frightening.

By the time she recognised the empty bottom of the pram for what it was, she was screaming.

Michael Evans' progression up the insurance firm where he had worked since leaving university had been fast and impressive, and the acquisition of a beautiful, clever wife at the age of thirty-four — a wife (as Michael hated himself for admitting he was a little impressed by) a notch or so above him in the social scale — had fitted neatly into a relatively smooth, happy and uneventful life. His Englishness, his emotional restraint — at that time enough to make some doubt that feelings of any real strength lurked under the dignified, correct exterior — attracted Juliet by its appearance of calmness and solidity. A man of few words, her mother had called him, not altogether disparagingly, and Juliet had loved that in him. His habit of thinking long and hard before replying to even the simplest question, bowing his head and placing his hands together against his lips like a praying saint in a mediaeval triptych, had amused her, and the reply that would eventually emerge was invariably coloured by a kindness and consideration for the questioner that contrasted comfortingly with Juliet's less serene and more dissatisfied outlook on life. At their first meeting at a party in Kensington they had quickly homed in on each other, her elegant beauty and apparent confidence thrown up in shimmering relief against the background of city suits, sensible ties and brightly coloured frilled cocktail dresses that could have gone straight on to enjoy a few dances at Annabel's before being gently but purposefully unzipped to allow a good grope in the taxi on the way home. Juliet's naturally blonde hair, bobbed into a swinging, shining pelmet, her white silk suit and expensive but understated jewellery spoke of subtler and ultimately more satisfying delights. She looked stunning but — at least in the immediate future — unzippable. Michael was entranced, and she in her turn was drawn to the oasis of peace and wry amusement that he had hollowed out for himself among the loud, over-confident voices around him. They found themselves spending the whole evening together. Several more had quickly followed, including a few outings to the cinema and to small Chelsea restaurants, until there had come a night when, after a visit to the London Coliseum to indulge Michael's taste for the less demanding operas, hesitant, respectful sex had followed in his small flat in Fulham. It soon seemed easier, and somehow the right thing to do, that Juliet should move in. Marriage followed within the year, and their lives settled into a predictable, comfortable routine.

Michael was a clever, honest and hard-working businessman, and Juliet's job in an upmarket firm of estate agents was well suited to her good taste and persuasive manner. She was a popular and successful member of the team, but as she and Michael had known from shortly after their first serious conversation that they both wanted children, she only gave it a limited proportion of her attention and effort. She was quite prepared for a time when she would have to set her career aside — at least until the little Evanses were happily ensconced in the obligatory boarding schools — to concentrate on the important tasks of running a good home, nurturing an admirable, high-earning, respectable husband and bringing up a brood of future useful Englishmen — or women.

When they first moved into the neat terraced house in Battersea a few months after their wedding they both mentally set aside a small light room on the top floor as a future nursery, assuming its occupant would arrive within a few years as easily and comfortably as everything else had so far done in their short, enjoyable courtship and marriage. As time went by and no hint appeared of impending offspring, a tiny little feathery sensation of fear began to flutter occasionally deep within Juliet. After some nine years of conventionally happy, sexually active if unexciting marriage, the flutter had become the beat of heavy wings — and Juliet began to admit to herself that something unspeakable was hovering on the edges of her well-planned, smoothly run adult life, threatening to throw it off balance with the strong gusts of unease it created.

Although she herself was becoming increasingly aware of this shadow lurking at the edges of her everyday life, it was the reactions of those around her that made it difficult to carry on as if no problem existed.

Her mother, in particular, made her feel horribly awkward about the lack of babies and, never the most tactful of women, was extraordinarily accurate in pinpointing the most humiliating moments to drop heavy hints about this shortcoming in her daughter's achievements. Juliet had once made the fatal mistake of quietly admitting to her that she and Michael were disappointed not to have so far produced any children, and she had regretted it ever since, sensing that — behind the show of sympathy and understanding — it had given her mother another little weapon to use against her.

'Well, after all it's not as if I had any grandchildren to leave it to when it comes to mine,' Mrs Palmer volunteered in the middle of a discussion about wills at one of her dinner parties. As the average age of her guests, apart from Michael and Juliet, was as usual somewhere in the seventies, this jolly subject was fairly typical of those raised around the Palmer table.

'Everyone should make one, of course,' added Michael, carefully ignoring the reference to his lack of contribution to the family dynasty. 'It's surprising how many people don't bother, and then leave their spouses with the most complicated situa —'

'Yes, but I don't have a spouse, you see. My daughter is all I've got,' ploughed on Mrs Palmer, turning to smile sweetly at Juliet as she underlined her point with the subtlety for which she was famous, 'all I've got. Apart from you, Michael dear, of course. It's not as if there were any young ones to benefit from my savings. I'd always thought there might be schooling and so on to help with, of course. Even my dear dog isn't with me any more.'

Michael and Juliet had adopted the Palmers' black labrador three years previously. Mr Palmer's death had meant a move for his widow from the large house in Hertfordshire to a London service flat, and to keep the family pet would have been impossible. Juliet, hating the idea of giving her away, had begged Michael to let the dog live with them, and in spite of it necessitating complicated arrangements for having her collected by a friend each day while they were at work, he had agreed. But Mrs Palmer saw the transferring of Lucy as entirely to their benefit, and had never once expressed any thanks for their having taken over the responsibility. At the time, Michael and Juliet had put it down to the recent bereavement, but as the years went by and Mrs Palmer still complained self-pityingly about the old dog's absence, Juliet found it increasingly irritating.

Her relationship with her mother was an extraordinary mixture of closeness and utter separateness, and it sometimes appeared to her that Mrs Palmer deliberately chose to hurt her in order to re-establish some kind of power over her. Juliet became adept at brushing aside the references to missing grandchildren, not only because she found them disturbing, but also because treating them with any seriousness made the awful possibility of a genuine problem more real.

But the afternoon she caught Michael looking longingly out of the window at some small boys playing football outside the flats that backed on to their house, she knew something must be done. She walked up quietly to stand just behind him, and followed his gaze towards the laughing children.

'What is it?' she asked, not needing an answer, but half hoping they could bring the unspoken problem out into the open.

He jumped guiltily when he became aware of Juliet behind him. 'I was just wondering if I needed an overcoat. It's clouded over again.'

'Oh Michael, for heaven's sake.'

'What?'

'You know.'

If Michael was worried enough to protect her from his consciousness of there being something wrong, then Juliet knew it was time she herself turned and confronted it. Later that evening she studied again the magazine articles and chemist's leaflets that she had hoarded in her bedside drawer.

'I've bought an ovulation thermometer,' she announced as she came in from work the next day.

'What?'

'It'll give me an idea when I'm ovulating, and we can make an extra effort, if you see what I mean.'

'I see exactly what you mean. It sounds delightful. I suggest you take your temperature this minute,' said

Michael, as he threw his jacket on to the sofa and began to undo his shirt buttons.

'Michael, what are you doing?' laughed Juliet. 'Don't be so silly. It isn't instant like that, as I'm sure you know perfectly well. No, stop it – I want to read the instructions,' she said as she wriggled out of his grasp and sat down, moving his coat on to the arm of the sofa. 'Now look – it's in a sort of huge scale – see? So I can —'

'Come here, my dear,' Michael interrupted, as he sat down beside her and slipped a hand inside her blouse, 'and I shall personally undertake a particularly thorough examination. I'm sure we can sort out your internal problems in a jiffy.'

'Darling, shut up. Listen. My temperature will go up immediately after ovulating and – hang on.' She read on to herself for a moment or two, frowning a little. 'Well, that's a fat lot of good, isn't it? We've got to make love like mad just before and during ovulation, and my temperature's going to go up just afterwards. What good is the thermometer if it's going to tell me when we've just *missed* it for God's sake?'

'I can see a perfectly simple answer. We make love more or less permanently until your temperature goes up, take a few days off to get up our strength, then start again. Don't you think?'

Juliet smiled but went on reading. 'I've got to fill in the chart and put in little crosses when it goes up. Yeah, yeah, I see the point. I'll get to know my cycle and all that. And I suppose at least I'll know that I *am* ovulating.'

She turned to look at Michael. 'I do love you, you know. Even if you haven't got me up the spout yet. Come to think of it, who's to say it's me? Perhaps your sperm are a bit wimpish?'

'Nonsense! They're absolutely first class. Now come here and I'll prove it to you.'

But after a few months of temperature taking, crosses on graphs and carefully timed sessions in the creaking double bed, Juliet appeared no nearer to producing the longed-for heir. Michael knew she minded more than she was letting on, and noticed an irritation creeping into her attitude towards him. For his part, the necessity of performing to order was becoming increasingly difficult and depressing: it became hard to remember a time when they'd had sex for the sheer pleasure of it rather than to meet the demands of a schedule.

'You're on,' Juliet said to him one night as she brushed her hair at the dressing table. After six months of attempts at timed conception, this succinct, if uninspiring, phrase had become part of their regular routine.

'Again? Are you sure?'

'Why, don't you want to?'

'Yes, yes of course I do. Do you?'

'Well, we don't have any choice, do we? I'm not going to waste another whole month.'

Michael resisted snapping back at her, and only sighed quietly to himself as he pulled back the sheets and climbed into bed, trying to marshal his thoughts into suitably erotic directions, but feeling more like a sperm bank than a lover.

The evening of the day she went to see her GP was the first time she cried. He had been so matter-of-fact, so sensible, and so horribly in agreement that 'Something should have happened by now.' She had half expected him to laugh it off, to jolly her out of it and tell her to go home and not be so silly (a healthily pragmatic approach he had taken to many of her minor ailments since she and Michael had become his patients on their move to Battersea), but he had listened quietly and seriously as she told him of her fears, and she had seen in his eyes that there was to be no quick answer.

'I'd like you both to go and see a Professor Hewlett,' he said as she came out from behind the curtains after the examination and moved to sit in front of his desk. He made notes as he went on. 'There's no immediately obvious problem, but I don't see much point in making you wait before taking this further. Standard advice after a first infertility enquiry is to go and try again for a year or so, as you may know, but having known you both for a few years now I'm sure you've been making love the right way up, so to speak, and certainly from what you tell me you've been trying often enough and at the right times for it to be surprising that nothing's happened yet. Your cycle's a bit longer than average, but it seems regular enough, and the chart seems to show quite clearly that you're ovulating regularly. Go and see

Bob Hewlett and we'll take it from there. There are plenty of good chaps in this field now, but he's seen a lot of my patients lately and won't take you round the houses. I'll get Jennifer to make an appointment and give you a ring.'

His mention of her periods took Juliet back to the time when they had disappeared, to memories of her anxious mother dragging her to the doctor at sixteen, painfully thin yet still refusing to eat normally.

'You do know I was anorexic years ago?'

'Yes, yes of course. You told me, and I have it here in the notes that Dr Chaplin sent on. That shouldn't have any bearing on this at all. Your weight has been perfectly stable in the – um —' he paused and looked down at the beige folder on his desk, flipping back several pages, ' —ten years you've been coming to see me. Your menstruation was re-established a long time ago wasn't it?' Juliet nodded. 'Don't worry,' he smiled up at her encouragingly, 'there's a long way to go yet before you need assume we have anything we can't cope with.'

She was calm all the way home, telling herself over and over again that the doctor had found nothing wrong; that she was to go and see a specialist and that there was every reason to feel positive. But when she had to face Michael, the dark creature that had so far only made itself known by occasional forays into her conscious mind seemed to grow and rise up and fly at her from the front. It was the way he looked up at her anxiously as she walked into the sitting room that made her give way.

'How did you get on? What did he say?'

'Oh Michael — there's something wrong with me. I knew it — I knew it. There's something horribly wrong.'

She threw her coat on to the sofa and sat in the armchair, leaning forward on to her knees and rubbing at her temples in an effort not to cry. Lucy padded over to her and sat down beside the sofa and licked her hand, sensing unhappiness.

'Why, what did he say? Juliet — tell me, please. What's wrong with you? Can they do anything about it?'

'He didn't find anything really wrong. It's just that —'

'Well then, that's OK isn't it? And who's to say it's you? It could be my sperm, you know. What did he say?'

'Oh do stop asking me that! I just know something's wrong, that's all. I told you there was. I'm never going to have children, Michael, I can feel it. Oh God, what am I going to do?'

She burst into heaving, sobbing tears, and the whole world seemed to be focused on her empty, useless womb.

It was hard for the policeman to understand what Anna was saying through her hysterical tears. When his radio had first alerted him two streets away he had assumed that yet another car had been broken into, or a purse snatched: the theft of a baby was quite outside his experience and the painful distress of the babbling, wild-eyed girl in front of him was deeply unsettling.

'Come and sit down for a moment, love,' he said as

he tried to shepherd her gently away from the doors of the supermarket. 'Then you can tell me calmly exactly what happened and we'll sort things out. Don't worry, love – we'll get your little one back, he can't be far.'

But Anna couldn't move. She was clinging desperately to the pram with one hand, and with the other she rubbed her cheek with repetitive movements that seemed to be trying to tear the skin from her thin, white face. The swollen eyes and blotchy, roughened complexion gave her the look of a wizened old lady and there was a bitterness set into the downward lines around her mouth that PC Anderson guessed had been etched there long before today's drama. She had clearly had to face obstacles before, but now she looked as though she might be torn apart by the intense suffering suddenly thrust upon her from nowhere. The dense black make-up around her eyes was smudged and running, giving her the look of a frightened panda.

'I've g-got to go and – and – and find him!' she stuttered in a strong Glaswegian accent, easily discernible in spite of her gulping sobs. 'My baby! My baby!'

As she let go of the pram and made a sudden, darting move towards the door, PC Anderson grabbed her by the shoulder and turned her back to face him. Her eyes were wide open and terrified and sweat was breaking out on her face and neck; he could see that she was in danger of collapsing if he didn't manage to get her to sit down quickly. He kept his hand on her shoulder and with the other behind her back, ushered her firmly through the checkout.

A gaggle of assistants was hovering around the tills, their excited faces alternating between interest and sympathy, revelling in spite of themselves in the drama of the situation and in the excuse for a break in routine.

'Stand back, ladies, please. Thank you. Now, love, where's your manager? I need a quiet room to go and have a chat with this young lady. And I don't want any of you to leave without telling me, all right? I may need to have a talk to you. One of you bring that pram with us, please.' He turned as he became aware of a large, flustered woman advancing towards them, wiping back a flopping piece of startlingly red hair from her forehead.

'Come with me, please, constable. I'm Mrs Paulton, the under-manageress. There's a room at the back where you can be on your own. I'll bring you both a cup of tea. Poor thing!'

Both Anna, still juddering and hysterical, and PC Anderson followed the comforting shape of Mrs Paulton towards the back of the shop. As Anna passed packets of cornflakes, rice and washing powder she could feel a part of her brain vaguely wondering how they could still exist in this new universe in which she now found herself. Did people still eat? Did they still wear clothes, and get them dirty? It didn't seem possible. If Harry wasn't with her then surely the world as she knew it had stopped, turned upside down and shown its murky underbelly.

As Mrs Paulton sat Anna gently down in the back room, the policeman waited outside in the corridor and radioed a quick message to his communications centre, aware that the simple words 'alleged child abduction' would ensure immediate action.

'Right now, love, what's your name?' he asked as he came into the room and squatted down beside Anna.

'Anna Watkins.'

'And tell me exactly what happened.'

'I only left him for a second. I just needed to get a few things and he — oh God, I'm sorry, I'm so sorry, I didn't mean to leave him, I love him so much. Oh Jesus, what am I going to do?'

'Come on now, love, there's no need to get so upset. The sooner you can tell me what happened the sooner we can get him back.'

'They'll take him away from me won't they?'

'No, no love, come on now, no one's blaming you for anything. Just try and tell me everything you can. What was your little one wearing? What's his name? Did you see anyone near the pram?'

The baby was starting to cry. As Juliet continued to walk quickly along Streatham High Road he began to twist and squirm in her arms, turning his face round and up towards her, his mouth sucking and puckering, his eyes open and filling with angry, hungry tears.

'All right, darling,' she muttered into his pink coil of an ear, 'it's all right, Mummy's here. We'll soon get you home.'

But even if it had been true, it wasn't home Harry was after, but food.

Chapter Two

'Please, *please* stop crying. Mummy's going to get us home very soon and then we'll wait for Anthony to come. Won't he be pleased to see you're safely back again? Mummy lost you for a bit didn't she, and Anthony was very angry. Everything's going to be fine now, sweetheart, and we'll all be happy again. Please try to stop crying, darling, please try. Sshhh now, quiet now, come on, stop it now, sweetheart. Stop the noise. Mummy's here.'

Juliet had reached her parked Volvo with an increasingly complaining baby and having placed him in a large shopping basket on the back seat was driving quickly out of Streatham in the opposite direction to the supermarket. His persistent wailing was disturbing her in a way that was more unsettling than anything she had felt for a long time and she couldn't understand why the stomach-wrenching sensation it produced in her was so familiar. She had been through this before, but in an altered form, in a world the mirror image of this one, darker and more closed in. Where was she when she had felt this, many, many years ago? As she drove on, carefully following her planned route, she remembered: it wasn't a child's crying that this terrible sound was dragging up from her past — it was her own. She could hear again the sound of her wailing as she had heard it echoing round her head while they had held her arms and legs in the hospital to stop her running. The more she had wriggled and screamed, the tighter they had gripped her emaciated body, bringing the spoon with its unacceptable contents time and time again to her mouth, pressing it against her lips until she could taste it, or tipping its load into her open, sobbing jaws until she gagged, choked and swallowed in spite of herself.

She turned around to look at the baby on the back seat, but could see only the brown wicker ordinariness of the basket, showing no sign of its extraordinary contents. It was comforting, and she shook her head a little to rid herself of the unwelcome memories that had broken through, unbidden, into the present. She would leave these thoughts till later, until she had reached safety for herself and the baby. Then she would have time to unpack her brain and slowly pick over the contents until she could face them properly and exorcise them; for the time being she would let them hover harmlessly in the pending section of her mind.

Anna had lapsed into a defeated, miserable calm, and was doing her best to give the policeman the information he needed. She was a girl of innate intelligence and a natural toughness which had stood her in good stead through a life that had not been easy. Had she been dealt better cards originally, she would have played them well and avoided the traps set for her by others who appeared to hold all the aces. She had been born into an area of Glasgow that had rid itself of the slums of the fifties and sixties, only to find itself inhabited by an even greater threat. A new, insidious culture was breeding and spreading in the perfect medium of unemployment and poverty, filling the dish that was this small pocket of crowded, inner city life with spores that were ready to break loose and find new areas to infect and ultimately destroy. The figures huddled in corners of Hyatt's estate no longer discussed the buying and selling of watches or gold jewellery, but of cocaine, crack and heroin. The drug scene had become a way of life: the added threat of HIV had brought a new edge of despair and hopelessness to its victims and even those on the fringes of this miserable, pervasive trade — such as Anna and her family — were touched by its contaminating effects.

She sometimes wondered if her early memories of her father, Ian, were imaginary. She was uncertain whether she had invented the times when the house felt happy; when he didn't shout at her mother, when she and her younger brother, Peter, were given hugs from him at bedtime and treats at weekends. Years of watching perfect families in her favourite television series — when she had wanted to be like them so much that she had sat in front of the set, screwed her eyes tightly closed and prayed and prayed to be taken into the screen and into their lives – had confused her.

But her memories were right. It was only after years of being unemployed since the closure of the tobacco factory where he had worked for over two decades that the morose, defeatist side to Ian Watkins' nature was released, producing a bitterness that resulted in a lack of kindness and affection to his wife and two children that amounted to cruelty. The bitterness had infected his children: Anna made no real friends at school, and alienated her teachers with the harsh cynicism she expressed with sharp intelligence.

She had always known she would get out of the family home at the earliest opportunity, and the continued daily diet of television for her and Peter had helped to instil in her the illusion that if she could only get herself 'down South' she would be able to make something of her life, and even return in glory after a few years, bringing back fame and fortune as in the fairy tales she had read to herself as a young girl.

At the age of fourteen she began to plan her escape. She took on an early morning paper round and started to save the small amount of money that it brought in, and in spite of her father's insistence that it was to be given to her mother to help with the bills, she managed to lie sufficiently well about exactly how much she was making to be able to put tiny amounts aside in a tin on top of the old-fashioned wardrobe in the bedroom she shared with her brother.

At sixteen she packed her few belongings into a carrier

bag in the middle of the night, emptied the tin into her purse and left, making her way down to London by hitching lifts and buying just enough food to survive. Her family made rather half-hearted attempts to find her, but deep down her mother recognised in herself an envy at Anna's freedom, and knew that even if they did succeed in tracking her down, they had nothing to offer which could persuade her to return. Only Peter was truly sad at losing her, and cried himself to sleep for many nights in their room. For months he waited for some news of her – a letter or call – but gradually began to face the fact that she was gone from his life for ever.

It didn't take long for Anna to discover the reality of trying to survive in a large city where jobs are impossible to find unless you have a permanent address, and where a permanent address is impossible to find unless you have the job to pay for it. Having no family or friends to turn to, she found that the helping hands she was offered tended to come with invisible and insidious strings attached. Not that she was sexually inexperienced, having had several rushed and unfulfilling encounters after originally losing her virginity at fifteen in the back of a van, but she was streetwise enough to be suspicious of every stranger she met.

She inevitably found herself clinging to the first person who spoke to her with what appeared to be genuine warmth and kindness, knowing that his motives might not be entirely altruistic, but unable to resist basking in the gentleness of his tone and the comfort of his arms around her at night. This was Dave, an eighteen-year-old from Brighton. Having made his way, like Anna, to the streets of London, he had found them paved not with gold but with crumbling, unwelcoming concrete. They met in Piccadilly Circus, where many of the homeless gathered to watch the world go by or to intoxicate themselves into a senseless, or at least differently sensed, stupor in which they could then see it through the comforting haze of drugs or alcohol. Anna, having run away from Glasgow partly to escape the effects of the drug culture, found herself straight back in it, and it soon became clear that Dave himself survived by pushing relatively small amounts of crack and ecstasy around Wardour Street and Soho Square. She added to their meagre finances by begging, something she could only allow herself to do by telling herself, in a piece of tortuous logic, that at least she was going out and finding the money herself, and that it was better than living off the state.

When every penny is a struggle to find, even the smallest expenses become difficult. Anna soon convinced herself that as Dave was sleeping only with her, and as she believed his tales of relative monogamy prior to their relationship, condoms were a luxury that could be dispensed with. She had a vague idea that they were being handed out free somewhere locally, but never got it together to find out where or to bother to do anything more constructive about protecting herself. As a girl who had grown up knowing several friends who'd either had full-blown Aids or were HIV positive, she knew

28

she was taking a calculated risk, but strangely enough the more obvious, and more likely, outcome of a pregnancy never seriously occurred to her.

She put off confronting her condition for months. Somehow in the mess of her life, the lack of periods and the sickness assumed an insignificance they would never have had if other more pressing physical problems hadn't had to be faced. Anna's priorities were finding her next meal and a place to sleep without compromising herself with what she saw as the 'system', and the momentous change taking place in her own body almost appeared to be part of someone else's life, belonging to a future that seemed unreal. Perhaps she also knew, without admitting it to herself, exactly what Dave's reaction to prospective fatherhood would be, and hoped that by ignoring her condition, she could make it disappear. But of course it didn't. Anna's impoverished and undernourished body nurtured the tiny uninvited guest in spite of her, and the embryo that was Harry grew and grew until, demanding more space, it began to make her belly swell.

She was right about Dave. Struggling unsuccessfully to take responsibility for his own life, there was no way he could countenance taking on another one, and as soon as Anna had reluctantly confirmed what he had been beginning to suspect, he was off. Anna wasn't surprised to find herself abandoned – she felt herself destined to be so, and it only seemed to fit into a pattern which had been laid out for her from the start. Perhaps it added another little brick of bitterness to the defensive wall with which she encircled herself, but she almost enjoyed the sheer predictability of it, and if she had believed in God would certainly have been tempted to congratulate Him on the thoroughness of His planning when it came to a life of unhappiness and hopelessness.

Her small effort at coming down to London in order to better herself had landed her in even greater trouble than before; now she saw no possibility of the imagined successful job or marriage, and resigned herself to a future of poverty and dependence. Since her arrival she had thought very little of home, managing to keep her mind carefully turned away from worries about Peter or her mother, frightened that to start on that road would lead her only too quickly towards a horizon of unbearable loneliness. But now the pull of the past was almost irresistible. She admitted to herself for the first time how much she missed not only the two of them, but also, to her own surprise, her father.

She considered an abortion, of course, but having let matters drift for such a long time she knew it was very late for that and, with the loss of Dave, she was already beginning to think of this mysterious lump inside her as her one ally against the world. She was also realistic enough to know that the existence of a baby would secure her some sort of housing, and for once she allowed herself to join the system and accept help. By the time she made the fatal shopping trip when her whole world was to be turned upside down, Lambeth Council had settled her in a high-rise flat in Streatham, where she managed efficiently, if uncomfortably, on benefits. And where she lived for one reason only – to love and protect the little boy who had come to mean everything to her.

The awe-inspiring medical charisma of the Harley Street and Wimpole Street names has been lent so generously to the lesser-known streets that cross them that over the years the houses using the addresses of their more illustrious neighbours have stretched further and further around the corners in a proliferation of 'A's and 'AA's until they almost meet halfway between the two streets, leaving only a handful of correctly named houses between them. The address of Professor Hewlett's clinic was officially given as 'Harley Street', and so it took Juliet and Michael several minutes to find the pillared white house round the corner in Weymouth Street, separated by at least four houses from the junction. They were surprised by its ordinariness, perhaps expecting the building to show some outward sign of the extraordinary events that took place behind its unrevealing walls.

It would have been hard to imagine a less clinical setting. The hall was carpeted and lit by chandeliers, but the air of luxury was mitigated by a large, practical reception desk placed across the entranceway, almost hiding the two computer screens and the smiling girl positioned behind its high wooden façade. 'May I help you?' she enquired, with scarcely a hint of the adult-talking-down-to-child tone that Juliet tended to expect from anyone in the medical world when addressing a patient.

'I'm Michael Evans, and this is my wife. We've come to see Professor Hewlett.'

Juliet looked up quickly, half anticipating a look of pity and superiority on the girl's face, but catching only a smile of genuine warmth and apparent understanding. She felt Michael's arm move to rest on her back, as if he sensed her wariness.

As they were ushered into the waiting room and towards a large, comfortable sofa, Michael was puzzled by his sense of being in a fast food restaurant. Why did he feel he should be ordering breakfast? He looked up at what he had been aware of on the edge of his vision: a series of framed photographs of the medical team and staff was hanging on the wall, each subject wearing a cheerful, positive smile and bearing a name, qualifications and a job description. They looked so extraordinarily ready to burst into efficient enquiries as to what Michael would like to order ('Eggs, sir? Will that be fertile or infertile, sir?' 'Just twins to go, please,'), that he had to shake his head to remind himself where he was.

In the armchair opposite sat a balding man of forty-five or so. He was leaning forward, resting his arms on his knees and holding one hand to his forehead, not moving or glancing up as the newcomers sat down. Michael reached for Juliet's hand and gave it a little pat. He wanted to say something reassuring but felt the sound of his voice would intrude on the quiet, slightly melancholy atmosphere, and contented himself with a small clearing of the throat.

'Don't,' whispered Juliet.

'What?' he whispered back, half aware of the man in the chair, who still hadn't stirred. 'Don't what? Cough?'

'Sorry, it doesn't matter.'

They sat on in silence for a few minutes. A nurse walked in and over to the man in the armchair. She bent down and murmured something by his lowered head. Michael heard a muttered 'Oh Christ,' then, 'Yes, yes all right. In a moment.' After a few more words in the man's ear, the nurse straightened up again and walked towards the door, turning to give him a sympathetic smile as she left. He raised his head and looked after her, then with a sigh rose slowly to his feet and stretched his arms behind him before giving them a little shake. He slowly walked out, still never glancing in the direction of the sofa.

'Poor chap.' Michael lifted his hand off Juliet's and, in order to have an excuse to do so, dusted some imaginary specks off the shoulder of his jacket.

'Why?'

'Oh, I don't know. He just looked a bit bloody miserable that's all.'

'What do you mean?'

'Well, I don't know, he just looked a bit miserable. You know.'

'How could you possibly know that? How could you possibly know that a man you've never seen before in your life and have only seen now for about two and a half minutes is "bloody miserable" as you put it? God, you're so irritating sometimes!'

'Julie, I understand how you're feeling, but there really isn't any need to be quite so unpleasant. I was only passing a conversational thought. It wasn't meant to be in any way serious and I—'

'Oh all right, all right.'

She dropped her head and Michael could feel the welling of despair in the slight figure next to him. He felt the familiar stab of the intense pity and love that overcame him every time he was reminded of just how deeply she was wounded by her childlessness, and of how much pain it caused her at the slightest provocation.

He put both arms round her and let her head fall on to his chest, laying his cheek on her beautifully dressed hair and smelling the familiar mix of perfume and faint shampoo. 'It's all right, darling. It's all right. We're going to sort it out, you wait and see.'

'I'm so sorry, Michael.'

'I know, I know.'

And she was. Sorry for her short temper, sorry for the way she snapped at him and took out her frustration on him — this kind, tolerant man she depended on and took so much for granted. Years of familiarity had made her careless of his feelings, but at times she could see only too clearly how she treated him, and she hated herself for it. The strain of the past months of making love to order had told on both of them. Even the simple gesture of holding each other had become inextricably linked with their determined attempts to conceive; it was hard to remember a time when they'd had close physical contact for the sheer joy of it.

'It's not you. I just can't bear myself, you see.'

'I know.'

'No, I'm sure you don't. You've no idea how I loathe myself most of the time.' She was looking up at him now, still in his arms but pulling away slightly, not crying but with such despair in her eyes that Michael thought it must be only seconds until she was. 'I feel so empty, and so foolish – it's hard to explain – as if I've just been pretending – how can I —'

'Pretending what?'

'I don't know how to – pretending to live. Pretending I was getting up, pretending I was going to work. No you don't know what I'm talking about, of course you don't. I mean – I'm a *sham*. I'm not real.'

Apart from the necessary discussions about the love-making cycle, it wasn't often that the subject of the non-existent child was touched upon openly now. For most of the time it was left as an unacknowledged hollow at the base of their marriage, only occasionally referred to obliquely by Juliet as in, 'Well, at least we don't have baby-sitter problems.' Or, 'I don't suppose we'd be able to afford this holiday if things had gone according to plan.' The small upstairs room had always been called the nursery, and the name had become so familiar and ordinary that neither had thought to stop using the word when it became less and less suitable. They had discussed things enough to confirm a willingness on both their parts to pay their way out of the situation if it were possible, but it always filled Michael with hope when he felt Juliet was trying to put across to him how she really felt. These moments often seemed to follow patches of intense irritation with him, as if something in her was fighting every inch of the way against revealing her true feelings until they burst out of her unbidden and released themselves in a wave of weeping.

It was this intense distress of Juliet's that made it so difficult for Michael to talk about his own sense of inadequacy and loss. For a man who liked to think he was rational and in control of his feelings it amazed him how much guilt he, too, felt at his failure to produce the required son and heir (it never occurred to him to wonder why he always imagined his offspring as male). But it was more than that – he had unexpectedly found a deep sadness within himself at the thought of never carrying his child in his arms, never kicking a football in the park with a miniature version of himself, never proudly watching the young Evans collecting his degree. As time went by his thoughts became almost biblical: phrases such as 'Fruit of his loins', 'Evans begat Evans', 'Thy seed shall replenish the earth' rattled round his head. The child became a clear picture in his mind until he could have described every detail of hair, figure, expression and face as if the boy really existed. Sometimes he felt he was going mad, but comforted himself with the realisation that this life of the imagination at least gave him a release of emotion which might otherwise have unleashed itself on Juliet.

Even at work he remained good-natured and out-wardly at peace. He sometimes envied the ability of his colleagues to release their frustrations in outbursts of swearing and shouting, marvelling at their capacity to show strong emotion on such subjects as parking fines or politics. He thought with amusement of how violent, on a scale ranging from parking meters to childlessness, the manifestation of his own unhappiness would be if it truly reflected the deep wells of despair buried inside him. Not that his restraint made him seem in any way weak or inadequate; on the contrary his gentle but slightly cynical analysis of office problems betrayed a wisdom and maturity that were clearly lacking in the overheated reactions of those surrounding him. His childhood in Nottingham, as the bright-eyed boy of the manager of a furniture shop and a piano teacher mother, had led him to be aware, from his entrance into the local grammar school to his departure from Manchester University with a degree in economics, of how much was expected of him. Ever since seeing his parents' anxiety at his admittance of any blip in the smooth upward curve of the life they had planned for him, he had learnt to keep his worries to himself.

But the distress over the non-existent child was differ-ent. For the first time in his life he felt the lack of any kind of real escape valve for the emotional pressure building inside, but was inhibited by his keen awareness of her own suffering from unburdening himself to the only other person who would be completely in sym-pathy. He found himself becoming increasingly attached to Lucy, the labrador, but consciously steered clear of imbuing her with too many human attributes, having seen in other couples how easily a pet can become a child substitute, involving, in his eyes, a lack of dignity for both parties.

As it was, he liked to think that Juliet was unaware of just how much he minded, and concentrated on supporting and cheering her.

This policy may have been a mistake.

Chapter Three

'And?'
'Polycystic ovaries.'
'Poly-what-ovaries?'
'Cystic.'
'Oh, right.'

There was a pause while Harriet let this mysterious information sink in.

'And is that bad?'

The two women stared at each other for a moment, then Juliet made a face. 'Well I suppose so.' She went on looking across at her friend, then they both laughed. 'Well, evidently.' They laughed more. 'How would you like cysts on your ovaries? Not just one, mind you, not just your monocystic, but the full poly. It's not madly glamorous is it?'

Harriet was giggling now, bending over in her chair, relieved to see the old Juliet emerging once more out of the midst of this alien affliction. And Juliet was laughing in relief too, knowing this was the only person she could ever talk to in this way, able to unburden herself without facing the over-solicitous reactions of Michael or the demanding worry of her mother. She was always smugly aware of Harriet's envy of her own happily surviving marriage, but Juliet's searing jealousy of her friend's two children counterbalanced it, giving them a spurious emotional equality. Juliet had sometimes imagined a world where the two of them could combine — a creature half-Harriet and half-Juliet; the perfect happily married mother of two. The other halves — merging to create a woman not only abandoned but also barren — could wander in some eternal limbo for those that don't fit, for those that break too many of the rules of social acceptability.

'No, but I mean what can they do about it? Can't they sort of scrape them off or something?' This produced another burst of giggling. Harriet scooped her long brown hair (too long for thirty-five as Juliet sometimes idly considered telling her) back behind her ears and wiped smudged mascara from beneath her eyes.

Juliet leant forward and spoke more quietly. 'You should see how they look inside you, it's really bizarre. They said I had to have a scan, so of course I thought it would be like the ones you had with Adam, but it's completely different.' She pictured herself back on the couch in the small dark room in Weymouth Street; the radiographer had explained what was going to happen, but she had still been taken aback by the jellied penis-shaped instrument with its ultrasonic eye inserted gently into her vagina to gaze unashamedly up and around her womb and ovaries like an all-seeing joyless dildo.

'God, I just feel so pleased that they've found *something*. I don't care what I've got so long as there's something I can do. I should be dark, fat and hairy apparently.'

'What?'

'The typical polycystic woman is large, dark and hairy. But not always. Obviously. Can I have another glass of wine?'

'Of course.' Harriet stood up and reached across the coffee table between them for Juliet's glass. 'It'll have to be the Bulgarian red now, that's all I've got left. Are you sure you're allowed to drink by the way?' She moved towards the small kitchen, collecting an old newspaper and abandoned toy gun as she went.

'Oh don't be so silly, Hattie. Believe me, if I get pregnant I shan't touch a drop, but at the moment they tell me anything that helps me to relax is good.'

'OK. Fine. So how did you get these things?'

'They didn't exactly say.' Juliet stretched in her chair and looked around the comfortable, untidy sitting room. Harriet's second-floor flat in Pimlico had been a refuge for many years now, in spite of the painful reminders of babies and then, later, of young children that were invariably scattered about. 'Where are the sprogs?' she asked.

'Peter's got them for the weekend. They're taking them to Chessington today I think. The ghastly Lauren likes fast rides apparently. She would, of course. Another point to her.' She was calling from the kitchen, and Juliet thought how little bitterness suited her even from a distance. Her voice always changed tone when the ex-husband or his new love were mentioned, reminding Juliet of the early days at school when Harriet's sneering and bullying had been so impressive and had made all the girls want to be in her gang. Only after the two of them had been friends for two or three terms had Juliet got to know her softer side which, as Harriet relaxed into the routine of boarding-school life, had become increasingly dominant – until eventually it was Harriet to whom Juliet turned for comfort and advice, and who took her completely under her wing and used her dominance protectively rather than aggressively. It was Harriet who had first realised that something was very wrong as she had watched the skeletal Julie undressing in the dormitory; Harriet who had seen the pocketed food, heard the retching and groaning from the lavatory late at night. Although she had been too young to put a name to it she had sensed very quickly that her friend needed help, and that something quite dangerous was inhabiting her, subtly changing her not only physically but also from within.

The pair had remained friends after they left school. Long indulgent letters were exchanged between Harriet's bedsit in Paris, where she was taking an interesting but unproductive Fine Art course, and Juliet's university flat in Exeter, descriptions of suitors dominating the narrative, detailing their prowess in activities ranging from electrical repairs to love-making. But when Harriet met Peter over coffee in the Louvre, a change in tone crept into the letters and Juliet soon sensed love in the air. Back in London a couple of years later they had married, and the original hard and dissatisfied little girl was buried beneath a mound of glorious and uncomplicated happiness.

Juliet had envied Harriet's complete abandonment in love. Peter was her world, and it was quite startling to see how Hattie adored him. It was the sort of love, Juliet supposed, that most people find only once in a lifetime, and some never find at all. Her own feelings for Michael seemed so contained in comparison, and Juliet often idly wondered if what she felt for him perhaps wasn't love at all, but a convenient liking and companionship which, overlaid with the glitter of lust, had appeared to be deeper and more important than it actually was. But when the phone call had come from Hattie late that night; when the strange, thick voice had told of her misery at Peter's infidelity and of her utter hopelessness faced by a future without him, Juliet had had enough of a glimpse into the open soul to see the torment that is always waiting on the other side of such all-encompassing love.

She had thought, gratefully, never to know it herself.

Juliet abandoned the car deep in the recesses of a public car park in Streatham and took from it a large brown holdall and the precious shopping basket with the thankfully sleeping baby in it, and carried them outside. It was almost dark, and she instinctively kept away from the streetlights as she walked quickly towards her destination. A lucky chance had led to her discovery of the semi-derelict house in Andover Road some weeks before; several wrong turns taken unthinkingly while coming back from a shopping trip had led her deeper and deeper into the unknown territory. She had pulled over to the side of the road and taken out her A–Z, but had soon found herself lost yet again in the thoughts that were then dominating nearly every waking moment. Gazing up at the row of abandoned houses alongside her she had sensed a solution, and had begun to formulate her terrible plan.

Now at last she was here. She had her baby back and all else would soon fall into place; when she was ready she would call Anthony and he would come, of that she was sure. Checking both ways to make sure that no one saw her, she slipped down the path along the side of the house and forced her way in through the broken door at the back, then climbed the stairs to the first floor. Once in the large front room she took a car rug out of the holdall, gently lifted the baby from the basket and then placed him carefully down on the tartan wool. He stirred a little in his sleep but didn't wake, dreaming now of food instead of crying for it; feeling in his dream, rather than seeing, the comforting embrace of his mother and the rush of sweet, warm milk. His brain was as yet filled only with sensations and needs, with emotions, pictures and desires, with no memories older than a few months.

Juliet undid the poppers of his baby-gro, slipped it off his shoulders and rolled it down over his arms and legs. She pulled open the sticky tabs of his nappy and slid it from beneath his body, wincing a little involuntarily at the strong smell of ammonia. He stirred and whimpered. She looked down at his naked form, lit only dimly by the orange light from the lamp post that stood a few doors down the street, and found herself quietly crying. She bent her head to kiss him on his rounded belly, then laid her cheek lightly against him, not letting any of her weight rest on him, but touching him just enough to feel the warm beating softness.

'Oh my dearest, dearest darling. Oh my sweetest darling. Oh my lovely baby.'

She lifted her head again to look down at him, seeing the gleam where her wet cheek had pressed against him, then as she gazed at him began to feel frightened. She sat up quickly and took off her blazer and laid it over him, panicking at the thought that he was cold. It was very quiet, and the silences between the baby's whimperings were only broken by the noise of occasional cars turning into the small street, throwing odd swinging shadows from their headlights on to the walls and ceiling of the room as they negotiated the nearby corner. The whiteness of their lights and the thrust of their engines cut through the orangey quietness in sudden bursts of intensity, stirring the unease inside her, and leaving her each time more threatened by the silent darkness in between. She had never before been inside the room, but had assumed it would be completely empty, and only now did she begin to wonder what unknown objects were lurking in the corners, or what remnants of human occupation might be mouldering in unsavoury piles in the shadows. 'Dear

Lord, let him come soon. Let him come,' she whispered, then closed her eyes, covered her face with her hands and swore quietly to herself, 'Oh fuck it, fuck it, I haven't told him yet have I? How can he come when you haven't told him? Pull yourself together, Juliet, think it through. He'll come when you tell him.' She kept her face covered and breathed in the warm sweatiness of her hands mixed with a sharpness from the baby's urine.

Then, as she knelt beside the baby, head still buried in her hands, eyes tightly closed, she heard something. Without moving her head, she snapped her eyes open behind her covering palms as she flinched and held her breath. She heard it again: a rustling behind her. Not daring to move for fear of what she might see, she kept completely still and focused every effort on listening, feeling her stomach clench in fear. Nothing. She could hold her breath no longer and began to let it out as quietly as she could, straining to listen as she exhaled, hearing only the smallest sound of her own breath escaping into the room, and of the baby's fast, even breathing. Then – something again – a whisper of a rustle this time, still behind her, and a small dragging sound. As she turned and brought the hands down from her face, she saw the large figure of a man rising up out of the shadows in the corner and at the same moment she opened her mouth to scream.

Chapter Four

Michael and Juliet were quite taken aback when Professor Hewlett suggested IVF treatment. Test-tube babies were something you read about in the newspaper; something that happened to other people, like plane crashes and lottery wins, even something to be slightly disapproved of as unnatural and unnecessary. Back in the large, comfortable consulting room after the results of all the tests had come through, Juliet had tried hard to listen once more to the details of the condition of her ovaries and the problems with hormones, egg quality and elevated levels of this or that substance, but it wasn't until towards the end of the consultation when the words 'in vitro fertilisation' hung in the air that she really tuned in. She sensed then that, although the professor was giving her and Michael every opportunity to feel they were taking some active part in the decisions and alternatives that appeared to present themselves at every turn, they were being guided inexorably towards a particular treatment and that if they did nothing but nod and appear to be following the arguments they would slowly but surely be set on the extraordinary course that must lie ahead.

'We've had considerable success with using IVF in cases such as yours, and thirty-five is a good age to be trying. After thirty-eight or thirty-nine the eggs do tend to be of lesser quality, as I think you know, and although we have many successes after that age — and indeed over forty — you stand a higher chance if you start immediately. My inclination is not to go through the laser or diathermy route with your ovaries, I have a feeling we'd be wasting precious time and there are other factors which lead me back to IVF. We'll have to monitor you very carefully as there's a higher risk of overstimulating the ovaries when they're polycystic, but as I say we've had considerable experience with other cases just like yours and I'm very happy to treat you along these lines. You'll obviously need to discuss this between yourselves and you may feel you'd like a chat with your GP, but I see it quite clearly as the best course of action . . . I'll get Sally to give you some leaflets and of course I understand that you'll need to consider the financial implications.'

A strange sensation in the pit of Juliet's stomach was puzzling her, exciting her, and she turned her thoughts inward to confront it. As Professor Hewlett paused and looked at her she felt she was expected to ask all sorts of intelligent, relevant questions, but for a moment she had to indulge herself in examining this little spark in the very middle of her being. She smiled to herself as she recognised it for what it was; something long forgotten but comfortingly familiar after such a long absence – hope.

Sensing that the appointment was nearing its close, she bent to pick up her handbag from the floor next to her chair, letting her hair fall forward over her face to hide the smile, then brushing it back with her hand as she straightened up again. 'I don't think we need even to discuss the money, do we, Michael? I'd just like to get going as soon as we possibly can.'

Michael nodded. 'Absolutely. It's not as if we're rolling in it or anything, you understand, but this is more important to us than anything else. We'd sell everything we've got.'

'Let's hope it won't come to that.' The professor smiled at them as he rose and moved from behind his desk. 'But it's very important that you understand exactly what you're doing and that it's not going to put too much strain on you both. Now, let me find Sally for you and we'll see if we can start sorting things out.'

Husband and wife walked back to the car in silence, both deep in their own thoughts but each comfortingly aware that the other was thinking about the same thing. Michael slipped his arm round Juliet's shoulders and she snuggled against him as they made their way along Weymouth Street and round the corner into Wimpole Street. When they reached the blue Volvo parked sedately in its 'Pay and Display' space, she looked at him across the roof as he took out his keys and pressed the button on the small black box that was attached to them. Nothing happened and he pressed it again, and then again, as he waved it vaguely around in the hope of directing its invisible beam more effectively.

She rested her hands on the car roof. 'What do you think, darling?'

'It's the bloody battery, it's —'

'What? No. I mean —'

'Oh, I see! Sorry, sorry.' He stopped pressing and looked at her. 'I think we're going to do it. I think it's going to work.'

'So do I.'

He pressed again and the locks lifted with a satisfying click.

After a week and a half of using a nasal spray containing a drug to 'shut down her system' as they put it, Juliet started the course of injections which was to stimulate her ovaries and start her on the journey towards egg collection. She was offered the choice of going to her own GP for the injections, going to the clinic daily or even letting Michael administer them, but she had chosen to go to the clinic, loving the feeling of having something positive to do every day, and each time looking forward to the contact with the nurses who were always happy to answer questions patiently and discuss the thrilling subjects of pregnancy and birth over and over again for as long as she wished. She went every day at eight-thirty in the morning before going to work. She would chat to other women undergoing treatment, some of them into their third or fourth try, and sometimes she would feel panic at the thought that this might be her in a year or two's time, growing ever older and more desperate, nearer every minute to the watershed of forty, and then reaching it and passing on to the downhill slope that would lead further and further from any hope of success. But on the whole it was comforting to be with others who understood and who had already been through the processes that still lay ahead of her.

Every day she was ushered into a small room subdivided by screens and she became quickly accustomed to watching the ritual of her treatment. The top of a glass ampoule would be broken off, the clear liquid it contained sucked up into a syringe, squirted back into a second ampoule of white powder which dissolved instantaneously, then sucked up again before a new needle was attached and plunged into her buttock where the magic liquid was slowly pushed into the waiting muscle. Then after a few minutes relaxing she would set off for the office, feeling better for being filled with a mysterious substance which would work silently inside her body, bringing the fantasy of the baby ever closer to reality.

As the days passed she began to feel quite bloated, and imagined huge sacs of eggs ever expanding inside her.

'I'm like a chicken, Hattie. If only I could just lay one of the bloody things and let it hatch in one of those incubators.'

'How do they know when you'll be ready?'

'When I'm ripe you mean?' Only with Hattie could she joke so lightly about this most important of all possible events in her life. With Michael it was too fragile, too serious to discuss in any but the most hushed and reverential of tones, and it was a relief to be having lunch with her friend again in one of their familiar haunts in Kensington, smiling over the lasagne and chatting about eggs and babies as if it were no different from discussing the weather or the government; just much more interesting.

'They scan me every few days to see how they're doing. More jellied eyes. I'm getting quite used to it.'

'And how's Michael?'

'Oh, he's fine. He's terribly worked up about it, of course. He thinks it doesn't show, but I can feel his tension zinging about inside him. To tell you the truth it really irritates me sometimes.' Juliet leant forward over the pink-clothed table. 'I mean it's not as if he's got to do anything but just wait – I'm the one who feels like a battery hen. And who has things stuck up her all the time.'

'Don't knock it, darling.' Harriet raised her eyebrows. 'Some of us could do with a bit more of that, I can tell you.'

'Oh no, you're not pulling that one on me! It's the most unpleasant experience and even you couldn't possibly find anything remotely sexy in it at all. Much more fun to produce them the way you did. Michael and I haven't had it for weeks now. It's really weird – all those times we were so careful when we were going out together; we'd have given anything not to have had to worry about condoms and all that, and now that there's no need, it — well, sex just doesn't seem to have any point somehow.'

'Mmm. I guess so.' Harriet took another swig of her wine, covering up the old familiar wince she felt at the reference to love-making with Peter. He had called her the previous night to talk about Adam's problems at school, and she had hated hearing the television on in the background, unable to stop herself picturing Lauren's horribly long legs tucked up on the sofa while she watched News at Ten; Lauren's large, long-lashed eyes fixed on the screen; Lauren's perfect pink ears half aware of her lover on the phone to his old, discarded, sagging wife.

Professor Hewlett was studying Juliet's latest scan report and smiled up at her. 'Well, Mrs Evans, we're ready.'

How strange it is, thought Juliet idly, that this man who has looked up, through and round me still doesn't feel he knows me well enough to call me by my Christian name.

'Oh good. So when do I —'

'Right, this is what happens. I'll make an appointment for you to come in tomorrow morning with your husband. We'll give you a very light anaesthetic and pop you under for a little while. Collect as many decent eggs as we can and introduce them to your husband's sperm, and then it's over to Nature for a bit. It's a very minor procedure and you'll feel absolutely fine once you've woken up and had a cup of tea.'

Chapter Five

It was a particularly beautiful October day; after a brief shower the sky had cleared and as the taxi took them up through Hyde Park the sun caught the few wet leaves still hanging on the trees in glints of liquid gold that were almost dazzling. Juliet had taken trouble with her hair and make-up and was wearing a cream jumper under a tan wool suit that, set against the yellow of her hair, echoed the autumnal colours around them. Michael glanced across at her and saw how good-looking she was. The lines beginning to settle into her skin around her eyes and mouth seemed merely to add to her beauty, giving her face a look of thoughtfulness and weariness that made him long to stop the car, take her in his arms and squeeze the unhappiness out of her until nothing remained but the carefree young girl he had first met. But he too sensed the solemnity and significance of the occasion and had put on one of his best dark suits and the blue patterned silk tie Juliet had given him the previous Christmas, as if the indignity ahead of him could be mitigated by an appearance of ordered formality.

They hadn't wanted to bring the car, not knowing how long they would have to be, and not trusting to their hitherto good luck in finding a nearby parking space. The taxi dropped them off on the corner of Wimpole Street and Weymouth Street and they walked the few yards to the door of the clinic. Although the building was familiar after Juliet's many visits for her injections, today it felt different and somehow threatening, and her physical discomfort added to her feeling of unease. Her abdomen felt more bloated than ever, and it frustrated her to carry round what felt like a grossly distended belly and to look down on herself and see a shape only fractionally more rounded than her usual flat contour. The feeling of fullness that she had longed for more than anything in the world was a sham – and to know she was filled not with a baby, but with a chemically induced swelling of her ovaries made it all the harder to bear. On the way there, she had found herself noticing, as she always did, just how many prams and pregnant women they passed on the way. The world seemed to be entirely populated by successfully fertilised females, and she could swear they smiled at her mockingly as she stared at them out of the taxi window. They seemed to belong to a club that was at one and the same time exclusive yet – for everyone but herself – easy to enter.

'Come with me now, Mrs Evans. The big day, eh?' Juliet was pleased when Janet's friendly face appeared round the waiting-room door. The friendly Irish girl was her favourite nurse, and she was relieved to find her on duty. 'I'll take you through to change, my dear, and Mr Evans — can you go and do your duty upstairs now?'

Juliet was whisked away and Michael was ushered upstairs to where he was to produce his sperm. This interesting and quirky little room wasn't new to him; on their very first visit for the initial consultation he'd had to come up here and produce a sample, but today he saw it completely differently. It was one thing to ejaculate for the purposes of investigation and diagnosis, but quite another to produce on demand the sperm that would be used to grow his child. The responsibility weighed heavily on him, and he sensed failure hovering like a nasty taste at the back of his mouth.

Juliet, too, was feeling tense. She was out of the smart tan suit now and wearing one of the strange white cotton gowns that open down the back. Her Irish friend had disappeared to attend to someone else, and another young nurse, new to Juliet, had to tie the tapes for her, adding to her feeling of being out of control and powerless. Perhaps that's why they put you in these things, she thought idly, so you can't even dress yourself, so you know you're completely in their hands.

'Right, Mrs Evans,' the nurse said to her briskly but sympathetically, 'let's get you along into theatre ready for Dr Northfield who'll be looking after you today. Just pop these little cotton slippers on and I'll take you through.'

It looked more like an office than an operating theatre. It was on the ground floor, only about twelve feet square and had grey Venetian blinds at the windows, a black articulated couch that reminded Juliet of a dentist's chair, a couple of television screens on a table next to what appeared to be a large glass box with a covered tray in it, and a further screen on the other side of the couch. The only obvious sign of the true business of this room was the pair of metal upright rods attached to the lower end of the couch, from which hung two leather loops. A picture flashed through Juliet's mind of her body stretched out on the couch, legs wide apart, feet strung up in the loops, and eggs being pulled out of her on a string like flags from a conjuror's hat. She shook the image away as the nurse laid a large sheet over the couch and settled her on to it, leaving her legs for the moment mercifully down and tightly held together.

'I feel a bit jittery, I'm afraid. I'm not very good at this sort of thing.'

'It's all right, Mrs Evans,' said the nurse, adopting a comforting, motherly tone towards this woman twice her age: her uniform, capability and the nervousness of her charge giving her perfect credibility as being at this moment the more mature and responsible of the two. 'It's only natural. But you've nothing to worry about. When the anaesthetist gets here he'll explain it all to you; they're very good now, you know, you'll only have a very light anaesthetic and you'll wake up feeling right as rain and it'll all be over. I'll have a lovely cup of tea waiting for you.' She slipped a black blood pressure cuff over Juliet's arm and closed the conversation by putting the ends of her stethoscope firmly into her ears as she began to pump up the pressure.

Juliet lay her head back on the couch and took a deep breath to try and calm herself, suddenly sensing, in a flash of insight, just how extraordinary this situation really was. Her husband was somewhere upstairs on his own and she was lying downstairs in an operating room surrounded by virtual strangers, and yet within the next few minutes both of them would attempt to extract from their bodies – or, in her case, have extracted – two small amounts of fluid that could change their lives for ever.

Dr Northfield turned out to be very young, very dark and very attractive. His short-sleeved blue surgical uniform made him look more like a doctor from an American television series than from a small Harley Street clinic and revealed tanned, thickly haired arms that set Juliet imagining a glorious future when the arms of her son would look just like this, and would carry her shopping, comfort her with manly hugs and one day hold her tiny grandchild.

His surprisingly deep voice snapped her out of her daydream.

'Hello there, Mrs Evans. I'm Anthony Northfield and I'll be collecting your eggs today. This is Dr Chang, the embryologist.' Only then did Juliet notice a small, oriental man in a white coat hovering just behind Dr Northfield. He nodded and smiled at her, then moved to sit at the table, on which stood a microscope, several glass dishes and the monitor screens.

Dr Northfield moved closer to Juliet. 'I've a couple of little gadgets here I'd like to fix up first if that's OK. Just relax back on the couch here and we'll get you comfortable. All right?'

He smiled encouragingly down at her as she settled herself, then picked up what looked like a small finger stall with wires attached, which he fitted on to the end of her finger. 'Just so's we can keep an eye on the oxygen in your blood. All clever stuff here, you know!'

Another boyish grin accompanied the fixing of the blood pressure cuff on to Juliet's upper arm once again, then young Dr Northfield sat back on a black plastic-covered stool and linked his hands in his lap. 'So. Now we wait for the great man.'

Juliet assumed that he was referring to Professor Hewlett. An unpleasant thrill of panic suddenly shot through her bowels from nowhere at the thought of what was to come, and involuntarily she gave a small gasp.

'All right, Mrs Evans?' asked the nurse, leaning over and putting a comforting hand on her arm.

'Yes, yes of course. Sorry, I'm not very good at all this,' Juliet said again, and then she noticed the green boots that both the nurse and doctor were wearing. She suddenly pictured them sloshing ankle-deep through blood, and had to shake her head to rid herself of the unwelcome image.

'You'll be fine,' smiled the nurse.

'Nothing to it,' added Dr Northfield, 'it'll be over

before you know it. Just a gentle little doze and we'll do all the work.' He smiled at her, and Juliet felt a little calmer.

The door opened and a grey-haired man entered dressed in a short-sleeved blue tunic similar to the young doctor's. On this larger, older figure it lost all connotations of American television and looked crumpled and well-worn, the material stretched tightly across a generous paunch and its modern styling thrown out by the pair of half-moon spectacles and dramatically untidy hair sported by the wearer. Juliet knew instinctively that this must be 'the great man' referred to earlier – no one could get away with looking so dishevelled and eccentric in such a setting without the power and kudos of status.

'Right, let's get the show on the road!'

He managed to exude bonhomie and pomposity at the same time in this one short sentence, and Juliet found herself taking an instant dislike to him.

'Got any good veins there?' He bent over and tapped at the back of her hand.

'Mrs Evans, this is our anaesthetist, Dr Andrews. Don't mind him – his bark's worse than his bite.'

Juliet felt grateful for this thoughtful introduction, and determined to withhold her instant opinion of the grey-haired figure still tapping at her blood vessels and give herself a chance to like him. 'I'm afraid I'm rather nervous,' she volunteered.

'Yes, my dear, I can see that.' The grey head, that looked as if it belonged to someone just in from a violent storm, bent over her as the strong, calm fingers fiddled at her arm. 'Not to worry, I'll soon have you sleeping like a baby. But you'll wake up crystal clear, I can guarantee that. Now then, I'm just going to – here we are now, just a little tiny prick and we'll – good, good. Pass me that cannula would you, nurse? Thank you. Now, give a cough for me, would you? Good, and another one.'

'I apologise, I'm not a very good patient, I – ow!' Juliet jumped as she felt a sharp pain in her arm.

'Just relax, you're OK. Well done, all finished. Keep quite still now or it might fall out again.'

Dr Northfield called from across the room: 'Just remember it was the anaesthetist that hurt you, not the gynaecologist!' Juliet found this far funnier than she would have in any other circumstances. Being so utterly dependent on them for her health and future happiness she was disproportionately thankful for any demonstration of interest or concern from the two blue-uniformed doctors, even if it took the form of a patronising, schoolboy humour that coming from anyone else she would have dismissed as puerile and unfunny.

'Having put the cannula in,' Dr Andrews was quiet and far less jovial as he spoke half to himself, 'I shall – heart only sixty-six p.m., Anthony. Right, my dear,' the jollying-along tone was assumed once more, 'I'm going to inject this stuff now, it works very quickly; think of something nice; your husband? Come on now, don't be frightened.' Juliet could see out of the corner of her eye the top of a large syringe being slowly pushed downwards. 'You're going to soak up quite a lot of this stuff if I'm not mistaken,' he added, as he looked down at her legs, which were still wriggling in nervous anticipation. A moment later they were still.

The atmosphere in the small room was changed to one of quiet but casual intensity now that Juliet's conscious mind was successfully switched off.

'Her oxygen level's down. We've knocked out her breathing, let's lighten her up a bit. That's better. Right, she's all yours, Anthony.'

With the help of the nurse, Dr Northfield lifted up Juliet's legs, slotted her feet into the hanging leather loops and pushed back her gown. He pulled a low stool on castors towards him, positioned it between Juliet's legs and sat down. He pushed the scanner (the jellied penis of her conversations with Harriet) into her vagina, and watched the screen in front of him while he began the search for ripe follicles. When he found a giveaway dark shape he carefully entered it with a fine tube attached to a pump and switched it on so that it sucked the contents into a test tube, which was passed to the waiting embryologist to examine under the microscope for possible eggs. As Anthony bent back down again to continue the search, the part of his mind not engaged in replaying sections of the previous night's football on Sky Sports was concentrated on listening for the call that would give him the news he waited for. After a short pause it came:

'Egg!' The call from Dr Chang was clear and definite,

as if he were bidding at an auction in a rather noisy hall.

'Good,' said Anthony, still peering at his screen.

And then again: 'Egg!'

Chapter Six

He had done it.

Michael gazed proudly at the evidence of his manhood in the phial in his hand, tucked and zipped himself neatly away and rang for the nurse. While he waited for her to come and collect his potential future offspring, presumably swimming vigorously but vainly in search of a suitable home, he sat back again on the chair, exhausted. As he cleared his head of the fantasies that had eventually produced his orgasm, he found himself staring at the magazines through which he had been riffling in search of excitement. He leant forward to shuffle them into order on the table, turning the topmost one over without thinking, to hide its cover, then smiling to himself as he realised what he was doing. What was he hiding from whom? This room existed for nothing other than its prescribed purpose, and nothing could disguise exactly what he had been up to behind its closed doors. It reminded him of times in his youth when he had hung about the door of the chemist's, burning with a mixture of excitement and embarrassment at the idea of going in and asking for a packet of condoms, and then amazed at the matter-of-fact reaction of the white-coated man behind the counter when he had finally plucked up the courage to do it. How easy it is for them now, he thought, these young boys. Boxes of them on display in garages; machines in the men's loos. 'They don't know they're born,' he muttered to himself out loud. 'They should try going in and asking for them, like a man. Namby-pambies.' He smiled again, and sighed.

He could hear the unsettling but strangely familiar sounds of the clinic corridor outside; crisp uniforms swishing past on sensible feet, the occasional trolley or wheelchair with chatty occupant being ferried to one of the myriad rooms that could be reached from this part of the building. How strange to think that every one of the voices he could hear was coming from a body that had begun life with this desperate search of a sperm for an egg. Would his son be quite the same as they? Would an arranged marriage of semen and ova in a test tube really create a human being as full and perfect as one begun with a spasm of desire into the warmth and softness of its mother's body?

He looked up at the window, where the open curtain revealed a freshly washed sky. From his chair he could see only the tops of the trees outside, and if he ignored the noise of brakes, revving engines and slamming doors he could make the street disappear, and imagine himself at home in bed, lying back after making sterile but comforting love to Juliet. An oddly sentimental post-masturbatory *tristesse* came upon him, and he almost laughed out loud at the absurdity of it all: should he stay a while and mutter sweet nothings to his glassy partner before slipping silently away into the promise of the day?

The door opened after a brisk knock and a dark-haired young man popped his head cheerfully round the door. 'Hello, Mr Evans, I'm Anthony Northfield, one of the gynaes here. I've been collecting the eggs from your wife, and you'll be pleased to hear that we managed to get five, and three of them are in excellent condition. Success achieved at last, I gather?'

He smiled waggishly as he nodded at the phial in Michael's hand, as if trying to invoke a bar-room masculine complicity, a knowingness that implied he, too, had laboured desperately for hours over girlie magazines and that as part of the same fraternity they both understood the difficulties and embarrassments involved.

'Yes, indeed,' muttered Michael, not sure whether to be proud or ashamed in front of this jolly young medic. How fresh and uncrushed he looks, he thought, how unworried and simple and clean. I bet he doesn't jerk off in quirky side rooms, all on his own. He'll make his baby by the direct route, no worries, bang bang, a few quick thrusts and sperm'll be swimming, eggs'll be cracking, breasts swelling and a firm young belly filling with his easy, boisterous, *natural* child.

Michael was to look back on this first meeting with Anthony Northfield with something akin to fascination. From the new perspective given him by those few short horrifying months that followed, he would find it hard to believe that he hadn't sensed anything. An instinct should have warned him, some male antenna should have picked up impending danger. But it didn't.

He handed over the phial and stood up, aware of his own creased trousers and unkempt hair. Funny, he thought, how uncombed hair is attractively tousled when you are twenty-five but depressingly messy when there's less of it and you're over forty.

Juliet could see her Wellington boots were not going to fit any more. Her feet had grown so quickly over the last few minutes that there was no longer any hope of being able to pull them on and she picked one up and threw it at Michael. 'Come on,' she heard him say firmly in her ear, 'all over now.'

When she opened her eyes, muttering and squirming as her conscious mind dragged itself unwillingly back to the reality of leather couch and bright lights from the strange, time-altered dream, she realised it wasn't Michael but the anaesthetist who was speaking, and she sat up suddenly in embarrassment.

'Careful now,' the wildly grey-haired head bent towards her and a scrubbed pink hairy hand was placed over her forearm, 'take it easy. You are a jumpy one, aren't you?'

Anthony's young, keen face appeared round the door. 'Five!' he announced triumphantly. 'Five! And three of them excellent. I'm really pleased — that's more than I expected.'

'Oh that's wonderful!' Juliet felt enormously proud and relieved. She was wide awake now, and could hardly keep from leaping up in her excitement, but paused for a second as she pushed herself up on one hand to close her eyes and examine the line of little Mabel Lucie Attwell babies that had assembled in an instant in her mind's eye; three of them plump, bonny and smiling, the other two more thin and serious.

The nurse, who had been hovering next to her elbow, took her arm and gently helped to ease her off the couch. 'Come and sit down in the recovery room and I'll fetch you that cup of tea,' she said, and guided Juliet out of the brightly lit room and back through the small corridor into the comfort of a small side room furnished with a couple of armchairs and a table piled with magazines. She settled her patient into one of the chairs, covered her with a rather old-looking blue blanket, and gave an encouraging smile before bustling out of the room.

Juliet wished she'd asked for coffee instead of tea, but didn't have the energy to call after the nurse. In any case, she was enjoying this moment far too much to spoil it by speaking. She wanted to examine the feeling of joy and elation inside her before the spell was broken. Stage one was achieved — she had made it! She dared now to unpack and look at the irrational thoughts that had been buried inside her beneath the recent layers of optimism — supposing there hadn't been any eggs there, after all? Supposing they had been bad, or broken, or addled or whatever happens to human eggs when they've gone wrong? '*Excellent*,' he had said, '*excellent*.' She saw the magnificent word rolling around her head like a ball of wire wool inside a kettle, cleaning out the furry bits of fear and uncertainty and leaving a shiny, refreshed brain, ready for the wonderful new thoughts that she would let creep into it when she was ready.

'Five,' she whispered out loud, 'and three of them excellent. Yes!' She wiggled her legs, this time in glee and impatience, and laughed to herself at the very thought of it all. She could sense the image of five cherubic little babies hovering again on the edge of her mind's eye, just waiting to be let in, but she resisted the temptation to look at it, and instead tried to picture the small glass dish containing the eggs that she supposed at this very moment was making its way down to the laboratory.

She was quite surprised to see Michael when he came into the recovery room, and realised she hadn't given him a moment's thought since she had come round from the anaesthetic.

'Hello, darling,' he said as he bent to kiss her. 'How are you feeling? You look fine.'

'Yes, I am fine.' Why didn't she tell him? What was stopping her shouting out the glorious news?

'Julie — they found *five*, darling, did you know? Isn't that wonderful?'

She felt cheated that Michael already knew. Not because she wanted the pleasure of telling him herself, but because she counted it as a personal triumph, a special secret between her and those hovering babies that she hadn't been quite ready to share, and she resented his hijacking the moment for himself.

'Of course I know. I was there, remember?'

'I didn't know how long you'd been awake. Anyway, it's great news.' Michael had grown so accustomed to Juliet's irritability over the last few weeks that he deflected it automatically, almost without being aware of it. 'Oh, here comes our tea.'

The nurse pushed aside some of the magazines on the low table between the two chairs and put the tray of tea and biscuits down on it. 'As soon as you feel up to it, you can get dressed, Mrs Evans, and go home. But take as long as you like, there's no hurry.'

'Thank you so much, nurse,' Michael called after her as she left the room. He stirred a large spoonful of sugar into one of the cups and then passed it to Juliet, miming a silent kiss at her as he leant across the table. She smiled back at him.

'I'm sorry I'm so ratty, darling. I don't know what's the matter with me.'

'I do. I feel a bit the same. You should have seen me up in that ghastly room – I was ready to bite anyone's head off half an hour ago.'

'Was it OK?'

'Yes. Eventually. In terms of head count a few hundred thousand or so, they tell me. Pretty good going compared to your five.'

'Yes, but three of mine were excellent, you know. I bet no one said any of yours were *excellent*.' She giggled as she sipped her tea, then put her cup down and reached out to stroke the side of his cheek. 'Thanks, darling.'

'What on earth for? For my magnificent sperm?'

'Don't be silly. Just thanks for being so good to me. I'm so bloody impossible at the moment.'

'I love you. You know that. You don't have to thank me. Just make sure it's a boy, that's all.'

Down in the lab Juliet's eggs were being cleaned of stray cells until the five little potential beings were ready to meet their future partners. An embryologist in a white coat used a large pipette to suck them up out of their dish and expel them one by one into tiny semispheres in yet another dish, then brought over the jar of Michael's washed and prepared sperm. As he added a drop carefully to each little indented container, hundreds of thousands of wriggling sperm were let loose to begin the frantic, mindless, instinctive race to be the one to reach the egg, penetrate it and begin the series of events which would fulfil its ultimate purpose of reproducing its genetic information.

'Now, Mrs Evans,' the nurse had re-entered the room and was lifting the blue blanket off Juliet's knees, 'do you feel like getting dressed now?'

'Yes, certainly. And what do we —'

'Yes, I'm just going to explain that. Give us a ring in

the morning, about ten-ish. We'll know by then how many of the eggs have been fertilised, and be able to give you an idea of when we'll need you in for implantation.'

'I see. Thank you. Do you think they'll be all right?'

The nurse was used to the eternal need for reassurance that the women in her care always demanded. 'You can never be sure, of course. Let's just wait and see, shall we. They did well to find five, you know.'

'Yes, I know,' Juliet said, irresistibly picturing a cardboard egg carton with one missing. 'Thank you. And thank you for the tea – it was lovely. Thank you so much.'

She knew she was being over-effusive, but couldn't help herself. She felt so grateful to everyone around her for their kindness, their compassion and their understanding, and she was loth to leave, wanting this moment of happiness and comforting hope to last, frightened that it would all seem so different once she walked out of the clinic.

'What makes you think it was my wife?'

Michael could hardly bear the terrible news that he had just heard. He thought the last few months had thrown everything possible at him, but this latest blow had come so unexpectedly that it hurt him more than anything that had gone before. The part of him that was at first relieved to hear news of Juliet became submerged in the horror of learning what she had done. He had known it was she who had taken the baby as soon as the policeman had begun describing the reason for his visit, but prayed that his instinct was wrong, that there had been a mistake, that Juliet had, after all, had nothing to do with this terrible crime.

'How do you know?'

'The young mother was able to give us quite an accurate description, sir, of a woman she saw near the pram just before the incident. We matched it with our missing persons file on the computer and the similarities between the person she described and the photographs we have of your wife, together with the clothes we know she was wearing, were too strong to be ignored. Of course it's perfectly possible that it wasn't her at all, but given the problems that your wife has been —'

'Yes, it's all right, you don't have to explain.'

Michael could suddenly see Juliet leaning over a pram, lifting a tiny bundle up and out of it, and cradling it on to her chest. He closed his eyes for a moment and turned his head away from the policeman as he spoke.

'It *was* her. I know it. You're right.'

'No, sir — I didn't say that, I only said —'

'Please let me meet her.'

'I'm sorry?'

'The woman — girl. Please let me meet her.'

All the misery and disappointments Michael had survived up till now were thrown up again and relived as he thought of the wretched mother of this stolen child. He felt his own losses echoed through hers, and an instinctive reaction to reach out and comfort her was what prompted his impulsive plea to the officer sitting in front of him.

'I'm not sure if that's really such a good idea, sir. She's very distressed, and —'

'Well, of course she is,' interrupted Michael bitterly. 'Don't you see how I understand that? She and I have a lot in common, you know. I just think I might be able to help. Please let me see her.'

The detective almost smiled at the idea of Michael and Anna having a lot in common. It was hard to imagine two more disparate types than the well-educated, quietly charming Michael Evans and the roughened young girl that was Anna Watkins.

'*Please!*'

Something in the way Michael looked at him was so honest, and so blatantly pleading that the detective hesitated. He could see no possible good in bringing these two sad people together and yet, somehow, he felt ashamed to come between them.

'I'll have a chat to the young lady,' he said at last. 'But I'm sure you'll understand, sir, if she doesn't want to see you.'

'Yes, I will. Just ask her though, please.'

Late at night, in a lab next to the one where Juliet's eggs and Michael's sperm were lying together in a dish considering their future, Dr Timothy Stark idly wondered, not for the first time, if he was God. It was not long since the thirty-year-old clinician had learnt the technique of intracytoplasmic sperm injection (or ICSI to its friends) and he still marvelled at his power to be not only a witness at the moment of conception, but also its initiator. His musings on his possible status as the Deity provided excellent material for conversations at his wife's dinner parties, where he would casually bring up the subject of what one meant by God, and gently steer it towards the definition 'creation of life'. At this point he would sit up in his chair, raise a hand in the air and with a triumphant cry make claim to his position as the Lord. This caused much amusement, and on a good evening perhaps a little shock among the more religious guests at the table.

As he bent forward to peer into the eyepiece of his microscope the shadow of his white-coated figure was thrown on to the cream walls of the lab by the light from an Anglepoise lamp on the table beside him. The only other illumination in the room came from the escaping reflections of the bright light under the microscope and the bluish glow from the monitor next to it. His one open eye focused on the magnified mass of squiggling sperm before him. Without raising his head, he reached for the handle that manipulated the tiny, sucking needle that he would use to pick up one of the sperm and inject it directly into a waiting egg. When he moved his hand a system of gears transferred his large, clumsy movements into microscopic adjustments and he watched closely as what appeared to be a large pointed stick entered his field of vision from the right. The stick quivered slightly as Dr Stark shifted his bottom on the stool and took a deep breath in preparation for the chase, aware as he did so in the silence of the room of the small rustling of the material of his coat and the remnants of a slight wheeze in his chest from a recent cold. He spotted a likely-looking sperm in the circle of light in front of him and sucked it up without difficulty, wriggling and tadpole-like, into the end of the needle. Gently he expelled it again and, before it could make a break for freedom, tapped it firmly on what he couldn't help thinking of as its head, until it was stunned, still and dormant. He always felt uncomfortable at this moment of sperm bashing, aware that too violent a tap could harm it, and too little leave it springy and keen enough to turn round and escape from the egg the moment he released it. But how simple it really was, he thought, this business of creation. That had been Frankenstein's mistake, of course, in combining ready grown and mature human body parts and attempting to invest them with life; how he would have admired the simplicity and intelligence of this method of the nineties. All one had to do was to choose and join up the components in a glorious pick'n'mix and then stand back and watch the miracle of creation take place. And the miracle would ensure that they grew into creatures every bit as fascinating and complex as the clinician who had given them life.

Whether his part in this extraordinary process added in any way to the sum total of human happiness, or brought any nearer the possibility of enhanced wellbeing in the world was not something Dr Stark felt necessary to consider. He was indeed not even particularly aware of the small surges of individual happiness that were caused by the fertilised eggs that left his laboratory going on to grow into healthy babies, or of the depths of despair that were caused by those that didn't. His world existed within the walls of his laboratory, and his successes and failures all took place in the small glass dishes in front of him and in the microscopic events that took place there.

Next door in one of the small indentations in the numbered plastic tray that lay in a glass-fronted cupboard, Michael's microscopic, wriggling sperm were approaching Juliet's eggs.

Dr Stark gathered up another of Mr Jephcote's inert sperm in the end of the needle and moved it across the micro-distance that separated the pool of sperm from Mrs Jephcote's cleansed and waiting egg. The fat, magnified needle hovered for a few seconds outside the wall of the *zona pellucida*, then moved suddenly towards it. The sharp stab forward merely made it bend inwards like resistant rubber. A second attempt broke through, and Dr Stark watched the immensely enlarged but in reality unimaginably microscopic drama as he expelled the still unmoving sperm into the very heart of the egg. He imagined his whispered comment to his wife later in the night when he would creep quietly into bed next to her drowsy body: 'Well, a few more miracles tonight.'

One of Michael's sperm, too, broke through the token resistance of the shell of one of Juliet's eggs and settled in to make its mark.

Chapter Seven

An old lady was very slowly manoeuvring two large bundles of what looked like pieces of rag into the only lift that appeared to be working in the block of council flats, so after a vain attempt to help her, which was met by an astonishingly vigorous burst of abuse, Michael and the policeman made their way up the stone steps to the fifth floor. At the end of a narrow balcony which looked down on to a concrete playground and rows of dustbin sheds was the door to Anna's flat.

Michael heard footsteps running to open it at the sound of the bell, and a young woman flung it wide with a half-suppressed look of hope on a puffy, white little face. Before she had time to speak the policeman forestalled her.

'I've brought Mr Evans, Anna, as we discussed. We won't keep you long.'

The look of crushing disappointment was there so briefly it was almost imperceptible. As quickly as Michael saw it, it was replaced by a clenching around the mouth and a look of what might almost be taken for hatred in her black eyes. She moved back to let them past her into the dark, narrow hallway.

'Go in,' she said quietly, and pointed to a door on the right which led into a small sitting room. The two men went ahead of her into the room, and stood awkwardly looking around, waiting for her. Red nylon curtains were half drawn across a small single window, and the sun shining through the narrow strip of uncovered glass revealed a thousand grey dots where the morning's rain had dried to leave the tell-tale residue of London dirt. The room was immaculately tidy, almost bare, and was furnished only with a small sofa upholstered in red Dralon, a worn yellow armchair, two wooden upright chairs with plastic seats and a low coffee table covered with a white lace cloth, on which stood two half-empty cups of coffee and a plate of biscuits. A television in the corner was showing an old black-and-white film with the sound turned down.

A policewoman had got up from one of the wooden chairs as they entered and, scooping up the coffee cups, moved towards a second doorway, through which Michael glimpsed a small kitchen.

'Can I get you some coffee or something?' she asked, throwing an encouraging smile at Anna who was joining them from the hall.

'Not for me, thank you,' said the policeman. 'Mr Evans?'

'No, no thank you,' said Michael, 'I'm fine.'

'Mr Evans, this is WPC Calvert, and this, of course, is Miss Watkins.'

'Hello, Mr Evans.' The policewoman nodded at him from the kitchen doorway, her hands, being loaded with cups, giving her the excuse not to have to cross back to him to shake hands. She moved into the kitchen as Michael turned to look at the pale young girl who was staring at him from across the room.

'Why don't you sit down?' she said.

As Michael sat down on one of the wooden chairs he noticed a worn-looking fabric cradle tucked behind the sofa. The vividly coloured rattle and tiny teddy that were lying in it seemed out of place in this quiet, ordered room, heavy with its atmosphere of strain and unhappiness.

The policeman stood by the window watching intently but tactfully as Anna sat in the armchair and stared belligerently at Michael. Michael leant forward and smiled back at her, trying to penetrate the barrier of fear and aggression that she had wrapped around herself like a suspicious animal.

'I'm Michael Evans, and as you know we believe my wife has taken your son. I don't know how to tell you how sorry I am – oh God, that sounds feeble. I mean I realise there's nothing I can say to make you believe that I understand how you're feeling. But I just want you to know that I am so, so sorry. I've lost a child too, you see, not in the way you have, of course – how could I ever claim that? My lost child hasn't ever really existed, you see, but – oh dear, I'm talking nonsense aren't I? Please forgive me. What I really wanted to tell you was that I don't think for one moment that my wife would do anything to harm the baby.'

For a split second Michael thought he saw a flash of something like relief pass over the girl's face.

'I know she wouldn't,' he went on. 'I'm sure she'll look after him. Just give me the chance to help you though, in any way I can. At least let me do that. Would you mind if I saw a photograph of him? How old is he?'

She didn't reply, but merely jerked her head miserably in the policeman's direction, keeping her bloodshot eyes always on Michael, as if by lowering her guard, even for a second, she would let in some unforeseen and dangerous threat to her precarious stability.

The policeman took a brown envelope out of a plastic document case he was carrying, and pulled out of it three small photographs, one of which he passed to Michael.

'That's Harry,' said the girl, squeezing the words out of a mouth compressed by misery and hopelessness. 'Three months. He's three months old.'

Michael took the picture and looked down at it. There was an odd pause for a moment, then, as he stared at the dark-haired infant in its blue knitted coat lying in a pram and smiling up at the camera, he quickly brought his hand up to his mouth to suppress a small gasp of puzzlement. The smile he had been bravely maintaining in the face of Anna's dourness was wiped from his face and he looked intently at the image in front of him as if trying hard to remember something.

There was a strange silence in the room. Anna's eyes held a new light of fear, as though yet another unexplained horror was creeping through her.

'Are you all right, sir?' The policeman, too, was puzzled, but as Michael stuttered something in reply, could only catch the words, 'this child'.

'I'm sorry, sir?'

'I know this child.'

The sound of footsteps from the kitchen as the policewoman moved from sink to cupboard broke the stillness as Anna stared even harder at the man in the chair in front of her. After a few moments she spoke.

'What do you mean, you know him? You can't do. That's my baby!'

She was almost shouting, outraged at the suggestion that this stranger could have any knowledge of her beloved child, any possibility of a previous acquaintance. She felt out of her depth, in some way outmanoeuvred. Her anger and fear made her look even younger than she was, the smudged black make-up round her eyes at odds with the rest of her pinched white face, like a little girl who's been dressing up and then turned round to find she's lost her mummy and doesn't want to play any more.

'No, you don't understand,' Michael lifted his eyes back up to Anna's, 'I *know* him. I've known him for years.'

Anna jumped to her feet and screamed at him, as the WPC came in quickly from the kitchen and moved towards her.

'Get out! Get out! I knew I shouldn't have let him come here. What do you mean, *known him for years* – you're as crazy as that fucking wife of yours! My baby's only three months old, my baby, oh! My baby! Oh Harry! I want him back, I want him back! Give him back!'

The policewoman had put a steadying hand on Anna's shoulder, and as the shouting turned to sobs she gently eased her back down into her chair, while her colleague turned and bent to speak gently in Michael's ear.

'I think we'd better go now, sir, if it's all right with you. We don't want to upset the young lady any more, do we?'

He straightened up again and nodded at WPC Calvert, who still had an arm round Anna's shoulders. The kidnapping of a baby was serious and rare enough to justify immediate and solicitous police attention, so Anna was being given every support possible. A media blackout had so far successfully protected her against intrusions from press or public, but the appointment of a Family Liaison Officer in the person of WPC Calvert was an added precaution. If there was anything further that could have helped to alleviate her distress, it would have been provided. There wasn't of course. Nothing could help Anna but a pair of soft arms around her neck, a fuzzy round head laid sleepily on her shoulder and the quiet, nuzzling whimpers of her own sweet child. The need for him was a physical hunger, and her guilt at what she saw as her wickedness in leaving him in the pram chewed at her continually like a dog worrying at a toy. A part of her was missing, and she felt that if she wasn't able soon to bury her nose once more in the warmth of the yielding little folds of his body, and breathe in the smell that felt as necessary to her as breathing itself, she would surely go mad.

Michael was ushered from the room and out of the front door on to the graffiti-strewn balcony. He felt foolish and ashamed. He hadn't even begun to say any of the things he had wanted to, hardly a word of comfort or understanding had been uttered. Perhaps the police were right; it had been a foolish idea to see the girl, and it had only served to upset her even more. But he had so much he wanted to tell her, so much sympathy to pour out to her. If only he hadn't seen that photograph. How could he explain? How to begin to make anyone understand that he had seen that baby every day and night in his thoughts and his dreams for the past ten years? How was it possible that the image conjured up again and again by his yearning imagination had been so uncannily brought to life in this tiny flat in a corner of Streatham? He hadn't just seen a familiar face in that photograph – he felt he had seen his own son.

'Oh hello, Mrs Evans, how are you feeling?'

'Well, I'm fine, but what I was—'

'Yes, of course. I know quite well why you're telephoning. Now, I'm sure you'll be delighted to hear that we have three of your eggs here that have been successfully fertilised and—'

'Oh, that's wonderful! That's just so wonderful. Oh thank you so much, thank you!'

'Well, my dear, you've nothing to thank me for, but I'm very glad to be able to give you such good news. Now, let me — I think Dr — yes, Dr Northfield said for you to come in this afternoon about four o'clock if that'll suit you?'

'Oh yes, that'll suit me beautifully. That's absolutely fine, thank you.'

'All right, we'll see you then. It won't take long and you can go home again later after a short lie-down.'

'Yes, right, thank you.'

Juliet said goodbye but kept the receiver in her hand and began to dial Michael's work number. As she pressed the first couple of digits she imagined the conversation she would have with him. 'Michael! Michael! It's worked! I've got to go back. They're fertilised!' She could hear herself shouting down the telephone and pictured Michael behind the desk in his small office in St Martin's Lane leaping to his feet, beaming and over-excited. Then she quickly squeezed her eyes shut to obliterate the scene. It was all too clear, too predictable and she didn't like it. She stopped dialling and pushed down on the cradle and released it again, lifting her eyes to look out of the kitchen window. She caught sight of herself reflected in the pane, the outline of her face highlighted by the weak London sun, but the features too dim in the watery glass reflection to be seen in any detail. She felt a sudden need to look at herself, to make herself feel real. She put down the receiver and walked over to the mirror that hung above the pine table that they had bought in an over-priced second-hand furniture shop in the Wandsworth Bridge Road when they first moved in. The face looking back at her gave no clue as to the extraordinary news that she had just heard. A sudden rush of despair welled up from deep in Juliet's belly and made her catch her breath.

'What?' she said out loud. 'What is it? What's your problem, for God's sake?'

She moved back to sit at a stool by the worktop where the phone was waiting, but this time dialled a different number and smiled to herself as she heard Harriet's familiar voice answering in her brisk but accessible tone.

'Four six nine two – hello?'

'It's me. Julie.'

'Oh, hi – how're you doing? I was just thinking about you. What news?'

'Great. Three! Three ready to put back.'

'You're kidding! That's fabulous! You must be thrilled. Hey, you clever old thing – this is really working out, huh?'

'Oh Christ, don't say that, there's —'

'I know, I still say it's working out great. Just wait and see. Mike must be jumping up and down – well, when I say *jumping up and down*, I guess I mean he must at least have stood up or something?'

'Mmm.'

'Isn't he? I mean, come on, the man's been almost as wound up as you, Jules, he must be pretty – Jules, isn't

87

he? Hey, what's up — you don't sound right, what's the matter?'

'I haven't told him.'

'Why not? Where is he?'

'He's at work.'

'Well, come on, phone the guy, for God's sake!'

'I'm going to, I just —'

'You just felt you had to tell your old pal first? I understand. They're so bloody — well, I don't know — it's just good to have these things inside your own head for a bit, isn't it?'

'Yes. Yes, exactly.'

'OK, but now you have to give him a break and phone him. Or I'll do it for you.'

'No, don't you dare, he's —'

'Don't be daft, I'm only kidding.'

'Hang on, I'm blipping.'

'You're what?'

'The phone's blipping. There's someone else trying to get through. I'll call you back.'

'OK. But remember, you silly bitch, it's great news, yeah?'

'Yes, yes I *know*. Bye.'

Juliet could never remember the sequence of phone buttons that would transfer her directly to the caller waiting on the line, so instead of trying she pushed down again on the cradle with her finger. It rang back almost immediately.

'Julie? It's me. Was that them? Were you on the phone to them? What did they say?'

'No, it wasn't. I already rang them before. It's good news, Michael, I've got three to put back.'

Michael had noticed before how often lately Juliet referred to 'I' instead of 'we', and this time, combined with the casualness of her tone, it got to him. He had been sitting next to the telephone in almost unbearable suspense for the last half hour or so, willing it to ring with their result, and the relief of hearing the good news released some of the resentment that had been building up in him.

'*We* have three to put back, Julie, *we* have three. Why the hell didn't you ring me straightaway?' He paused in silence, then took a deep breath and went on. 'But it's wonderful, darling! Oh, that's so wonderful! I told you, didn't I?'

Juliet didn't answer and there was a moment's silence.

'Who were you talking to just now?'

'Harriet.'

'Jesus.'

'No, Harriet.'

'Don't be cheap, Julie. Did you tell her?'

'Of course I did.'

'How could you? Why didn't you phone *me*? Don't you realise what this means to me? I just —'

He was interrupted by a knock on the door, and looked up to see his secretary's face peep round it.

'Mrs Rutherford is here, Michael.'

'Give me a couple of minutes, then show her in.'

The face disappeared again and Michael lowered his head to speak into the receiver. 'I just don't get it. Are you deliberately trying to hurt me, or —'

'OK, OK, I'm sorry, don't make such a thing of it . . .'

'Yes, well that's what you always say.'

'No I don't.'

'You do, you know.'

There was another pause.

'Anyway, what time do we go in?'

'About four o'clock. But I want to go on my own, Michael, please let me do that. I'm sorry I didn't phone you, but really I'll be fine. I don't want to make an outing of it — just let me get it done and I'll see you tonight. We agreed, do you remember? Oh God, I wish it was right now. I just want to get going, darling. I want them in there, do you know what I mean?'

'Look, I'll come back and take you —'

'No, no, don't. We agreed I could do this bit on my own. It's terribly simple they said, remember?'

'No, I think I ought to take you. I'm sure it's best.'

'Michael, I really don't want you to. I'm fine, really I am. I'll take a taxi.'

'So are they going to put all of them back?'

Before he could hear her answer the door opened again and he covered the mouthpiece of the phone as a smartly dressed middle-aged woman was ushered into the room. 'Oh, I'm so sorry, Mrs Rutherford; do forgive me, I've just had some rather good news. Will you bear with me for just a moment?' He gestured at her to sit in the chair in front of his desk, then turned away from her and spoke into the phone again, more quietly. 'Are they going to put all three back?'

'Well, of course they — no, I don't really know. I assume so. I'll know when I get there.'

'All right, darling, if you're sure. I'd much rather be with you, but—'

'Michael, do stop fussing. It's as simple as having the injections. I'm better on my own. Don't make such a thing of it, it's fine. I keep telling you.'

'I know. I just want to be part of it — you know.' He had lowered his voice a little and turned further away from his client, who had tactfully started rereading the details of the policy documents she was holding in her gloved hand.

'Well, you can't. None of the others do — oh Michael, I don't want to talk about it any more. Don't spoil it, you always spoil things by fussing, I—'

'All right. Look, I must go. Let me know how you get on, won't you?'

'Of course. I'll ring you when I'm home. Bye, darling.'

'Bye.' He put down the phone and turned back to his client. 'Sorry about that, Mrs Rutherford. Now, your contributions.'

'Do you need to go somewhere, Mr Evans — do feel free to—'

'No, no thanks. Everything's fine. Indeed, it's wonderful.' He couldn't help smiling, and felt suddenly benign towards this lady seated in front of him. 'Your insurance. I know you're very keen to make provision for your children, Mrs Rutherford. Very important.' He was grinning broadly now.

At four-thirty that afternoon, Juliet lay with her legs apart and raised uncomfortably in stirrups, fully awake this time and not liking to imagine the undignified picture she made. She felt an almost irresistible urge to bring her arms down over her hips and cover her exposed crotch with her hands, but forced herself to take a few deep breaths and produce a kind of superficial calm. She detached her mind from her surroundings and indulged herself for the thousandth time in the dream that inspired her life, that gave it meaning, that gave it hope; she clutched at the thrilling, terrifying thought that had become her mantra. She saw herself lying like this in nine months' time, not emptily waiting to have a millilitre of fluid inserted into her, but straining to expel that very same substance changed by time and the succour of her own body into a human baby.

'I'm just inserting the pipette now, Mrs Evans.'

Dr Northfield's voice brought her back to the clinic and to her lonely discomfort. She glanced at him as he spoke, seeing only the top of his head as he bent over her, his arms reaching towards that most private part of her that seemed to be everyone's property these days but her own. She thought wryly of how shy she used to be and a part of her floated to the ceiling and looked down on this extraordinary scene; the vision she saw of herself with this young man grappling between her straddled legs gave her a twinge of excitement, and her tension disappeared for a moment and her thighs relaxed even further apart. She felt wanton and uncaring, aware of her sexuality and of the doctor's hand playing around the entrance to her vagina. Would he be able to see that it was swelling and reddening with the thoughts that were beginning to race through her head? She pictured his arm pushing up inside her until it reached the neck of her womb, and she moved her hips slightly down and forward to encourage him.

'There we are, Mrs Evans, all done! Nothing to it. I'll leave the nurse to look after you now, and I'll see you in my office in a few minutes.'

He was gently unhooking her legs from the stirrups as he spoke, and Juliet felt almost disappointed as he stood and pulled off his latex gloves. He looked about twenty-eight, still boyish, with a large nose and dark eyes and skin that reminded her of a waiter in their local Greek restaurant. He smiled across at her as he threw his gloves into the bin, then walked towards the doorway, where he turned to look back at her, one hand holding the side of the open door, the other pulling off the green hat he had been wearing over his dark hair. 'Good luck,' he said, and smiled again, then paused, still looking at her, as if waiting for her to say something. A strange but not unpleasant sensation rather like pins and needles crept upwards through Juliet's body as she looked back at him, then he suddenly turned and was gone. She forced herself to concentrate on her inside again and imagined her three beautiful eggs finding their place in the lining of her womb. Was it to be their home, or just a tragically temporary shelter?

'Good girl!' whispered the nurse kindly in her ear.

How it took her back, that reassuring deadly voice,

that caring, vicious, cruel-to-be-kind tone that was always followed by some unbearable act of vandalism. She was there again, in that room: horrifying; clean; smelling of antiseptic and floor polish. They were stuffing her; the smelly brown rubber tube almost choking her as it was forced down her throat. Couldn't they see how gross she was, how she had to be left alone to be thin, to be light, to be human again? Nobody understood; they were coming at her again with that tube; she couldn't stand it; the pain, the fear.

How old were they, these memories? Twenty years? More? It was all still so clear: the misery she had felt when her mother first began to make the stinging remarks that had set her on the strange course she had followed relentlessly for so many agonising years. 'Puppy fat', it had been at first, then 'podgy', then the undisguised nastiness of 'ugly', later maturing into the full-blown phrases that hurt most of all: 'You'll never find anyone to take you out while you're carrying all that weight.' Or, 'There's no point in buying you any decent clothes while you look like that.' Hours spent inspecting herself in the mirror had only confirmed the eagle-eyed truth of these maternal observations, and once she discovered the magic that a couple of fingers down the back of her throat at night could achieve, inevitably she became addicted to the cycle of overeating and vomiting, interspersed with intense periods of starvation, that came to dominate her life.

When her weight dipped so low as to be dangerous, her doctor had insisted on her being admitted to hospital, the diagnosis of anorexia nervosa (in the days before the concept of bulimia was generally recognised) necessitating positive action. It was there that, after weeks of being alternately threatened and cajoled to eat without success, she had finally been force-fed. It was the mid-seventies, and such treatment was already becoming rare – as she was told, several years and several doctors later – but she was unlucky enough to catch the last remnants of the barbaric and humiliating practice.

'Come on now, Mrs Evans. Just relax and lie there for a minute or two. It's all over now. Nothing to worry about. We'll get you dressed in a minute and I'll get you a nice cup of tea.'

Juliet squeezed her eyes tight shut and pulled herself back into the present. She was gripping the sides of the narrow bed as if hanging on for life, and the screwing-up of her eyes had released a tear which was now hovering around the top of her cheek. 'I'm so sorry. I seem to have got a bit panicky.'

'That's quite understandable, dear. Everyone gets a bit emotional about it, it's not easy, we all know that.'

As Juliet opened her eyes and met the compassionate gaze of the nursing sister, she wondered how she could possibly have been reminded of the terrifying person who had monitored her treatment all those years ago. This one was kind, positive, on her side. Does this woman go home to a husband and children? she wondered. Does she tire of them, complain and shout at them? How pathetic she must think me, so anxious to produce what she takes for granted.

The comforting smell of soap powder on the white gown that she wore, and the plastic wristband giving her a spurious sense of belonging, were enough to steady her for the moment. She would play along and force herself to believe in the reality of it all and drive away the feelings of hopelessness that hovered destructively at the edge of her mind. She had always known she walked on the very edge of a pit of despair, now she must look only upwards and not countenance the possibility of a fall.

Juliet wanted a bath. Suddenly more than almost anything she could imagine she longed to sink back into warm, soapy water and let the dirt and hospital smells float off her.

Chapter Eight

Anna was looking at Harry's vest. It was white terry towelling, with short sleeves and a piece that went down between the legs and joined with press studs. It had been getting a bit small for him lately, and she knew that, one way or another, he would never wear it again. She almost laughed out loud when she remembered how sad this had made her the last time she had looked at it, two days ago was it? No, it couldn't be, could it? Was it really only two days ago that she had watched Harry, lying on his yellow stretch cotton sheet, blowing raspberries at her, and seeming suddenly far too long in the torso to fit into the vest? She had tickled his tummy and blown a raspberry back at him, wondering if she should try to squeeze his chest, shoulders and chubby arms into the vest and then cut the rest of it off at the waist, but she'd had an immediate vision of the tight fabric stretched across his small body. Lifting him up and out of the cot, she had kissed him, and said, 'Oh, to hell with it. You'll be getting a new vest today, son, if I have anything to do with it.' And she had tossed the scrap of material on to the floor.

Now she sat on an upright chair next to the cot in the small bedroom that she shared with the baby and pressed the vest hard to her face, breathing in deeply to try and find his smell. She rubbed the fabric into her eyes and nose, as if she could become part of it, just to be where his flesh had been, press against what he had pressed against with his fat pink tummy and round shoulders. She kept her head buried there while she pictured the clothing stall in the market where she had intended to buy the new vest. If she had gone there first, instead of to the supermarket – she wouldn't have lost Harry then, would she? She could still do that, surely? She saw herself walking along the street to the supermarket with the pram, saw herself nearing the entrance, beginning to turn towards it and slow down – *Don't stop! Don't stop!* She tried to force her own image past the glass doors and rows of steel trolleys, and on up the high street to the market. But the Anna of her imagination insisted on reproducing reality and stopped and pushed the pram through the doors; then as present-Anna followed her, pressed down on the old-fashioned brake with one foot and picked up the battered black knapsack by the feet of the sleeping Harry. *Pick up the baby too! Pick him up too! Never mind the fucking bag, pick him up, you stupid thoughtless fucker!*

How could she see it so clearly? Where was she watching from now to be able to see in every detail her own inexorable walk towards disaster? OK, she couldn't make her earlier self go on to the market, she couldn't make her pick up the baby, but at least she could force her to come back to the pram those few seconds sooner, surely? She didn't need that bloody bottle of chocolate sauce, she didn't even like chocolate sauce – she'd actually stood there looking at it for what must have been almost a minute, trying to decide whether to pop it into her trolley, pricing what she'd already chosen and vaguely working out what she had left. *Don't stop at the chocolate sauce*, the wise Anna in the little bedroom screamed in her head to the innocent Anna in the supermarket – *oh please God, don't stop*. But nothing she could do, no effort of will could prevent it. For the hundredth time she saw herself pushing the trolley down the aisle towards the till (*Go on! Go on!*), then pausing, her eye caught by the tempting row of brown plastic bottles under the deadly sign 'NEW!' And she had stopped. At this point the Anna in the bedroom flew to the checkout just in time to catch a pair of hands lifting Harry from the pram. Why couldn't she grab those hands? Why couldn't she stop the blonde bitch in the blazer she was now convinced had taken him? Why couldn't she follow her to see *where* she had taken him, as she could follow the memory of herself? She mentally looked away then suddenly back, trying to surprise her own vision into revealing more of the stranger who was stealing her baby. But all she saw when she did so was the empty pram. She had reached this stage so many times in the replay of that terrible morning, and every time she thought she would surely be able to see just a little more, but she never did.

She sighed from the pit of her soul, then she lifted her head up and was back in reality. She pulled her eyes into focus and saw a tiny hole in the fabric of the vest in front of her, and knew it reminded her of something. But the picture of the hole it conjured up wasn't empty like this one, it had pink flesh showing through, and an echo of anxiety attached to it. She shook her head to clear the remnants of the supermarket, closed her eyes and tried to look again at the remembered hole. It had frayed grey material round it, and was low in her field of vision. Black; black leather next to it. A shoe! A black leather shoe and a grey sock with a tiny hole in it — yes she had it. The man who had come to see her yesterday — the husband of the cow who must have taken Harry. She remembered looking down for a second as he had leant towards her, but hadn't realised till now that she had noticed anything at all about him. She tried to picture his face, but couldn't, only aware that it had looked horribly sad and worn, too much like the way she herself had been feeling, and she had wanted it gone out of the flat. Why had he wanted to see her? She hadn't been able to understand when the police had told her, and had felt wary and threatened, but now she suddenly understood. He was *involved*. However kind the rest of them were, however sympathetic, experienced and professional in dealing with her, they all went back to normality at the end of the day. She had assumed the unrelenting horror was hers alone, but perhaps, just perhaps, that sad-faced man bore a little of it too. She knew her own despair was blinding her to everything else, and she struggled to put him in perspective, to see him as another suffering human being rather than a part of the giant, crushing weight that seemed to be the rest of the world.

Anna stood up and let the little vest fall back on to the bed. She was still wearing the long tee-shirt she had slept in, and her uncombed hair fell over her face in lank strands. She pushed it back with one hand and tucked it behind her ear as she moved to the sitting room, where the ever faithful WPC Calvert was half dozing on the sofa. Anna looked down at her for a moment, then turned away as the policewoman opened her eyes and lifted her head. 'Oh, hello, Anna. You're awake. How are you feeling? Can I get you anything?'

'No, no thanks. But I'd like to get in touch with the guy who came here yesterday. I want to ask him something. Can you arrange that for me?'

The policewoman looked taken aback for a moment. 'Are you sure? You were very upset yesterday and—'

'I know. I shouldn't have been so – no, I'm sure. I'd like to see him. He might tell us something more. You know, something that – oh I don't know – I just think I ought to see him.'

WPC Calvert knew that the husband of the suspected abductor would have been questioned exhaustively for any possible clues that could help in the search, but as her priority was to give whatever help and comfort she could to the bereft mother, she was pleased to find there was something concrete to set in motion that might occupy Anna's thoughts while the real search went on.

She was well used to handling sensitive situations, and had often had to indulge emotional and irrational requests.

'Yes, I'm sure that can be done. I'll ring Detective Inspector Graham. He'll sort it out for you.'

'How do you feel?'

'Just the same. But the bloated feeling has gone down a bit more, I think. How do *you* feel?'

'Paternal. I know I shouldn't say it, I know I'm tempting fate, but I just can't help it. I do. I feel *paternal*. Protective. And I love you.'

Juliet smiled. 'I love you too. Paternal, eh? Yes, that sounds good, doesn't it? Mind you, I don't really think I could say I feel maternal yet, or at least no more than usual. I don't —'

She stopped as a waiter arrived at the table to take their order. After a greeting as effusive as only the Italians know how, he reeled off the specials and stood back, glowing with apparent pride at the magnificent range of delights he had offered them, betraying only the merest hint of disappointment as they ignored his suggestions and ordered only a simple pasta for Juliet and a veal escalope for Michael.

They felt secure in this small local restaurant, a bolt hole they always escaped to when neither of them felt like cooking, or when there was nothing much in the house and they had no energy to shop. The large blown-up photographs of the Amalfitana coastline, framed to give the impression of being views of the outside world from wooden-silled windows, had remained unchanged – if a little dustier – since they had first moved into the area. The red checked tablecloths and Chianti bottle candles had a reassuringly old-fashioned and timeless cosiness, and both Juliet and Michael felt an unspoken truce descend on them whenever they ate here, as if their differences were left at the entrance with their coats.

She hadn't been entirely open in her description of how she felt. She didn't feel just the same. There was a change, slight but unmistakable, but it was too tiny and too precious to be shared just yet. She withheld it not because of any coldness towards her husband: on the contrary, she was feeling extremely benign and warm towards him, but the minuscule flutter of fullness that she sensed at the base of her belly was so subtle that to betray its existence by putting it into words might just allow it to escape in a tiny puff of smoke, leaving her empty again. She would leave it a few days, then attempt to voice her secret conviction that she was – oh, how could she even dare to *think* the word – that she was – no, she wouldn't say it, even in her head.

'What were you going to say?' asked Michael, as he reached for a packet of breadsticks and tore the paper off one end.

'Oh, only that I don't suppose I should expect to feel anything yet. Not quite as desperate as I did perhaps, but I know that's just because we're actually doing something, if you know what I mean. It's – oh Michael, do look!' She lowered her voice on the last few words and gestured with her head to a table a few feet away, where a large Italian family was halfway through a meal, noisily and cheerfully tucking in to huge plates of pasta, gesticulating and laughing.

'Yes, they're very jolly, aren't they?' Michael smiled at her.

'No, no, look – I meant the little one.'

Michael looked back in the direction of Juliet's gaze and saw then what had caught her eye. An older woman at one end of the table was holding a tiny, black-haired baby over her shoulder, rubbing its back and rocking her body slightly as she chatted to the young girl next to her. The baby's eyes were open, dark in its little pale face like two currants pushed into an uncooked bun, and it seemed to stare at Juliet, unblinking and serious, as if by looking hard enough it could begin to understand some of what it saw.

'Isn't it sweet?' she whispered. 'So little!'

'Yes, isn't it,' answered Michael. He reached out and took Juliet's hand across the red checks and gave it a fond squeeze. He had left unasked so much about the day, not liking to break the mood of content and calm in which he had found her on his return from the office, but now he felt able to ask some of the questions he'd been holding back. He gently lifted his hand from hers as the drinks arrived and were put in front of them, tactfully not commenting on the fact that, unusually, Juliet had ordered orange juice instead of Campari. He leant forward again. 'How did it go today, darling? I mean, was it all as good as they hoped? Did they put all three —'

'Yes, oh yes it went well. Much easier than I thought actually.'

Juliet was looking almost beatific in the candlelight, Michael thought. When the edge of bitterness and unhappiness left her face, it softened into that of the girl he had married. She was wearing a blue sleeveless linen dress that scooped just below her collarbone and fitted gently over her breasts and waist, following the slender contours of her frame without hugging it, giving her the classy yet irresistible sensuality that he loved in her. A fine gold chain that he had bought for her when they were on holiday in Greece two summers before twinkled at her throat, and she had brushed her blonde hair over to one side so that it swung in a yellow shiny cascade over one eye as she, too, leant forward, hiding one of the pair of gold-framed pearl studs that she wore in her ears.

'You look gorgeous,' he said, and kissed her cheek.

She smiled and went on, 'I didn't have any kind of anaesthetic this time. It was more like the scans they keep giving me. Quite simple really, all over very quickly.'

'Not the plastic thing looking up you again?'

'Yes, but I'm getting used to that. I hardly mind it at all now.'

Michael acknowledged within himself a tiny stab of jealousy and at the same time a burst of astonishment that he could be so childish. 'Oh really?' he said, raising one eyebrow in mocking roguishness, 'Enjoy that do we?'

'Oh Michael, don't be ridiculous! You should just see how unsexy it all is. For heaven's sake, you're as bad as Harriet — if I was after that sort of thing I could do a bit better than a plastic probe. Here am I, going through all that and you think I'm enjoying it! Mind out, your tie's in the butter—'

But they were both laughing at it all, luxuriating in the teasing and the relief of the moment.

Anthony Northfield was telling his girlfriend about his day. He had showered and changed into beige slacks and an open-neck white shirt, his hair slicked back and still wet, cuffs rolled up to reveal his forearms. She loved him like this: relaxed and apparently self-confident; tired by his day at work but with the stresses of it washed away and with only the echoes of minor power remaining to bolster his hopes for the golden future that was expected of him. He leant back in the cream-covered sofa, secure in his good looks and reasonably so in the progress of his life so far, and took another sip of whisky. A childhood in Hampshire, surrounded by an adoring family of doctor-father, musician-mother and two bright younger siblings had brought him up to assume his life would be success-ful; the only small cloud on his horizon being the secret fear that he was not quite up to scaling the heights his parents had projected for him. It was unspokenly taken for granted in the closed confines of the family that, being the first-born son, he would continue the medical tradition of his father and grandfather, and he knew they had never really appreciated the sweat that this expectation placed on him. Where his younger brother and sister sailed calmly through homework and exams, he battled through storms; where his parents moved smoothly about the Hampshire social set, whether at local dinner parties or in French ski chalets, he bumped and staggered. But the smooth good looks were a huge asset and, combined with hard work and late nights struggling to master the complexities of the human body, he scraped through medical school with an acceptable degree. By this time he had learnt to use his physical attractions to good effect and to combine them with a not entirely manufactured charm that, together with good use of his father's influence in the old boy network still prevailing among the medical fraternity, secured him a post in a large London teaching hospital. There the effectiveness of his bedside manner was soon spotted and exploited to its full potential, and when offered a move to the hospital's infertility unit, he jumped at it, sensing that his talents would be used to best advantage if employed in the care of women.

When Professor Hewlett left the hospital to set up a private clinic in Weymouth Street, he invited Anthony to join him, and in the ensuing six years he made himself a valuable member of the team; technically competent, and in style and manner impressive. The clinic flourished, and everyone involved began to reap the financial and emotional rewards of being part of its success. The only shadow hovering over the sunny upward slopes of the path Anthony could see ahead was the secret, niggling fear that still came to him at unexpected moments – in the middle of a dinner party, halfway through an egg removal, deep in the darkness of the night – that he was not quite up to all this; that in some unknown way he would one day be found out as a sham, as lacking in some essential ingredient, as a pretender to the throne of the golden few who went on to consultancies, brass plates and knighthoods. He could not have foreseen that it was the physical attributes that had, in no small part, led to his progression, which would cause the biggest threat to his stability so far.

He looked across at Andrea as she sat in the armchair opposite him, shoeless feet tucked up under her neat thighs, and stretched out one arm and arched his back as he felt the warmth of the whisky taking the edge off any lurking uncertainties.

'And what about you, sweetheart?' he said. 'How did it go?'

Andrea worked for a P R and marketing agency, handling the accounts for several major food manufacturers; as successful in her promotion of new ready meals and repackaged canned vegetables as Anthony was in his pursuit of pregnancies. Any qualms she had at abandoning her original dream of working in journalism and vigorously pursuing truth and revealing injustice had been shelved at about the same time that Anthony had convinced himself he could contribute more to the overall good of mankind by working in private practice at the clinic, than by leasing his skills to the NHS. They'd first met when she was sent to research the subject of infertility as part of a promotion project for a vitamin manufacturer – later abandoned. Andrea's interviewing technique was immaculate. The long legs were beautifully displayed as she leant her elbow on one crossed knee, pencil in manicured hand hovering delicately around her mouth, the rubber-tipped end occasionally but provocatively gripped between even white teeth as she listened, rapt, to the intricacies of sperm mobility. It didn't take long for Anthony to suggest that they continue the discussion over lunch, and within a week they were exploring sperm mobility far less theoretically.

Two years on, their relationship was steady and fulfilling, although even in this Anthony worried that it was a little too good to be true, and that Andrea might one day see through to his buried uncertainty. She had no such hidden twinges, and her outward confidence and satisfaction were a true reflection of what lay beneath.

She still worked in the same agency as when they had met, and had recently been briefed to upgrade the image of packaged pizzas, which were still selling in vast quantities but which were now manufactured by such a large number of different companies that the client, Middlesex Foods, feared for their market share.

That day she had made a presentation to the marketing director of her proposal for a nationwide pizza competition, in which readers of a major national newspaper and of one of the leading women's magazines would be invited to send in ideas for new pizza toppings, at a charge of a pound for each entry which would then be given to charity. Andrea was pleased with the plan: it had a satisfactorily triple-pronged attack. Pizzas would be mentioned for three consecutive weeks in the national press, always linked with the brand name of 'Pizza Pete', a few hundred new ideas for toppings would be gathered for the price of a prize weekend in Italy, and the charity connection would, as usual, add some warmth to the whole operation.

'Yeah, I think it went well. They wanted me to suggest the charity I had in mind, and I haven't really got round to that yet, but I said I'd got a list which I was considering. There must be something that works well with the whole idea of pizza. Aren't there diseases when you can't taste or something, so that we can say all the money we raise will go towards helping children taste these wonderful toppings for the first time?'

Anthony's medical expertise came in very useful from time to time, just as Andrea's work complemented his when advice was occasionally needed on the careful handling of a sensationalist press story about eliminating embryos or disposal of eggs.

'Well, of course there are conditions where you lose all sense of taste — strokes and things like that, but it's more likely to be in adults, and probably associated with other problems.'

'Oh God, no! I can't have pictures of old men with

heads on one side and drool coming out of their mouths,' laughed Andrea. 'It's got to be children, and they've got to look sweet.'

They were quiet for a moment, each riffling through their mental filing system of unfortunate medical conditions; tossing aside images of mongolism, blindness and crutches in a search for the perfect tie-up of picturesque human suffering and pizza.

'There's a ghastly skin disease where you get to look awfully *like* a pizza topping,' Anthony said, raising his eyebrows at Andrea in mock disapproval as she burst out laughing. 'No, you really do, it's quite awful. Perhaps you could have a picture of someone on the packaging, just to bring it all to life a bit?'

'Oh, shut up!' Andrea giggled. 'You're not being any help at all. Maybe I'm on the wrong track; d'you think it should be Romanian orphans again? Or have they been done to death? Anyway, I'd better get changed if we're really meeting Rachel and the others. What time did you say?'

She got to her feet and smoothed down the front of her skirt. Both she and Anthony generally changed down in the evenings, abandoning their neatly suited work uniforms for jeans or slacks, and designer sweaters or Calvin Klein sports shirts.

'I said we'd meet at The Lion at eight,' Anthony answered. And as she walked out of the sitting room he called after her, 'I think one of today's fancied me, by the way.'

'Not another one!' she shouted back from the

bedroom, enjoying the sureness she felt in their relationship as she did so. 'Pretty?'

'Not bad, bit old for me, of course, but then you know what they say about women of experience. She couldn't help enjoying it, I could see that. They always think I can't, but I always can.'

'You're outrageous. Where's your clinician's impartiality and disinterestedness?'

'Oh, it's there really. I just felt like annoying you, that's all. Hurry up, darling, or I'll come and examine you in a minute. I'm getting bored.'

Chapter Nine

Juliet was missing her regular visit to the clinic. While she'd been going through the course of daily injections to stimulate her ovaries, she hadn't realised how much she had become dependent on the ritual it involved, and how much it meant to be able to talk regularly to people who understood what she was going through. Now she tried to reimmerse herself in her work, knowing there was nothing more she or anyone else could do except wait, but finding it almost impossible to keep her mind on anything; using every excuse to try to be alone with her private thoughts, willing the time to pass more quickly, and yet dreading the moment when she would know. The clinic had presented her with yet another sheet of information the last time she attended, which she read and reread when she could find a moment to sit alone at her desk in the office. It included the unachievable advice: '*After the embryo transfer we suggest that you conduct your life in a routine manner.*' And ended with the request that, '*You will kindly get in touch with us when you know the outcome of this attempt, whether successful or otherwise.'* 'Try and stop me,' she muttered to herself.

She would often silently rehearse the phone call she would have to make to the clinic: 'Oh hello, this is Mrs Evans. I just thought you'd like to know that I'm pregnant . . . Yes, it is good news, isn't it? We're thrilled . . . oh, about July the fourteenth or fifteenth they think — a summer baby . . . Well, thank you, that's very kind of you . . . yes, of course, I'd love to . . . the day after tomorrow? Yes, that's fine, I'll see you then.'

She never stopped to wonder why it was always Anthony Northfield she saw herself talking to, or considered it odd that in her fantasy he should ask her to come back to the clinic for a special check-up. In reality it had been made quite clear to her that if the attempt at pregnancy should prove successful, it would be up to her GP to find an obstetrician to look after her and deliver her, and that her relationship with the clinic would be satisfactorily closed.

There were just under twelve days to go before she could expect the physical evidence that would send her hopes crashing, or the lack of it that would allow a trip to the Pathology Lab for an early blood test and the unimaginable joy of a positive result. Although she knew it was far too soon, she found herself once again checking the gusset of her underwear for signs of blood each time she went to the lavatory, and gazing earnestly down at her nipples in the bath for evidence of swelling. At least now she felt there was more justification for the repetitive searching and checking; no one could deny her the knowledge that inside her was an embryo, and that the possibility of its growing and developing was real. She didn't like to think that it might already have died and shrivelled and been expelled from her body, unacknowledged and unmourned – only in her nightmares did she sometimes see a tiny white body with lifeless webbed hands, eyes open and clouded like a dead fish, slithering helplessly from between her legs in a smear of water and blood. She would wake from such dreams sweating and frightened, not wanting to confront them for fear of making them too real to tolerate, and instead shaking Michael awake and asking him to fetch her tea.

Juliet already sensed in him a newly cherishing attitude towards her, a metaphorical arm on her elbow permanently guiding and guarding her, which, instead of making her feel nurtured, tended to verge on the edge of patronage. When she caught him looking at her anxiously as she got up from a chair or ran down the stairs, it irritated her – as if his premature assumption of the need for any special treatment was tempting fate. *I'm probably exactly the same as I ever was!* she screamed at him in her head. *Don't look at me like that! I can't bear it! We don't know yet, we don't know!*

But she never said such things, merely looked away from him and came out with one of her brisk, practical remarks which just added to his concern and made him treat her more carefully and gently than ever, which in turn annoyed her more.

Juliet had got into the habit of dropping in on Harriet

on the way home from work. She told Michael that she needed a buffer between office and home, and that a half hour or so of her friend's chatter relaxed her and took her mind off the self-analysis that was dominating her thoughts. In fact the real reason was more to do with the shops that, by making a slight detour, she could pass on the short walk from the office in Sloane Square to Harriet's flat in Pimlico. Several of them had become magnets: Boots, where she could stand for several minutes gazing at boxes of Farley's Rusks and packets of disposable nappies; the small newsagent's opposite, where she couldn't resist a quick glance through *Mother and Baby* or *Parents*; the Early Learning Centre — tiny chairs and wooden toys; even Gap had become a place of pilgrimage, thanks to the soft and simply designed tracksuits which she remembered Harriet wearing through both her pregnancies. Juliet would stand looking at the choice of colours, seeing her own swelling belly instead of Harriet's pushing out the fabric and stretching the waistband, picturing herself in aquamarine one day, navy blue the next, but always smiling and always enormous; Mother Earth in pure cotton.

'Darling, you're doing too much — you must both come and have dinner, I insist.' Her mother's voice on the telephone was concerned and understanding; a little too much so for comfort.

'Mother, it's very kind of you, but I've got so behind

with work I really daren't spend an evening out this week—'

'Nonsense! You've got to put yourself first now you know, not just for your sake, but for the baby's. It's good for you to relax occasionally. You're being very foolish if you don't do everything you possibly can at this stage – you know how you'll feel later if anything goes wrong.'

'Mother, you don't understand, they told me at the clinic it makes absolutely no difference if I—'

'Don't be so foolish, Juliet. Why do you think there's so much of this unnatural birth business nowadays? You know how I feel about it, it's obviously not right to be working when you're trying for a baby. When I got married, I—'

'Yes, yes, Mother, I know.'

Juliet couldn't face hearing her mother's views on working women yet again: in *her* day women gave up work when they got married; in *her* day they were satisfied to look after their husbands and homes and bring up children; in *her* day you didn't talk so much about sex and all its problems; in *her* day babies were conceived 'normally' as she called it. Juliet knew the list by heart. From the way her mother talked it would be reasonable to infer that her marriage had been happy and her only daughter a loved and well-balanced child; the reality had been drastically different, and Juliet's memories of the miserable period of anorexia were not the only traumatic ones. Her father had always been quiet – a lifetime of successful work in the Civil Service had taught him to be adept at keeping his head well down, avoiding confrontation and staying silent rather than risking a remark that might in future be quoted back at him — but even before Juliet's nervous problems began to manifest themselves he had retired still deeper into his shell. Taking the line of least resistance, he would leave matters of discipline to his wife, who was only too happy to take on the rôle of guiding her daughter on to the path *she* saw as correct. The unhappy girl had longed for a firm hand from him, and missed, more than he ever realised, the physical displays of affection, and even of anger, that she saw in the fathers of her friends. She had sensed, too, the deep misery underlying the apparent contentment of the marriage and was far more aware of the resentment masked by the civilised exchanges between the two parents than either of them appreciated.

'You know it's only because I care about you, darling.'

'I know, Mother. It's very kind of you, we'd love to have dinner.'

Why had she given in? Why did her mother always manage to make her feel guilty enough to do things *her* way? It was all too like her childhood and Juliet could feel uneasiness growing inside her like a cancer.

'Thursday?'

'Lovely!'

Liar.

'Mr Evans? It's Detective Inspector Graham speaking. I'm sorry to trouble you at home in the evening, but I thought it better not to contact you at work. I've had a call from Miss Watkins. Now, I don't know how you'll feel about this, but she seems rather anxious to make contact with you again.'

'Oh, does she? Is she all—'

'I think she feels she behaved rather badly when you met at her flat.'

'Oh, poor thing, poor thing. She doesn't need to feel anything like that at all. I understand. My God, I should do.'

'She's very anxious to make amends, as it were, and if you did feel you could spare a little time to—'

'Of course, of course.'

'I think anything that helps her stay calm can only be a good thing, if you see what I mean.'

'What shall I do? I mean shall I go to her flat again or what?'

'I think that'd be the best, Mr Evans, yes, if you don't mind. She naturally doesn't want to move from home at all, in case there's any kind of news, as you can imagine.'

'Is there any? Is there anything else? I spoke to one of your men this morning, but he didn't seem to think—'

'No, I'm afraid there's not really anything concrete since I last spoke to you, although I do have a couple of sighting reports which may prove interesting. They tend to confirm that it is indeed Mrs Evans that we are looking for in connection with the missing child.'

'He will still be all right won't he? You don't think he's in any real danger?'

'As I said to you before, it's always very hard to say in these situations, but my instinct, like yours, is still that your wife will be doing everything in her power to look after the baby and keep him safe.'

Juliet was getting worried about – how strange. She couldn't think of the baby's name. It was extraordinary; how could she have forgotten? And she noticed that when she tried to remember his birth she couldn't somehow picture it. She *had* given birth, hadn't she? Well, obviously, she must have. It was all very confused in her mind. Simon. That was it, wasn't it? Anthony had wanted him to be called Simon. Yes, of course. And now she could see the delivery room; Anthony was smiling, saying something about how excellent she was, or the baby was, or something. He'd looked so proud and pleased.

But now she felt anxious about Simon. He'd gone so quiet, and he had a sort of floppy look which made her frightened. She hadn't thought it would be like this; it had all sounded so easy. Where was Anthony? Why didn't he come? She had told him where to find her, hadn't she? She had seen him coming for her only last night, hadn't she? Suddenly she couldn't remember. Why did it all seem so mixed up? She felt suddenly angrier than she could ever remember feeling. Why did everyone have to make things so difficult? Michael knew she hated the dark; why was he leaving her here like this? She reached over from where she was lying next to the baby and pulled another bottle of milk from the holdall. She wasn't sure it still smelt too good, but as she pushed the rubber teat into his mouth he sucked greedily at it, and she lay back again on the rug and closed her eyes while she kept the bottle still held in one hand.

Anthony's face appeared again before her, as it always did when she closed her eyes. He was smiling at her. She could see how much he loved her, just by the way he was looking down at her. 'I love you,' he whispered, 'I need you, I love you, darling.'

'I know, I know,' Juliet whispered back. 'I know you do.'

Her anger lifted and she laughed out loud, jerking her hand as she shook. Simon gave a small whimper beside her.

Anthony frowned. 'What's that?'

'It's the baby of course, darling. It's our baby.'

'What do you mean *our baby*?'

'It's our baby, the one we lost. It's Simon. It's all right now, it's fine, I've got him back.' Why was Anthony looking so angry now? Why was he making that ugly shape with his mouth and looking away from her? 'What's the matter, darling? What is it? Oh don't, Anthony, I'm frightened, why are you looking like that? What's wrong?'

'You silly bitch!' He was leaning back down towards her now, staring at her again and whispering fiercely,

'That was Michael's baby, that was your fucking husband's baby, wasn't it? We agreed about all of that, didn't we? This isn't mine, either, is it? IS IT?'

Why was his face so big? It didn't even look like Anthony any more; it looked like her mother. The head was too red, it was frightening her, she didn't like it, she wanted Michael. No, no, not Michael, it was Anthony she wanted; she wanted Anthony back. 'Don't, don't, please!'

The face was even bigger now, a few inches from her own, the male mother spitting the words out at her. 'You stupid little bitch, you lazy, stupid, fat little bitch.'

'Who are you?' she cried out loud. 'Who are you? Where's Anthony? Anthony's coming, leave me alone, Anthony loves me, he needs me, Anthony's coming.'

The face leant even further down towards her, until she could smell skin.

Juliet screamed.

Simon turned his head and moaned.

Anna's room seemed smaller at night. The curtains were closed against the window and the light of the standard lamp was thrown on to the floor by a dark yellow shade that reminded Michael of his father's study at home. He sat on the sofa with his arms resting on his knees, head bent down looking at the floor, while he talked quietly and gently to the tense and worn-looking girl in front of him. Without looking up, he was aware of her sitting anxiously forward in her chair, all her energy focused on listening, as if with enough concentration she would understand everything, and it would all fall into place. Her hands were clasped in front of her, a damp, screwed-up tissue showing in the hollow between the palms, the sleeves of the old blue chenille dressing gown she wore falling over her wrists and making her look younger and more vulnerable than ever.

'And we'd tried for so long, you see, so very long. I don't suppose I realised just how much it all affected her. I should have been more tolerant, I realise that now, but I just didn't understand.'

'I see, yes, I do see,' Anna answered. It came out as a whispered croak; tight and rusty; seared by too much crying, and Michael gave a little instinctive clearing of his throat as though helping her to find her voice.

'I can tell now that everything that happened was part of an illness, really. I should have been more sensible, I got upset, though, and I didn't keep control of the situation as I should have. I blame myself dreadfully for what's happened, I should have been looking after her more.'

'You can't blame yourself. You can't afford that luxury. That's one thing the police have helped me to understand.' Her voice was clearer now, but still hoarse and strained. 'If you think you feel guilty, believe me, you haven't even started. I thought I'd go mad for the first few hours after he went. How could I have left him like that? How *could* I? I didn't even want to survive. It's only knowing how much he needs me that's keeping me going. Of course you're to blame, of course I am — so what? All that matters is finding him. I don't give a shit about anything else. I won't blame you, I won't even fucking blame your wife, I won't do anything. I just want to get him back and I shall never, never let him out of my sight again. *Ever*.'

Michael surprised himself by feeling a jolt of shock at her language, and glanced up at her. How tough she looked, like a cornered animal protecting its young; the little girl he had seen out of the corner of his eye shown now to be an illusion. This was no child; this was no vulnerable innocent needing help and reassurance: he saw in her a primitive and basic instinct for survival that was more than adult in its intensity.

'Anyway, I just wanted to apologise really,' she said, 'I treated you badly yesterday and I shouldn't have.'

'You don't have to say that.'

'I know. I wanted to. It was kind of you to come and see me – and brave too – and I shouldn't have let go at you the way I did.'

'Please, you mustn't —'

'No. *Let* me say I'm sorry. I've enough to worry about without upsetting you even more. I *am* sorry. Now, let me get you a cup of coffee or something. I haven't got any drink I'm afraid.'

'You don't have to get me anything – I'm OK.'

'Look, I'm nearly going mad here. I'm not even sure I'm real any more. For Christ's sake let me do something normal, let me make you a coffee, for fuck's sake. Sorry.'

'Yes, thanks, yes that's fine. Just black with one sugar.'

124

Dinner with Juliet's mother followed the same pattern every time. As Michael and Juliet changed – even though her mother had reluctantly had to abandon the formality of black tie she still expected a minimum of lounge suit and smart frock – the evening inevitably began with Juliet's rhetorical but demanding question, 'Why are we going?'

This time was no different.

'No, really, Michael, I mean why *are* we going?' she said, as she sat at the dressing table fastening her necklace. 'You know how I hate it, why do I let her do this to me? She could always get me to go to places *she* wanted, even when I was at school. When I think of all the ballets she dragged me to, just because she thought I ought to like it. Somehow it always felt like my fault that I was bored stiff. I really don't want to go, you know. Do you think we could ring and make an excuse?'

'Come on, darling, you know we can't. It'll be all right. She really does love to see you; just relax a little – she gets you so wound up. Feeling OK? You're not sick or anything?'

'No, no, I'm feeling good. It's not that. It's just her smug, irritating attitude – God, I don't have to tell you, surely. You know how she gets me going. I can't think why I always give in. I'm turning into my father, you know, that's what's happening. Now she hasn't got him to drag all over the place, she's using me instead.'

'Don't be silly, darling. She's not nearly as bad as you paint her. I'm really quite fond of the old bat.'

Juliet looked suddenly serious for a moment. 'You

don't know anything. How dare you say that? You don't know what I went through.'

'Yes, I do. We've been over it a thousand times.'

'But I tell you, you'll never really understand. She was the one who put me in those hospitals, Michael, she —'

'Yes, yes, Julie, I know. Now, don't get in one of your states. You're really overreacting, darling, we're only going to dinner, for God's sake. Just get this one done and we needn't see her for a bit. She can't hurt you now.'

'I wouldn't be so sure.'

Michael smiled at her. 'Don't be so melodramatic.' Then he took her by the shoulders and smiled again. 'You look completely wonderful in that outfit, darling. You're gorgeous and I love you.'

It was true Juliet was looking particularly glowing. She had put on a straight black velvet skirt topped with a boned black silk strapless top which pushed up her neat white breasts into semicircular mounds either side of the pearls she wore, like two little moons half eclipsed by the dark curves of the material. She had twisted her hair up into a sleekly pinned coil and Michael leant over and kissed the back of her neck.

'Let's go and do battle,' he said. 'I wonder what scintillating guest she's dug up for us this time. It can't be any worse than the American stockbroker.'

'No, it wasn't stockbroking, he was something in property, wasn't he?'

'Oh yes, I think you're right. Anyway, he holds the boredom record. She'll never top that one.'

'Don't bet on it,' she laughed. 'Mummy has hidden depths of talent; reserves of energy for creating the dinner party from hell that can *always* top the last one. I think she keeps these people in a cupboard somewhere. I can't believe they function anywhere outside her gatherings, they'd have been murdered years ago, surely. She keeps them filed on different shelves I expect. Dull, boring, super-boring and mind-blowing.'

'Just when you thought it was safe to go back in the dining room.'

'OK,' Juliet sighed. 'Let's get it over with. Dear Mama — here we come.'

Mrs Cynthia Palmer (since being widowed at the age of sixty-eight she had, correctly, insisted on reinstating her own Christian name in any correspondence) lived in a flat in a large, well-maintained service block in St John's Wood. Michael always felt a slight sense of unreality as he walked into the marble-floored, halogen-lit hallway, to be greeted with a nod and smile, tinged with an almost imperceptible edge of superiority, from the immaculately uniformed porter. The small lift, furnished like a tiny drawing room with red embossed wallpaper and a gilt-framed picture of grazing cattle squeezed on to one wall, took them to the third floor, where Juliet's mother waited in the narrow gap between the old-fashioned metal lift gates and her open front door. It always amused Michael and Juliet that Cynthia insisted on coming out of her flat to welcome them effusively in this particularly awkward space, where the three of them would invariably entangle with each other and the heavy lift gates while attempting to kiss cheeks and exchange greetings before eventually moving into the marginally less cramped conditions of the flat's own hallway.

'Darling, you're looking absolutely wonderful!' she beamed at Juliet, who was edging her way out of the lift past her mother's dauntingly large bosom. 'And Michael, dear, you're well, too, I see. I'm absolutely thrilled you've both made it, because there's someone I particularly want — oh, sorry darling, mind the — oops, sorry — there's someone I particularly — damn that's my shawl, can you just open the gate a bit again, Michael dear? That's it, thank you — yes, I was saying, there's someone — oh, what lovely perfume, Juliet darling, is it a new one? Now do come in, both of you.'

The stream of chatter didn't slow until they had moved from the lift, through the narrow hall — negotiating their way gingerly past the wobbly marble table covered with little silver boxes and china cherubs — and into the small, warmly lit sitting room. In the visual confusion of the ornament-encrusted room it took Michael a few moments to register the small man, dressed in a dusty-looking black suit, attempting to prise himself out of a velvet-covered armchair in one corner. Michael knew that chair only too well; it had been so heavily depressed over the years by Cynthia's not inconsiderable bottom that the springs had long since abandoned any attempt at normal suspension, and the seat now almost touched the floor, creating a deep bowl of velvet into which guests would innocently lower themselves, unaware of the feat of strength it would take for them to get out again.

Michael moved quickly across the red Persian carpet towards the struggling figure and held out his hand: 'Oh, please don't bother to get up. I'm Michael, Cynthia's son-in-law, and this is my wife Juliet.'

'This is Henry Pulford, a good friend of mine, Michael,' added Cynthia. 'Michael, can I get you a sherry, or will you have a gin and tonic?'

'A sherry, please, Cynthia.'

The look of relief on Mr Pulford's face as he allowed himself to relax back into the red depths of the chair was immediate. 'How do you do?' he smiled at Michael, reaching forward and upwards to shake hands. 'I'm very pleased to meet you. And you, Juliet. Your mother has been telling me all about you both.'

Juliet, in turn, leant over and grasped the dry, cool hand and smiled back down at him. 'Yes, I can imagine,' she said. 'I hope she hasn't been boring you with our entire family history.'

'Not at all,' Mr Pulford answered. 'In fact I think we may have quite a lot in common. Your mother tells me you have quite an interest in —'

'Juliet darling, do sit down — you shouldn't be standing so much you know. Put your feet up, darling, and

I'll get you an orange juice or something. Or would you like a glass of milk?'

Her mother's capacity to interrupt someone in mid-sentence without any apparent awareness of the havoc she invariably caused in the conversational process never failed to take Juliet's breath away, although she had long ago ceased trying either to point out this fault or to persevere with the original thread of dialogue. Any attempt at ignoring the interruption would simply result in her mother repeating the offending phrase, in progressively loud tones, until she was answered. Both Juliet and Michael had come to accept that it was simpler, and ultimately less destructive to the other participants, to abandon any attempt at conversational flow, and simply negotiate the sharp turns involved with as much control of the route as possible.

'I'll have some mineral water, please, Mummy, if you've got some,' answered Juliet, annoyed that her mother should assume on her behalf that she would not want to risk drinking even a small amount of alcohol, and even more annoyed that she was right.

'Yes, I was saying,' continued Mr Pulford, 'I think we share a common int —'

'Fizzy or non-fizzy?'

'Fizzy, please, Mummy.'

'—we've got quite a lot in common. I believe you are interested in minerals, Juliet, and —'

'Do you want ice? I've got some in the tray thing, if you want some?'

'Yes, OK. Thanks.'

Michael sensed from Mr Pulford's smooth handling of the imposed breaks in his attempt at an opening gambit that he was no stranger to Cynthia's company, and that, far from being offended, he had already become adept at keeping his train of thought retained in a sort of temporary limbo until able to re-release it on command. As he saw Pulford opening his mouth to go for a fourth attempt, Michael found himself toying with the pleasingly suitable phrase 'suspended sentence', and stored it away to amuse Juliet with once they got home.

'I am a geologist, or used to be. I'm semi-retired now. Your mother tells me you have quite an interest in minerals?'

Juliet turned and sat on a small square pouffe in front of the gas log fire. 'You really couldn't possibly call it an *interest*, I'm afraid. I think my mother's been exaggerating a bit — Mummy, whatever did you mean about me and minerals?' she called into the kitchen. After a brief wait, filled only with the distant sound of an ice tray being violently hit against a hard surface, she continued: 'I suppose she's thinking of the little plastic boxes of stones and rocks I used to keep in my room — some of them were from the Science Museum I think, when we went on a school trip. I don't even think I could remember half the names, now.'

'Well, it's actually a fascinating subject.'

Michael saw an evening of fossils and quartzes stretching ahead. As he rose to move to the kitchen to collect the drinks he surprised himself by realising that he was looking forward to it.

Chapter Ten

Anna was starting to cry. Very quietly, almost as if she were unaware of it, a small sob escaped from her throat and a tear spilled over from one of her brimming, glittering eyes and made its way down the side of her nose. She continued talking while she rubbed at it with the crumpled tissue, making an even redder patch in the blotchiness of her skin. Michael watched her as she talked on, curbing his instinctive desire to rush forward and cradle the distraught girl in his arms, knowing that he must continue to listen to every word, that only by allowing the misery and guilt to flow up like bile through her body and out of her mouth could he be of any help to her.

'He's all I have, you see. All I have. I shouldn't have left him, even for that minute – I know what people think of me. I don't care. I know how they look at me. But I'm not a bad mother to him – I'm not what they think. Now they'll take him away; they'll say they were right. They are right. I left him. But it was only a minute you see, I just can't think how I – I've never done anything like that before, I haven't really. I loathe myself.'

As she whispered on and on, Michael looked at her young, ravaged face and wondered how anyone could survive such an onslaught of unhappiness. He felt strangely close to her, almost as if he had known her before somewhere, and he sensed that he was probably the only person in the world that she could talk to in this way. He knew he could never tell her the whole truth about what had been going on during the last few months, but he wanted to try a little more to explain the instinctive empathy he felt with her.

He leant forward and placed a hand gently over one of hers. 'I told you that Juliet and I have been trying for a baby for years now,' he said earnestly, 'and we've been through some very bad times over the last twelve months or so. It doesn't in any way excuse the terrible thing she's done, of course, but I suppose what I'm trying to tell you is that I feel in some way that I have lost a child, too. Because of some of the things that have happened to us, I know now I shall never have the son I always thought I would – and I don't say that because of self-pity, Miss Watkins—'

'Oh for Christ's sake, call me Anna, this is—'

'All right, Anna, of course, and you will call me Michael won't you? You see, Anna, I only say it because the loss of Harry – and I know it's only for a very short while, I do believe that very strongly, you must believe that too, Anna – the loss of Harry somehow means much much more to me than seems rational. When I said yesterday about knowing him — and I can't think now how I could have been so thoughtless . . .'

'Oh, don't, it was nothing, I was just—'

'No, it was a ridiculous thing to say. But — I can't explain it — I feel I've lost him too. I'm sorry, I'm not explaining this very well, it's hard to put into words. I feel the most extraordinary sense of loss, not only because of Julie — that's frightening, of course, and very distressing, but because of Harry. I like to think I may be one of the few people who understands what you're going through. And, Anna, I know it's going to be all right.'

She looked straight at him for a moment, then suddenly buried her head in her arms and burst into loud, heaving, heart-rending sobs.

'Do you never drink, Juliet?'

Mr Pulford was accepting another glass of Puligny Montrachet as he spoke. Juliet lifted her own glass of water with a wry smile: 'Oh, yes, indeed I do. I'm very fond of wine, in fact, and I do miss my evening glass or two very much.'

There was a small pause, with the implied question hanging in the air for a moment.

'I'm trying to get pregnant, you see.'

Juliet's mother gave a small, nervous laugh, which Juliet ignored as she continued: 'Some people think it may be a good thing not to drink alcohol even before you conceive, you see, Mr Pulford, or in the early stages of pregnancy; and as Michael and I want to give this every possible chance I thought it better to lay off altogether for a bit.'

'Ah, yes, indeed. Still, you're having jolly good fun while you're trying anyway I daresay; keep practising, and you're bound to get it right eventually!' Mr Pulford had used this very phrase only the other day when talking to his nephew and recently acquired wife when hearing of their plans to start a family, and it had gone down extremely well, producing a roguish wink of understanding from his nephew and a satisfying fit of giggling from the young lady. He couldn't understand why it now met with such an unappreciative and humourless reception.

'Hah!' volunteered Mrs Palmer, as if in triumph.

'I beg your pardon, Mummy?'

'Nothing dear. I was only thinking what a funny business it all is, in my opinion.'

Mr Pulford suddenly had the feeling he had stumbled on something rather more than he had bargained for, and attempted diversionary tactics by beating a hasty verbal retreat.

'My nephew and his —'

'What do you mean, funny business, Mummy?'

'Oh, nothing, dear, I'm sure it's all perfectly marvellous, but it just does seem a bit — well, *unnatural*, if you know what I mean.'

'My nephew has recently —'

'Mr Pulford, I must explain, as my mother is obviously rather embarrassed about it all. Michael and I can't conceive naturally, so we've been on the IVF programme for a few weeks.'

Mr Pulford looked a little nonplussed.

'Test tubes and all that.'

'Ah. I see!'

'Test tubes,' muttered Mrs Palmer darkly, 'quite extraordinary. There certainly wasn't anything like that in my day.'

'My mother doesn't really approve, Mr Pulford,' said Juliet quietly. 'I don't want to embarrass you, but there's no point in pretending otherwise; she thinks it was somehow meant that we shouldn't have children and —'

'Juliet, that's complete nonsense,' interrupted her mother. 'It isn't that at all. I just don't think this testtube business can be quite right somehow; it doesn't seem natural, that's all I'm saying.'

'Yes, I know, Mummy, that's what you keep saying. I don't know what you mean by it. I don't know at what point your God, or your molecules, or your genes or whatever else it is that you think is planning your life draws the line and decides it's "not natural". And I don't know exactly how you are privy to that knowledge and what makes you so certain of it. Or how you can be sure that your personal index of what is and isn't "natural" should also apply to *my* life. Who gives you the guidelines? How do you put together your list of *natural* events?'

'There's no need to be rude, Juliet. After all, I've supported you through this extraordinary business. And with your medical history I'd have thought you'd be the first one to know about being sensible, and not mucking about with your body. Remember I was there, through all those ghastly years; just remember who looked after you. I think I've every right to say how I feel. It's not just me, you know, I'm not the only one who thinks you should let Nature take its course, I've read many artic —'

'Is it *natural* for you to dye your hair?' Juliet was leaning forward intensely, raising her voice. 'Was your hysterectomy *natural*? Was it *natural* for you and Daddy to have separate rooms after I was born? Was it —'

'Julie, really, that's enough.' Michael put a hand on her arm as he spoke. 'Don't, darling, just don't.'

'Was it *natural* the way they fed me in the hospital? You allowed that. It was you! Yes, you were there, all right, you bet you were. Who was it always told me how overweight I was? Who kept telling me how ugly I was? Oh yes, Mummy, you certainly were there. Don't forget, I've been through all those therapists, counsellors, I've been told only too clearly where the root of my anorexia lies. Just be careful, Mummy, just be careful . . .'

'Look, I really think I should make a move.'

Mr Pulford began to rise awkwardly from his chair, but Michael put out a restraining hand and encouraged him to sit down again. 'Don't worry. It's all right. I'm sorry about all this.'

'Yes, I'm so sorry,' added Mrs Palmer, 'I'm afraid my daughter gets a bit over-sensitive. It's a difficult time for her at the moment. She doesn't mean most of the things she says in this mood. Please don't go, Henry, I do apologise.'

Juliet turned towards him, and her eyes softened and lost their intensity for a moment, 'Yes, I'm sorry too. I don't mean to be rude – I'm sorry, Mummy, I'm sorry. I just want you to understand so badly. What came so naturally, as you put it, to you and Daddy, and to millions of people all over the world, didn't happen to me and Michael. If we let Nature take its course we would never have children; I know that now. Is that natural? Is there some natural law that says I should never feel a baby growing inside me? That I should never let a baby suck milk from my breast, cry in my arms, smile as I rock it to sleep? Should Michael never watch his son play football, go fishing with him, kiss him goodnight? Yes, you can smile, Mummy; they may be clichés, but it's what we want. We want a little girl in pink ballet shoes who plays with dolls; we want a little boy with a train set; we want babies in pink, babies in blue, a son at university, a daughter getting married in white. I can't help it, I can't help what I want. I don't ask for anything special, I just want what you've all got. I won't complain if my children aren't clever, or beautiful or successful; just let them *be*, oh dear God, please, please, just give them a chance to be. Is it Nature's plan that Michael and I should be alone for the rest of our lives?'

She stopped for a moment and looked round the table at each of the others in turn. Her mother made as if to speak, but appeared to have second thoughts and raised her napkin to her mouth instead and wiped it delicately.

Juliet leant towards her and went on, in a voice taut with the effort of genuine communication. 'Mummy, listen to me. I need to have a baby so badly I sometimes think I shall go mad with it; I dream I have a baby in my arms, that I'm kissing his sweet face, that I can smell him, see his smile, taste his tears, dress him, wake him in his cot, change his nappy – just hold him. I can feel his round arms, I can feel his cheek as I bury my face in his neck.

'Do you know what it's like to wake from such dreams? I once read that for a person who's lost the use of their arms and legs in an accident the worst thing is the dreams. You dream you're running, or walking, or making love; then wake to find you can't move. I feel like that. You can tell me I'm selfish and ungrateful, that I shouldn't dare to put myself even for a moment in the same position as a person who can never walk again, but that's how I feel when I wake from *my* dreams. As if I've lost something so important, so vital, that I'm incomplete, that there's no point in my going on, that something has been torn from me and killed, hurt, finished. I don't expect you ever to understand, but I wish – oh God, how I wish – that you'd try. Don't you think I hate myself enough for having to try and conceive in this horrible, humiliating, sordid way? I don't need you to despise it, Mummy, I can do that for myself.'

There was complete silence.

Michael was watching Juliet, aware that much of what she had said was in him too, that she had, more than she knew, spoken for both of them.

Mrs Palmer sat up, took a little rehabilitating breath, then turned brightly to Henry Pulford, who appeared to be concentrating intently on following the pattern round the edge of his wine coaster with one fingernail.

'Now, how about some more casserole?'

'Hi, is that Chris? Chris, it's Michael. Look, it's about Lucy, sorry to let you know so late but I don't think she's well enough to go. No, she's in the hall. I'm sure she's waiting for you, she always knows the time, doesn't she?'

As Michael talked to the friend who minded Lucy for them, he lifted the phone and moved to the kitchen doorway where he could see her still, quiet body lying on the carpet by the front door. 'I took her to the vet last night and he thinks she's had a minor stroke. Let's leave it for today and I'll pop back every now and then from work.'

He apologised to Chris again, put down the phone, walked into the hall and called up the staircase: 'Julie? Jules, where are you?'

'I'm up here. In the bedroom.'

'Are you all right, darling?'

The wait over the last twelve days had been interminable. Now that the time for a result had almost arrived, Michael found himself constantly checking on Juliet's wellbeing and condition, almost unable to hold himself back from demanding hourly bulletins.

'Yes, I'm fine, why? I'm just coming down. What did you decide about Lucy?'

'I don't think she's well enough to go. She's looking very odd. I've rung Chris and put him off.'

'Well, I can't stay here, I've got a couple of meetings later and I've promised to be in the office most of the day.'

'No, it's all right, I'll be able to keep an eye on her. Do you think I ought to take her round to the clinic again?'

'No, I should – look, hang on, I can't keep shouting, I'll be down in a minute.'

Michael heard Lucy give a breathy grunt, and walked quickly over to kneel down beside her. The dog was breathing steadily, but her eyes were half closed, and the pupils tilted upwards into her head so that only the whites were showing. As Juliet came down the stairs, Michael told her, 'She really doesn't look good, I think we ought to take her over there again.'

Juliet also knelt down, and tilted her head sideways to look into Lucy's face. 'No, she doesn't, does she? I don't think we should move her, though. What time is it? I really must go in a minute. I'll just give them a ring first.'

As she stood up and moved towards the kitchen, Michael kept muttering, 'Poor old girl, poor old girl.'

Something in the way he said it made Juliet glance at him, and she was startled by the tenderness on his face.

He'd always been so brisk with Lucy, so conventionally masterful and controlled that it was quite unnerving to see this exposed emotion. Juliet found it oddly disturbing. The air of mortality, sadness and sentimentality that clung round man and dog stirred up twinges of dread in her. But she knew that if she indulged herself in wallowing in this sad scene on the hall carpet there was no telling what unfaced horrors would be conjured up; and she had to float above it with her usual mixture of efficiency and practicality or be doomed.

'There's nothing more we can do here at the moment,' she said. 'Michael, do get up, I'm sure she'd like a bit of breathing space.'

But Michael didn't want to leave her. As Juliet briskly picked up the phone, he stayed squatting down next to Lucy and stroked one silky ear carefully, feeling the warmth of her skin and a slight sluggish pulsing underneath. 'Poor old girl,' he repeated, and thought of all the times she had leapt up at his homecoming in this hall, the undeserved total devotion she had shown him ever since they had taken her over.

He could hear Julie now, using her customary tone of patient bossiness with the young receptionist at the veterinary clinic.

'No, I'm afraid we can't bring her over. I've already explained she's extremely unwell and any more lugging about would be out of the question. Couldn't you —' she broke off to listen, then gave an exaggerated sigh of quiet exasperation, 'Yes, yes all right. Yes, I see. Thank you.'

She raised her voice as she put down the phone and crossed over to fill the kettle. 'She says the vet'll ring us in a minute and try to come round. He's in the middle of an operation apparently. I guess I can wait a few more minutes anyway. Do you want a cup of coffee? Michael? Michael, I said do you want a coffee?'

Juliet frowned and walked back towards the hall, but stopped abruptly in the doorway of the kitchen. Michael still sat on the carpet, his head buried in the thick coat of the dog's back, his arm protectively cradling her head.

'Oh for God's sake, Mike, do get up. Give the poor animal some air — you're not doing her any good lying all over her like that.'

'She's gone.' Michael's voice was muffled and indistinct. 'She's dead, Julie.'

As he lifted his head and looked up at her, she could see Lucy's tongue lolling sideways out of her mouth. She didn't know what to say. 'Are you sure?'

'Yes. She gave a few sort of shudders and tried to get up — then she just . . . stopped.'

'I'd better go and tell the vet — put him off coming.'

But as Juliet made for the phone, she was suddenly hit by the most desperate sadness. It was like a blow to the throat, and without warning she let out a loud and violent sob that wrenched itself so unexpectedly from her body that she grabbed the frame of the door to steady herself.

'Julie, are you all right?'

'It's just so sad, that's all. It's so sad.'

'I know, darling. But she didn't suffer, did she? She had a good life. Poor old girl.'

'What do we do now?'

'I don't know. We'd better stop the vet coming, though, like you said. Do you want me to ring him?'

'No, I'll do it. I'm OK, I'll do it.'

Juliet dialled the vet's number and got the same receptionist as before. 'Hello, this is Mrs Evans, I spoke to you a moment ago. I'm afraid everything's changed, we won't need Mr Archer any more . . . No, she's dead . . . Yes – the dog. Well, of course the dog, who else do you think I'm talking about? Sorry . . . so, really I need to know what we do now . . . What, Yellow Pages, you mean? Right, thanks for your help. Yes, thanks . . . goodbye.'

She bent down and picked up the large London Central Yellow Pages from the shelf below the telephone and carried it out into the hall. 'Apparently usually they'd come over and collect her, but they haven't got anyone available. There should be a service that can come round though. What do you think I look it up under? Dogs – Dead? Animal bodies – Disposal? Animal Funerals, or what?'

'God knows.' Michael was smiling at his wife, aware just how much pain her cool cynicism was hiding. 'Try Cremations – Canine.'

'Oh, don't be silly, Michael,' she laughed back at him. 'Here we are, Animal Services . . . I'll try this lot. Hold on.'

Michael could hear the faint digital tones as she dialled

a number, then the slam of the receiver back down on its cradle. 'Oh, this is ridiculous,' he heard her mutter, then she reappeared. 'Look, let's take her round to Archer's ourselves. That's the best thing. We can't stay here all day sitting with a dead dog, for heaven's sake. And I'm sure those people charge a fortune.'

'Yes, OK, Julie, you're right. Fetch the blanket out of my car and we'll wrap her in that.'

Chapter Eleven

'Are you sure you should be doing this, darling?' As they lifted the dead weight of Lucy's hairy frame on to the car rug, Michael glanced up at Julie anxiously.

'It's OK. She doesn't feel heavy like this.'

They carried the awkward bundle out of the front door and on to the top step. Juliet had always hated the wide, pillared stone entrance with its pretentious promise of an interior far bigger and grander than the rather modest hall on to which it opened, and now the steps seemed steeper and more daunting than ever as they hauled the dog's body down them and towards the car.

'Hang on, darling,' said Michael, 'I'll just have to get the keys out of my pocket. Can you manage her for a second? Look, prop her up against the bumper — that's it.'

He unlocked the boot of the blue hatchback and began to pull up the door. As he did so, a corner caught on the fringe of the Gordon tartan rug and the large, still warm parcel began to tip ominously towards the asphalt surface of the road.

'Oh, help! Michael — she's going to unroll, for Christ's sake — quick! Catch the corner of the—'

Michael let the boot door slam down again and lunged to catch the top of the bundle as it fell. 'OK, OK I've got her. Darling, can you open the boot again? I think the rug's shut in it. That's it, well done. Now, let's lift her in.'

Juliet checked that the door of the boot was safely opened to its upper limit, then stooped to lift the other end of the rug-wrapped dog. 'God, she does seem heavy now,' she said, as she tried to slide her hands further beneath the weight.

'I know,' answered Michael. 'Are you sure you're OK? I can probably manage her.'

'No, it's fine.'

'OK, now when I say *go*. One, two, three — go!'

Moving together, they managed to haul the bundle over the raised lip of the boot space and on to the rubber-lined interior. Juliet walked round and slipped into the front passenger seat as Michael tucked the ends of the rug in and closed up.

'Are you sure you want to come? I can perfectly well do this on my own,' he said, as he stooped to sit in the driving seat next to her.

She turned her head and smiled at him. 'Thanks, but no, I'd like to come. I don't feel I've quite said goodbye, if you know what I mean. Anyway, I don't feel like being on my own.'

The vet's smart little Georgian house was only ten minutes' drive away, and they were able to find a place to stop on a single yellow line immediately outside. Juliet opened the glove compartment and pulled out the small paper pad and pencil she kept handy for just this purpose, and scribbled a note '*Visiting vet — back 5 mins*' which she tucked behind the plastic case of the resident's parking permit on the front windscreen. As Michael opened the boot, she came round the back of the car and grabbed one end of the rug.

'I think if we carry it like a hammock it'll be easier,' she said. 'You take the other end there and we can sort of sling it between us.'

'All right, darling, let's go.'

Holding the gathered-up edges of the rug in one hand, Michael locked the car with the other, then together they made their way up the front steps of the vet's and pressed the bell. A buzzer sounded as the automatic door release was pressed from the inside, and they heaved their weighty burden over the threshold. As they moved through into the waiting room, Michael glanced up and for a split second lost his balance. The hammock tipped slightly to one side, and suddenly Lucy's large, lolling head slipped out of one end and hung out, tipped backwards as if the neck was broken, eyes half open and tongue protruding grotesquely.

'Bring her through here, Mr Evans,' said the white-coated nurse sharply from the doorway at the other side of the room.

As he obediently began the trek across the space between, Michael became aware of the row of quietly waiting clients in the chairs against one wall. An elderly lady in skirt and cardigan with a shivering Yorkshire terrier on her knee; a large, red-faced man with a wicker basket on the chair next to him, out of which a black cat peered ferociously; a couple holding a large cage between them, in which a hamster relentlessly trod its endless, squeaking wheel.

A small yelp made Michael look round, and he quickly registered three or four more people, each sitting with an animal on or next to them, and all gazing at Lucy's protruding head with the same look of fascinated horror.

'Can I give you a hand, Mr Evans?' asked the nurse, with a hint of desperation, as she moved towards him.

Michael glanced round once more and suddenly felt the urge to giggle. The outraged audience clutched their assorted charges tightly to them, pulling in their knees and pursing their mouths, as if trying to edge as far as possible away from the reminder passing through their midst of their own pets' final destination.

'Sorry,' whispered Michael breathily to the nurse, 'not really the best advertisement for your services, is it? Carrying a large, dead dog right through the waiting room?'

Juliet caught the slight quiver in his voice and looked across at him; then she too suddenly saw the funny side of it and brought a hand quickly up to her mouth to stifle a laugh. This left her holding her end of the package with only the remaining hand, which threatened its precarious balance even more.

Just as Lucy's tail began to emerge from Juliet's end of the rug and threaten to flop on to the floor, the nurse rushed forward, tucked it in and took firm control, hurrying the little procession out of the waiting room and into the surgery at the back.

By the time they emerged from the house, Michael and Juliet were in hysterics. Finding a parking ticket on the bonnet of the car merely made them laugh even more.

'Oh, God,' said Juliet, wiping her eyes with a tissue as she still gulped with the effort to stop laughing. 'Did you see the couple with the hamster? I thought they were going to explode. They looked so indignant, as if we were parading Lucy to make some sort of point or something. And the lady with the Yorkshire terrier looked absolutely terrified. Somehow I don't think we'll be very welcome at that vet's again.'

'I know,' said Michael. 'Now let's get home. Do you really have to go to work, darling? Why don't you ring them and take the day off? Tell them you've had a bereavement.'

This produced another burst of giggling, which continued on and off until they reached the house.

'Now,' said Michael as they walked into the kitchen, 'where's that coffee you offered me? How are you feeling, darling?'

'Wonderful,' beamed Juliet, 'I can't think why, but just wonderful.'

The next morning, as Juliet stepped into the bath, she felt blood trickling warmly down the inside of her thigh.

Andrea was sitting behind her chrome and melamine desk at Chewton PR in Baker Street, swivelling on her bright blue stress-reducing patented executive chair and thinking about tomatoes. The competition plans were going well, and having presented Middlesex Foods with a list of five possible charities, she was making a start on drafting a press release, attempting to link the three aspects – pizza, prizes and do-gooding – into one telling headline. She was pleased that the client had opted for the blind children – or the visually impaired, as she was trying hard to learn to call them. She wasn't sure just how much she could capitalise on the angle that particularly pleased her: she liked to think that those in whom one sense is non-existent or not up to par, as with these youngsters, must surely develop heightened awareness in the other four, with particular reference, from Andrea's point of view, to the sense of *taste*. She scrawled idly with a pencil on the pink pad in front of her. 'They may not be able to see – but you can help them to a great taste!' and 'They don't need to look to know it's great pizza!' Much as they pleased her, she knew that such phrases would never get past the charity officials, so she tried to temper her natural enthusiasm for a tie-up of ideas and concentrated instead on more subtle wording. She began a list of possible useful material, and had got as far as 'sight', 'insight', 'topping toppings' and the pedestrian but ever-popular 'win a holiday for two', when the phone rang. 'Andrea Williams,' she answered, in what she liked to think was a suitably intriguing mixture of the businesslike and the warmly inviting, while she added 'light to their darkness' to the list with her free hand.

'Darling, it's me.'

'Hi!'

'Hi. Look, I'm going to stay a bit late so if you want to go ahead to Janet and Toby's do, I'll meet you there.'

'Sure. Everything OK?'

'Yup, it's fine. I've just got to chat to Juliet Evans — the one I was telling you about the other day. The embryos didn't take and apparently she wants to see me personally before she decides whether to start again.'

'Oh, OK.'

'Bob feels she needs to talk to someone today — it's hit her pretty badly I think. I'm in theatre this afternoon, so I've said I'll see her after that.'

'Why you? You don't usually come in at this stage do you?'

'Just my natural charm and skill, my love. No one else will do.'

'Of course, silly me.' Andrea laughed. 'I'll see you at Janet's, then.'

She sat for a moment after she had put the receiver

down, aware of how much she enjoyed manipulating Anthony. She felt no jealousy whatsoever of the patients who, every now and then, showed interest in the tall, attractive doctor. She was well aware of just how strongly the doctor-patient relationship could work as the equivalent of an aphrodisiac, and accepted the prospect of any infatuations that might develop in female clients, knowing that Anthony's need for her was strong enough to prevent him taking the risk of succumbing to temptation. Andrea was more aware than he knew of his buried insecurity, and liked to use her power over him by frightening him just a little with the thought that she *did* mind. There was an unspoken acknowledgement between them that he was the more dependent of the two on their partnership, which left her free to enjoy his love for her without feeling that she would necessarily always need it, whereas he felt he had made, unofficially, a lifetime commitment.

She sighed with the fun of it all as she scrawled, 'Keep your eye out for a new pizza topping!' on the pad.

'No, maybe not,' she said to herself as she reluctantly crossed it out.

'Now, Mrs Evans,' smiled Anthony across the desk in his second-floor office in the clinic, 'I quite understand how lost and disoriented you're feeling; it's only to be expected. You really should give yourself a few days to recover from the disappointment before you even begin to think about the future. You do know, don't you, just how many attempts end like this? Specially the first time? It's not really my particular area to counsel you about choices and so on, but I must stress how typical it is for the first try not to take, and—'

'How do you know it didn't take?' interrupted Juliet, staring at him intently.

'Well, I'm sorry, I rather gathered that . . .'

'No, I mean what makes you think that it didn't take, rather than that it *did* take and that I lost it? Did something to dislodge it?'

'You mustn't think that, Mrs Evans, you really mustn't. It won't be anything you've done, I can—'

'How do you know?'

'Well, I just know,' Anthony returned, feeling a little uncomfortable under the fierce gaze she was giving him, 'there's no doubt in my mind that as you began to bleed on the twelfth day, the embryos hadn't implanted.'

'I think it had. I think *one* of them had.'

'Look, Mrs Evans, it's a terribly common feeling among women who've had a failed attempt that they must have somehow caused an embryo to abort, but I do assure you that it just isn't the case. If the embryo had taken fully then I'm sure nothing you've done would have caused it to leave the womb. Just think of all the extraordinary things women get up to to try to rid themselves of unwanted pregnancies. I know that's hardly the sort of idea that you may wish to be listening to just now, but it really is relevant. People talk a lot about stress and health and so on, but I can assure you, half the population of the planet wouldn't exist if babies were that easy to dislodge. Do reassure yourself . . .'

'I can't. You see, our dog died and I was stupid enough to let my husband persuade me to lift her body into the car — and out again. She's very heavy. I knew I shouldn't, but my husband—'

'Please, please, you mustn't let this cause problems between you and your husband. The IVF programme is extremely stressful and difficult for you both, and you need each other's strength and support if you're going to continue with it. Whatever you do, don't start blaming each other for anything to do with these attempts. I've seen so many couples walk in here at the start of their treatment, happily facing it together, and then watched the strain come between them. Don't let that happen to you. I can only say again, Mrs Evans, categorically, that nothing you have done in this case will have started the bleeding. From all the evidence I would assume that unfortunately the embryos just didn't embed properly into the wall of your uterus. We still don't understand why they so often don't under these circumstances, but I am completely satisfied that's what happened in your case.'

'But you see, I *felt* pregnant. I really did. I didn't want to say it to anyone because it seemed like tempting fate, but I just felt different. I know I'm right. If only that bloody dog hadn't died—'

'Oh, *if only, if only*! Now, you know that's the one thing we never say here. That's just too easy. My advice to you is to go home and have a quiet evening with your husband, and not think at all about—'

'I don't know quite why you're pushing my husband at me so strongly all the time. Nor why you're so anxious to defend him, it's perfectly obvious to me that—'

'This isn't getting anywhere, Mrs Evans. I completely understand why you're so upset, it's only natural, but do please take my advice and put all this out of your mind as much as you can for a few days. Then, if you want to, come and see us again and we'll have another talk.'

Juliet looked at him for a moment. Throughout the conversation she had been watching and listening for the signal that she was waiting for, and knew that this was the moment when it might happen. She waited for a few seconds, thought of saying something, then smiled a little. If he was going to play it this way, she might as well go along with it. He still made himself crystal clear to her, and that was what mattered. 'I do wish you wouldn't use that word "natural" so much,' she said, 'you're beginning to sound like my mother.'

Anthony was relieved to see the smile softening the corners of her mouth. 'Quite right, Mrs Evans, not a word we tend to favour much around here, with all its misunderstood implications. Now, I hope you'll forget this nonsense about blaming someone – yourself *or* your husband – and concentrate on thinking about what you'd like to do next. When you're ready of course; take your time.'

'No, I've decided. I want to try again straightaway. I never had any doubt about that.'

'Don't you think you ought to discuss this with your husband first?'

'No, no, of course not, it doesn't — I mean, we have. We both feel the same. We want to try again. As soon as possible.'

'OK, Mrs Evans, just give the girls a ring in the morning and we'll sort out your schedule.'

'Thank you. And thank you for seeing me this evening — it's very kind of you. I'm sorry to have made you so late.'

'Not at all, don't worry. That's what we're here for. I'll see you out. Don't hesitate to get back in touch if you need me. I'll always be happy to see you.'

And there it was. Spoken at last.

Juliet's mind was whirring as she walked along Weymouth Street in the cold November air. She huddled her coat around herself and smiled, knowing now that what she had begun to suspect at the first egg collection three weeks ago was true. Now it wasn't only in a look held a fraction too long that he had let her know, it had been in his words as well. She almost laughed out loud; how clever he was not to let anyone else know; how she admired his restraint in the way he was handling it. He would not have to wait too much longer, she would make sure of that now.

'He said I should never have lifted Lucy into the car. He said I should have been more careful. Why didn't you stop me? I told you she was too heavy. I knew something like this would happen.'

'Oh, darling, that's awful. You mustn't feel like this, you mustn't blame yourself. Yes, you're right, I should never have let you lift her; but do remember, darling, that Professor Hewlett told us quite clearly that you should lead a completely normal life and that nothing you could do would cause th —'

'Well, I don't know how you're suddenly such an authority. I don't know why you think you know so much about babies. It was a stupid, stupid thing to do to lift her, and I shall always blame myself. I know I was pregnant; I just know it and now I've killed it. I shall never forgive myself.'

Juliet was trying to remember when she had last fed Simon. He was still sleeping, but a pool of foetid liquid was seeping out from under the coat. 'Can you change him, Michael?' she called out loud into the darkness of the room, then listened intently to the whisper she thought she heard in reply. 'What?' she whispered back, then 'What?' again, more loudly. 'Who is that? Michael, is it you? Can you change the baby? He smells. I don't like it. Oh God, *no*!' The face was back. The large, menacing, red face had burst into her vision suddenly from above, speaking horribly close to her and making her retch with its breath that smelt of shit.

'Shut up! Michael can't hear you. He isn't here,' it breathed down at her.

'Who are you?' Juliet asked it again, in a half-swallowed whisper. 'Please, please tell me who you are. Where's Anthony? Did he come? I thought I saw him. Please don't hurt me, I'm really sorry, just please, please don't hurt me.' She shuddered, then relaxed for a moment, then shuddered again, and this time it went on, becoming a protracted shiver that rattled her teeth and shook droplets of cold sweat down the sides of her face and into her ears.

Juliet knew someone was ill, but couldn't make out if it was herself or the baby. The face was still close to her, but seemed less unfriendly now, and she decided to appeal to it one last time. 'Can you help me? The baby needs changing and I don't think I feel very well. Could you put the light on and ask Michael to get me something to drink?'

Something was rustling in her ear now and she tried to turn to see what it was, but could only make out the pink blur of the baby's head. 'What is it?' she said to the sleeping infant, 'what do you want? Are you hungry? Is that you moving?'

The tiny form looked very still, and suddenly she heard the rustling again, but this time on her other side. It was a thick, warm sort of noise, and Juliet thought if she turned her head suddenly she might be able to catch whatever it was before it stopped again; but when she looked round there was nothing but the empty floor of the room, stretching from the unfocused foreground away to the dimness of the walls in the distance.

'It's something that you're doing, isn't it?' she whispered to the face that she felt sure was still hovering somewhere above her. 'I don't understand. I don't feel well. Stop the noise, please, I don't like it.'

Chapter Twelve

So the interminable round of tests and injections began again. Juliet and Michael settled back into their everyday work routine, dovetailing it with clinic visits, shopping and a minimum of socialising. The dog incident was never referred to again, although Michael felt sure he occasionally saw a flicker of reproach in Juliet's eyes when he caught her looking at him. But as her mood appeared to be one of quiet, positive satisfaction, he left well alone and referred to the treatment only when absolutely necessary. There was no discussion at all as they neared the time for egg collection, but Michael felt a dreary anticipation at the thought of facing the walls of the small room where his ejaculatory prowess would once more be on trial. Juliet had taken to coming straight home from work most days, no longer wanting to stray into the tantalising shops which had given her such unjustified but thrilling feelings a few weeks before, and too bound up in her inner thoughts to be distracted by anything external. It was more important than ever that this cycle of fertilisation was successful and, coupled with the secret knowledge that had to be contained just a little longer, she could think of nothing else. She still looked in on Harriet occasionally, but even her friend, with whom she was usually more relaxed than anyone else, found her less talkative and more serious than she remembered her being for a long time.

'Come on, darling, don't let them get you down!' Harriet beamed at her, as she poured tea for each of them. Juliet had arrived on her doorstep after an absence of several days, and Harriet immediately registered the mood her friend was in, sensing that to talk about anything other than the clinic, the injections or the latest scan, would be out of the question. Gossip about past acquaintances or bitching about Lauren or her ex would have to wait. When Juliet was like this she could think about nothing but herself, and Harriet willingly accepted her rôle as absorber of her friend's self-centred obsession, remembering clearly how, when the situation had been the reverse in the months after Peter had left her, Juliet had listened uncomplainingly to hour after hour of her own woes.

'You've only had one go, for pity's sake, let the old eggs have a chance. God, if you can produce five so easily, you must have thousands more brilliant ones just longing to be given a go. Chin up, old girl, no one said it was going to be easy. Remember, you're absolutely no worse off than you were when you started all this stuff. In fact, if anything I should think it's better now, because you know all the routine and so on, and you're bound to be more relaxed, don't you think? That must be good, surely?'

'Yes, I suppose so,' said Juliet. 'Although, no, I don't really think so — I only said that to try to agree with you, come to think of it. I don't actually believe that at all. It's supposed not to make any difference whether you're relaxed or not. One minute everyone's telling me nothing I can do will make any difference and I mustn't blame myself if things go wrong and all that, and then you're all saying that me being relaxed is going to be a help. You can't have it both ways, you know.'

'No, I suppose not. Sorry, Jules, I'm only trying to help. You really mustn't get so down you know, it doesn't do any good.'

'I'm not exactly "down". It's far more complicated than that.' She picked up the steaming mug and took a sip of the comforting liquid, noting as she put it down again the inscription 'Father's Tea' on the side. She raised an eyebrow at Harriet over the kitchen table.

'Yes, yes, I know,' said Harriet. 'I should have thrown it out ages ago. The likelihood of the father drinking his tea out of it in this case is about nil. But why the hell should I give it back to him to sip tea from with his beloved in their love nest? I bought it as a Father's Day present from one of the kids. Father's Day indeed! Don't make me laugh.'

It was almost a relief to see Harriet climbing back on to her bitter bandwagon, and Juliet smiled reassuringly at her over the rim of the offending mug. 'Never mind, Hattie, at least you didn't give me a Mother's cup — that might have been less than tactful under the circs.'

'What? Oh, yes, I see what you mean. What's on mine?'

As she turned her mug they both saw at once the legend, 'Don't Worry – It Might Never Happen!'

'Yes, well. It depends on your point of view, doesn't it?' sighed Juliet. 'That's exactly what I'm worried about. That it's never going to happen, I mean. Why can't your stupid mug say, "Don't worry – it *might* happen"?'

'Because, you clot, it means "Don't worry – it might never happen that your stupid egg doesn't get fertilised".'

'No, no, I'm not having all this double negative stuff! I'm absolutely clear that the mug has a message for me. It means, "Don't worry – it might never happen that you get pregnant".'

'Listen, you pathetic misinterpreting idiot, I've always had a much more instinctive understanding of the nuances of the English language than you, and I'm telling you that you're misjudging the message on this mug. In any case it isn't a message for you at all; it's for me. It sits on the hook on the bottom shelf of the dresser ready to cheer me up whenever I begin to harbour unpositive thoughts. What it actually means of course is, "Don't worry – it might never happen that Lauren Stuart takes her clothes off again tonight, reveals her perfect size thirty-four tits, gets into bed with the man who professed undying love for you and fucks him stupid." As it happens, the mug is wrong, but I take comfort from its positive and completely unbiased opinion.'

'Ah,' said Juliet, 'I see we're back to Lauren.'

'Yes,' sighed Harriet, 'it all comes back to Lauren, I'm afraid. She's one of God's creatures to whom everything comes back. Other people's husbands, children, money – she has a special magnetic device that draws things to her. Frightfully clever girl, our Lauren.'

There was a short pause, then, after another sip of her tea, Juliet whispered across to her friend: 'Shut up, Hattie. Just shut up.'

Harriet smiled, smacked her lips open and threw her head back, then nodded two or three times before answering. 'Yes. OK, yes. I'll shut up.'

They both looked at each other for a moment, then Juliet started to laugh. 'Why do you always get that funny look in your nose when you're upset?' she asked.

'What do you mean?' said Harriet. 'I told you your English was terrible, how can you get a funny look in your nose – it's not physically possible. You could get a funny look *to* your nose, I suppose, but not in it.'

'Well, you do,' said Juliet, 'it goes all flared and twisty, especially when you talk about you-know-who. Obsessive, my girl, that's what you are. We always swore we'd never get that wound up about men, didn't we? Look at you – you're doing just what we promised we wouldn't. Pathetic. Here's me can't think about anything except babies and here's you can't think about anything but your wrecked marriage. Honestly, Hat – shouldn't we be beyond all this? Those poor sods who chained themselves to railings and threw themselves in front of galloping horses or whatever must be turning in their graves.

Aren't we supposed to be more concerned with self-image and empowerment or whatever that ghastly word is? We didn't do all that heavy work on Pythagoras and calculus to end up moaning about babies and husbands. Where's our pride? Remember how we were then, Hat, remember how you were going to be Prime Minister and I was going to run the stock exchange. Dear God, what have we come to?'

'But we didn't know, did we?'

'Know what?'

'It's easy to think you don't need all that men and children stuff before you *know*. Before you know that later on that's all you'll want in the world, I mean. I don't have to tell you, Jules. It's all very fine pretending that your job is important and all that, that you're happy to feel independent and earning your own money, and that you and Michael share the washing-up, but you know perfectly well what you want more than anything else in the world, and what your whole life feels as if it's been leading up to from the word go. Don't you?'

Juliet looked down at her hand and sat silently for a moment, bending and stretching her fingers and watching the way the skin moved over the knuckles, the skeletal white of the bone showing through the flesh as she pulled them into a fist. It reminded her of the shiny end of a jointed chicken leg.

'Of course I do.'

'Hello? Is that Dr Northfield? . . . Oh, yes, good, it's Mrs Evans here . . . I was just wondering if I could pop in and see you for a moment, I'm coming in again tomorrow for another scan and I wondered if . . . oh, I see . . . won't you? Oh well, in that case perhaps I could take up just a bit of your time now, if you don't mind. You see I'm due for egg removal very shortly and I wondered if it would be you who would be – oh . . . well, of course, I realise that, it's only that, as you know I did get rather nervous last time and – yes, yes I know . . . yes, of course he'll be there too, or will you be using some of the frozen sp— Oh I see, yes. Well, then of course he'll be there too, but then that's hardly the point in the circumstances, is it? I felt sure you wanted to see me yourself this time, so we could have a talk . . . I do know all about it, you see. Oh, all right then. All right, thank you . . . yes, thank you very much. I hope so too . . . I will, thanks, goodbye.'

Anthony Northfield put down the receiver after his conversation with Juliet feeling slightly uneasy. Like all the doctors at the clinic, he was well used to patients becoming emotionally dependent on him during their treatment, but there was something in this particular woman's tone that made him wish he didn't have to deal with her himself, and that he could pass her on to one of his colleagues. He knew, however, the strong feelings that Professor Hewlett had about keeping the patients happy, and that even if he tried to wriggle out of this one, it would only take a call or letter from her to Hewlett's office for Anthony to be summoned and instructed to humour her and try wherever possible to be the doctor to treat her if she so wished. He pictured Andrea answering the phone at home in the evening, the time when Hewlett inevitably called with any problem that needed tactful discussion outside the hectic and closeted atmosphere of the clinic. He saw her face, frowning as she passed the phone to him, then watching him as he spoke to Hewlett. And he felt a small clench at the base of his belly at the thought of even a tiny threat to his life with her.

He tried to think what it was in the call that had bothered him; he was not immune to flattery, and normally quite enjoyed the attentions of those patients that obviously found the combination of youthful good looks, blue uniform and stethoscope mildly stimulating, but this time he knew something had been said that niggled at the back of his mind and wouldn't quite come out into the open.

'Oh well,' he sighed out loud, 'no doubt it'll all be all right if we can just get her up the spout.'

He pressed the handsfree button on his telephone and dialled an extension. After a couple of rings Sister Bentham's crisp voice answered over the speaker.

'Oh, sister,' said Anthony, 'how's Mrs Evans doing? How long to egg collection do you think? And what's her emotional state like?'

'Fairly stable, I think, doctor, although as you know she does tend to get a little tense. She has another scan on . . . just a minute, I think it's —'

'Tomorrow. She told me that.'

'. . . Yes, tomorrow evening after work, so we'll know more then, although I think she's pretty near. Anything I can help with, doctor?'

'No, not really, sister. It's just that Mrs Evans particularly wants me to do her egg collection, so I'm trying to sort out roughly when it might be so I can be around.'

'Another smitten one, doctor?'

Anthony could hear the smile in the older woman's voice, and realised she expected him to come back with one of his usual roguishly amusing replies.

Instead there was a slightly awkward pause, and after a moment she continued, 'Righto, doctor, I'll tell Janet, too, so that she can keep an eye and try to fit it in with your schedule.'

'Fine, thank you, sister.'

What the hell was it that had worried him like this? Why did he have the instinctive feeling that he wanted to be shot of this Mrs Evans and let someone else deal with her? 'Come on, old boy,' he said to himself as he stood up from his desk, 'you're getting paranoid, that's all. Too many neurotic, desperate women can send a chap a bit haywire. Press on and think of the knighthood, as my dear old dad used to say.' He chuckled as he walked to the door and flipped off the light switch.

Juliet was showing a prospective client round a flat in Eaton Square, her mind half involved with the details of lease, freeholder, vacant possession and ground rent, and half concentrated on the area of her ovaries, where

cramping fullness was a constant reminder of the chemically induced swelling that once more pushed out the
belly of her skirt beneath her sweater.

'I think you'll find this is extremely good value for
the area,' she was saying to her Iranian client. 'I'm sure
you know just what a demand there is for this particular
street, and I haven't had a flat as well situated as this
on such a long lease for a very long time. It's available
immediately, as I explained to you this morning, and
the seller is happy to discuss terms for the furniture and
fittings if you're interested. I think there's a divorce
involved, so it's well worth your making a quick offer
– I'm sure they'd be willing to consider any reasonable
amount.'

Mr Amjardi looked round the room and took in once
more the thick cream carpet, distressed gold wooden
chandelier and Adam-style marble fireplace. He glanced
across at Juliet, who was looking suitably upmarket in
her beige slub-silk skirt and loose white sweater, gar-
nished at the neck with a cleverly tied scarf.

'I like this very much,' he said in his polite, accented
voice. 'I shall go and consider, Mrs Evans, and telephone
you at your office, if I may.'

Juliet knew this was the moment when she should
use her experience and skill to net him. She could always
sense a potentially fast buyer, and was aware that it
probably required merely a small but firm effort on her
part to secure a verbal offer on the spot. If she let him
go now it was perfectly possible that he would come
across one of the many other vacant flats in the area,

and to lose him through a mere lack of trying would be absurd. This was her speciality, the homing in for the capture after the preliminary days or weeks of sifting through details to find the perfect tie-up of client and space. She knew this was right for him – she had felt it as soon as he walked in ahead of her and nodded quietly to himself, and now she mentally gathered herself up for the assault.

But she felt so weary of it all. She couldn't begin to retrieve from within herself the sense of excitement that she usually felt at such moments: the thought of clinching a deal seemed so unimportant; the prospect of a bonus from a good sale so irrelevant. The conversation with Harriet came back to her, and although the actual words were confused and distant by now, the meaning of what they had both been trying to say came through clearly enough: none of this mattered. It never had and it never would. Only one thing mattered, and she must concentrate all her energies on it until her goal was achieved; everything else was mere play-acting and must be abandoned and pushed aside.

'Yes, that's fine, Mr Amjardi. Take your time and give me a ring when you've considered it properly. I'll show you out.'

As they walked down the white stucco steps, Mr Amjardi gave a small nod of the head and bade her goodbye. Juliet walked towards the car where the junior, Tony, was waiting (it was company policy not to let any of the female members of staff show unaccompanied men round a property without a colleague waiting outside) and opened the door on the passenger side.

'Well?' asked the keen young man, 'did he bite?'

'No, he didn't,' she admitted, 'but he may very well in the near future. Now, back to the office, please, I want to get home early.'

The car pulled out from the meter bay and accelerated into the darkness of the December afternoon.

Anthony lay in bed with Andrea that night only half listening to her plans for a giant children's pizza party. It annoyed him to be aware of a tiny hint of unease still fluttering almost imperceptibly at the back of his mind, like a tired moth. At this point in the evening he had forgotten which event in his busy day had originally inspired this *frisson* of discomfiture, and he tried to sift mentally through all the appointments, telephone calls and conversations of the past eight or ten hours in order to pin down the source of this irritating distraction.

'So I thought maybe Hyde Park in the summer; a sort of jamboree of pizzas. We could have catering vans to heat them up and a lot of chefs dressed as Pizza Petes to hand them out. What do you think? I've got loads of underprivileged kids I can call on, and we'd be bound to get some good coverage if I time it right. I know it's a long way off, but it would give us plenty of time to get all the entries in and to work round the magazines' lead times. A celeb or two and a six- or seven-year-old with a huge slice of pizza touching each ear would be really cute, don't you think? Or maybe even smaller –

hey, yeah, what about a little toddler, just a two- or three-year-old? That'd help to make the pizza look bigger too. They're a bit too small to photograph well normally and — Hey, are you listening to me?'

'What? Oh sorry, Andy, I was miles away. Move your foot a bit, darling, will you? Your toenails need cutting.'

Andrea pulled the Habitat striped duvet up under her chin and rolled over to face him, curling her legs up and moving her feet away from his thigh.

'Why are you looking so serious?' she said.

'I was just thinking . . .' Anthony gave a sort of shivering shudder and shook his head briefly but violently.

'What?'

'Oh, nothing, I just can't settle somehow.' He grunted as he reached down over the side of the bed for the *Independent* which was lying on the floor in scattered sheets. 'Is there anything worth watching?'

'God, I forgot to return the new packaging proofs for the perfume. Oh, bugger! Never mind, I'll do it tomorrow. There's Newsnight in a minute.'

'Oh, yes, bung it on.'

The neat new combined television and video was positioned on Andrea's side of the bed, and when she couldn't find the remote she rolled over again, away from Anthony, and reached to the front of the machine and flipped it on. As the strident voices of two politicians discussing the relative merits or otherwise of the single currency flooded the small bedroom, Anthony suddenly remembered when it was that this niggle that still clouded his thoughts had begun. It had been during his telephone conversation with Juliet Evans. As he searched his mind yet again for the particular phrase or inflection that had worried him, he gazed round at the comforting reminders of his everyday life. Only a single bedside lamp was on, and the low, yellowy light it threw out softened the crisp lines of the neat fitted cupboards and modern furnishings. The colder light from the streetlamp outside slid through the half-closed slats of the wooden blind in diagonal stripes across the pile of Andrea's neatly folded clothes that lay on the small chair by the window. While still half-heartedly sieving his brain for the elusive seed of his unease, Anthony found himself lazily wondering if he could be bothered to make the effort to persuade Andrea into making love. He turned towards her and reached a hand out to stroke the back of her neck.

'Hey, pudding —' he began, then suddenly stopped short.

'What?' she answered, swivelling her head round to look at him.

'Wait a minute, I've, yes. Yes, that's it — I've got it.'

'What? What have you got?'

Now that he knew what it was, Anthony half wished he hadn't alerted Andrea, and for a split second considered inventing something, but the habit of unburdening himself to her was too strong, and he knew it was only by talking it through that he could exorcise it. 'Something that Evans woman said to me today. It's been vaguely worrying me all evening, and I couldn't remember why until just now. I was reassuring her about her egg collection – she's very tense – and she'd rung me up to ask for me to be the one to do her collection.'

'Oh yes . . .' said Andrea wryly, and turned over in bed again to face him, '*that* one.'

'No, shut up, Andy, let me think a moment. I explained it might not be me, and I told her that of course her husband could be there for as much of the time as she wanted. And she said something really weird. She said it didn't matter about her husband and that she assumed I'd want to be there so we could *have a talk*, because she *knew all about it*. What the hell did she mean by that? What talk? What does she know about?'

'It doesn't sound particularly weird to me. She meant that, I don't know, that the eggs were the important thing, I guess, and that she wanted to talk to a professional – yes, I suppose she meant that her husband isn't really the one to be especially useful in that situation because, well, because, you know – it's all a bit medical or something. And that she knows all about the treatment or whatever. Anyway, it doesn't sound odd to me.'

'Doesn't it? I still think it's a really strange way of putting it.'

Chapter Thirteen

Juliet stared at herself in her dressing-table mirror. 'Only two,' she muttered out loud, 'only two. It's pathetic!' She had leant forward until her nose almost touched the cold glass, and spat out this last word at her bitter reflection. A moist screen of condensation washed over her image as she breathed hard through her mouth, and she pulled back and wiped it away with her hand. 'God, you look awful,' she whispered, and slumped back in her chair and made a long, silent examination of herself. Her hair was lank and unwashed, her skin pale and dry, and the make-up beneath her eyes had blurred into long creases that ran outwards to the tops of her cheeks. She let the muscles of her face relax completely, feeling the weight of flesh sagging downwards and watching the small pouches of fat settle relentlessly round her mouth and jaw. She sighed loudly, sat up a little and pushed her hands into her hair on either side of her face, lifting the contours of soft skin and pulling her face and eyes up into an expression of youthfully oriental surprise. She gripped her hands even more tightly into her hair and leant on her elbows, staring malevolently through slitted eyes at the stretched image confronting her.

'All that bloody effort for two measly eggs,' she shouted, 'pathetic! Oh God!' She sighed again as she dropped her hands on to the dressing table and laid her head on her crossed forearms, feeling the flesh sink back downwards to pool once more round the bottom of her face. 'What am I going to do? What hope do I have with two? I've had my chance. I was given it and I screwed it up. He won't want me any more now, I know it. *Five* — that was the time I should have done it. You fucking idiot — you've lost it, haven't you?' She lifted her head again and looked into the mirror. The picture of self-pity that confronted her only reinforced her feeling of self-loathing, and she rose quickly from her chair and walked across the room to look out of the window. She leant her head against the pane and gazed down at the street as wearily as she had looked at her reflection, the cold of the glass against her forehead echoing the feeling of the mirror. She watched a woman holding an open umbrella in one hand and a dog lead in the other walk briskly along the wet pavement below, followed by a large, lazy black labrador, whose gait inevitably reminded her of Lucy.

'No!' she snapped at herself as she pulled back from the window and turned into the room. 'No! Not again! I can't start going over it all over again — *I can't*!'

'Darling, are you calling me?' Michael's voice rose from the floor below as he shouted up to her.

'No, I'm talking to myself,' Juliet shouted back, 'just ignore it.'

'You're not still worrying, are you, Jules?' Michael was climbing the stairs towards the bedroom. 'Now, have I got to go through this again? There have been many, many times that they've had babies born when even just one egg has been taken, let alone two. They told us that, quite clearly. Oh, darling – you look dreadful—' he said as he came into the room.

'Thanks a bunch.'

'No, you do, you silly old thing. You've been getting yourself into a state. Come on now, this is ridiculous. We've been through so much, don't start getting moody now – there's no reason to. We're on course, they've got two good eggs . . .'

'Not *excellent*, though, are they? No one said they were excellent this time.'

'Oh Jules, that's childish.' Michael was sitting on the edge of the bed now, watching Juliet as she paced the room without looking at him. 'Don't play with words – the eggs are perfectly sound and everyone was very pleased. There's a very reasonable chance we'll be lucky this time.'

'*This* time? We were lucky last time – how can you expect it to happen twice?'

'Well, as far as Dr Northfield is concerned—'

'Don't bring Anthony into it.'

'What? What did you say? What do you mean?'

'Nothing. Just don't talk about what you don't understand.'

Michael sprang up and grasped Juliet's shoulder, turning her towards him. 'Listen — no, *look* at me — I'm getting fed up with all this. I'm doing my best to be understanding and all that, but you're pushing things too far, Juliet, you really are. Don't you dare ever again to tell me not to talk about—'

'Oh, Michael, don't be so dramatic! Honestly, you're pathetic!'

'Shut up!' Michael shouted at her. 'Just shut up! I'm sick of trying to keep you sweet all the time, I'm *sick* of it. Try and grow up, Julie, you can't treat this as your private problem any more. I'm as much a part of this as you are, and I won't have you talking to me like that.'

'Oh you won't? You won't have me talking to you like that?' Juliet mimicked his voice as she spoke to him, 'Oh dearie me! Well, I'm so sorry, I'm sure.'

'That's it, Jules. I've had enough.'

Michael turned and walked out of the room and down the stairs again, leaving Juliet smiling oddly to herself as she moved to the bathroom to start washing her hair.

'Would you stay here tonight?' Anna looked seriously over at Michael as he sat opposite her on the sofa. For the third day running he had visited her, both parties finding more hope together than apart. Now he shook his head at her, the well-worn yellow jumper and old brown corduroy trousers that he had hastily put on when Anna had telephoned making him look younger and more vulnerable in her eyes than when he had dressed in his business suit the days before.

'No, Anna, you don't want me. You've got your wonderful police lady. I've no right to be here.'

'Right? We're in limbo, Michael. People in limbo don't have the need for rights, they just float about letting things happen to them. There are no rules now, don't you understand? Since they let Harry be taken, they've lost any hold they ever had over me. You don't need a right, you're lost, like I am. You can do what you want.'

'God, Anna, sometimes you sound like an old lady. You shouldn't be talking like this. You're so young. It's terrible to see what —'

'Oh no, don't start that. Don't start all that "tragedy has aged you beyond your years" sort of crap. I was always like this, don't you kid yourself. Yeah, maybe in your comfortable, middle-class life young girls are sweet and innocent . . .'

'I didn't say that.'

'But, believe me, I was never sweet *or* innocent. And I'm not sorry. I'm not complaining. And don't come here with your clichéd ideas about working-class girls who come to London from the North being stupid. I read; I watch the television; I know a bit about what goes on in the world — in fact I'm bloody sure I know a good deal more about it than you do.'

'I'm sure you're right,' smiled Michael.

'No, don't give me that patronising smile; I mean it.

Your world is a fraction of the real world. Mine's a huge part of it. And growing. And now I've lost Harry I've learnt about another reality. I thought I knew it all before, but I hadn't even started. You knew even less. Now I'm really living. So are you, perhaps for the first time. Crap, isn't it?'

'Oh Anna!' Michael stood up and crossed over to where she sat on the small, hard chair. 'Don't. Don't.' He squatted down in front of her and put a hand over hers. 'Yes, of course, if you'd like me to stay I will. I'll let the police know and they can call me here if they need me. I'd like to stay. Thanks.'

The window rattled a little as a gust of wind blew against it.

Anna smiled at him, then very suddenly bent down and brushed her lips across his forehead, the cold moistness of her mouth feeling like damp fingertips against the heat of the skin. 'Thank you, too,' she said. 'I'll tell Susan she needn't stay. I'd much rather be alone with someone who understands.'

'Are you sure that's all right? Shouldn't she stay? I mean, don't you think it looks a bit . . .'

Anna buried her face in her hands and groaned. 'Oh, for God's sake, man! Don't be so fucking stupid! Don't you understand what I've been trying to tell you? Everything's "all right". Nothing's "all right". It doesn't matter. Just get through it as you can, that's all we can do. If I find it comforting to have you here, and you want to be here, then that's it. That's fine. If they think you're fucking me, that's fine too. Perhaps you will.'

'Oh, Anna, really!' Michael protested quickly, but was at the same moment aware of the overwhelming wave of sexual excitement that had instantaneously washed over him at her words. 'Don't make things more difficult. There are men who can care for you without having to go to bed with you, you know. I'll stay here as your friend, and because I care about you, and need your company. Father figure, that's what I am,' he smiled.

'Sorry,' said Anna. 'I know, I know. I'm sorry. Anyway, you couldn't be my father. You'd have had to be about fourteen or something.'

'Thanks, but I'm much older than that. And anyway, how do you know what I was up to at fourteen? I'd be honoured to be your father.'

Michael knelt up and put his arms around her in a gentle hug, grateful that the seat of the chair came between them at the level of his hips, separating her from the tangible evidence of his own body's betrayal of his comforting words.

Anna pulled carefully out of his embrace, sat back a little and tilted her head as she looked down at him thoughtfully. Her jet-black hair, though still uncombed, looked a little less matted and lifeless than Michael remembered it, and her pale face was for the first time unmarked by streaked make-up and the puffy evidence of ceaseless crying. It looked scrubbed and a little raw, and the lack of even remnants of eye liner made her appear defenceless. Her black V-neck jumper and black leggings reminded Michael a little of the guests at bottle parties he used to go to as a youth on Saturday nights, where black-clad, long-haired young women with scarlet lips and Juliette Greco pouts had fascinated him with their air of foreign sophistication and incomprehensible existentialist ideas. But Anna didn't look sophisticated – for all her worldly-wise airs and cynical expressions. As she gazed earnestly down at him he felt he was handling a young creature with the fragility of an anxious little girl.

'Did you keep sleeping with her?' she said. 'I mean, after all the trouble, did you ever still make love to her? Did you share the same bed?'

Michael sighed, letting himself sit back on to the worn carpet and resting his arms on his knees. 'No. No, we didn't. You see, there's something I haven't told you. Worse than the Northfield business. Something I haven't really told anyone, except the ones who had to know of course, and that made – no, I can't really explain at the moment, Anna. I'm sorry. Not even to you. There are still some things I can't quite bring myself to face. But, no, we didn't make love after it all began.'

'Poor you,' she said, almost smiling at him.

'Yes,' Michael smiled back, 'poor me.'

'You really could sleep with me tonight, you know.'

Michael shook his head, still smiling.

'I know exactly what I'm doing, Michael. And I know you're the only person in the whole world I could say it to who would understand. Can you imagine? Her baby's snatched and disappeared and the woman wants to have a fuck? Who could possibly begin to understand that?'

Michael was looking away slightly.

'Do you want to? I mean it.'

'Anna, I'd do anything to help you, anything, I'm sure you know that now, but no, of course I won't make love to you. You think it would blot out your pain and misery for a while, but afterwards – then how do you think you'd feel? We'd both regret it, feel – I don't know – guilty, I suppose.'

'I wouldn't.'

Something in the simple way she said it made him look back at her, and her serious, saddened expression made Michael feel that she was right, that nothing could touch her feelings in that way. She had put herself through such torments of self-punishment and recrimination that she was inured to all further pain, except for the ever-present, gnawing, burrowing, disembowelling agony of the loss of Harry.

'Anna, I'm sorry. You may be right. It might be a help to you, and I know it would to me, but I just can't do it. You're very young, and my feelings are so mixed up by what's going on that I can't possibly trust myself to take an important step like that.'

'It's not an important step,' Anna snorted disdainfully, 'it's just a fuck, for God's sake, man. Don't treat it like a marriage ceremony or something. OK, that's fine – if you can't do it I understand, but don't make such a big deal out of it. It's nothing.'

'OK. Now drop it, Anna. Do you still want me to stay?'

'Yes, of course – what do you think? That I'm only after your body?'

'No,' whispered Michael, 'no, I don't think that's very likely.'

'Right then,' said Anna, 'I'll get some sheets for the sofa.'

Juliet walked down the front steps of the house and hailed a taxi to take her to Harriet's flat. As she opened the cab door, a gust of wind blew open the flap of her camel-hair coat, letting in a reminder of winter to whip across her chest.

The driver sized her up as she grasped the door handle and shouted her destination against the noise of the wind, and then climbed into the back, closing the door after her. Shopping trip, thought the cabbie; shopping with a girlfriend – Harrods probably – then out to lunch.

Juliet sat back in the cab and thought through what she had done. She had acted almost without thinking. After telephoning the office to confirm that she wouldn't be in, she had dressed quickly and left home without a word to Michael, who had been shaving when she had made the call to work, and the one before it to the clinic. It was simpler this way. He didn't need to know – he would understand, in the end. This time he mustn't be allowed to interfere – she had to give it every chance, not only for her sake but for Anthony's – surely that was obvious?

She looked out of the window. The trees in Sloane Square were draped in the hundreds of white bulbs that appeared every December, reminding her just how near it was getting to Christmas. For the first time in a long while she didn't find the prospect daunting; so many Christmases had been ordeals of pretended jollity; the lack of children to hang stockings for barely acknowledged at the family gatherings round the dining table. Now there was once more a flicker of hope, and she found the prospect of the festive season surprisingly welcome.

Both the eggs had fertilised. There was still a chance. If she could just handle things properly this time — if she could just be left alone to manage things then it might still be all right.

'Yes?' Harriet's voice sounded blurred and indistinct over the intercom.

'Hat, it's Jules. I need you. Can you take me to the clinic?'

'Oh God, what's the matter? Are you ill?'

'Look, can you take me? I'll let the taxi go if you can, otherwise I'll go on my own, and —'

'No, of course I'll take you. Can you come up first?'

'Yes, OK. Hang on, I'll just get rid of the cab . . . see you in a minute.'

'What is it? What's the matter?' Harriet asked as she let Juliet into the flat moments later, taking in at a glance her friend's brittle expression and unusually bare face.

'Nothing. I told you. I just need to get to the clinic to get the embryos put back that's all, and I—'

'Oh Jules! How wonderful! They've fertilised again, have they? Why didn't you go on in the taxi? Where's Michael?'

'Michael's at home. He's busy. And I wanted someone to take me, that's all. Do I have to explain everything?'

'Sorry. Sit down a minute and I'll get my coat.'

Juliet looked at the mess of toys scattered over the floor as she sat on the edge of the kitchen table. She was surprised not to feel the familiar pang of envy as she gazed down at them, and idly wondered why. She turned her head and looked over at the pile of unwashed crockery and saucepans sitting by the side of the sink, and half thought about getting up to rinse them and stack them in the dishwasher but decided against it. Everything from now on must be done to put herself first. Nothing must be allowed to come between her and this chance that had been allowed her. She mustn't even think of anything but herself, her body, and the positive effort of preparing.

'Where are the kids?' she shouted.

'They're both in Jessie's room, playing on the computer. It's OK, I can get the woman downstairs to come and sit with them while we're out,' Harriet answered as she bustled into the kitchen, pulling on her coat as she spoke. 'Now, where the hell are the car keys? And my bag? How long will we be, by the way?'

'Not long. Thanks, Hat.'

'It's OK.' Harriet smiled back at her. 'Just make it worthwhile this time, huh?'

'Sure.'

After a brief goodbye to the children, who were too distracted by computerised lemmings to pay much attention, Harriet arranged for her downstairs neighbour to go up to the flat within the next few minutes and stay with the children until her return. As she and Juliet made their way down the stairs, Harriet heard the distant sound of her telephone ringing. 'Jessie, will you answer that?' she yelled up the stairs. 'Oh, never mind. They'll never hear me with the TV on. They'll ring back, who-ever they are.'

Michael put down the receiver and frowned. He had felt sure Juliet had gone round to Harriet's, guessing that she might have already telephoned the clinic and been too upset to talk to him. He was becoming so used to her unpredictable moods that he wasn't in the least surprised to find she had left the house without a word, but not to find her at Harriet's perturbed him. Had there perhaps been good news after all? Could she have gone to the clinic on her own again, but this time without even telling him? He dialled the number and felt comforted by the familiar, friendly, efficient voice that answered.

'Good morning, can I help you?'

'Good morning. It's Michael Evans here. I just won-dered if by any chance Mrs Evans was with you?'

'No, Mr Evans, she hasn't arrived yet. Is there a message I can give her?'

'No, no that's fine, thank you. I just wanted to know if she'd got to you.'

In spite of everything, Michael felt hurt and alone. He had thought he was used to the way Juliet shut him off from her feelings and – increasingly – from the physical aspects of the treatment, but there was something in the way the receptionist had assumed he was included in the knowledge of what must be the successful egg fertilisation that made him suddenly aware just how isolated he felt.

'For God's sake, they're my embryos too,' he muttered out loud. Feeling suddenly angry and full of unresolved energy, he stood up and moved into the hall. He grabbed his dark blue overcoat off the peg and his keys off the table and went quickly out of the front door, slamming it behind him.

Chapter Fourteen

As Michael walked into the waiting room in Weymouth Street he stopped short at the sight of the woman sitting on the sofa under the window reading a magazine. Hoping he was mistaken in recognising the cut of her hair and the way she sat, he coughed discreetly as he made his way over to one of the armchairs. She looked up, and he was dismayed to find he was right.

'Harriet,' he said quietly. 'For God's sake, what are you doing here? No, I know that of course. I suppose I mean — why? Why are you here? What did Juliet say to you?'

'She said you were busy, Michael. I'm sorry, are you — I mean, did you want to bring her yourself? She didn't — oh dear, this is embarrassing — I don't quite know what to say.'

'No, no it's all right, Harriet. It's not your fault. I didn't mean to — things have been a bit strained recently I'm afraid, and I suppose she just felt like coming with you, that's all. It's not important, it doesn't matter.'

'She's been really strung up lately. I'm sure you're well aware of that, of course,' Harriet smiled, a little shame-faced. 'It's not surprising. I think you've both been marvellous. It can't have been easy.'

'No, it certainly hasn't.' Michael sat down in the armchair and looked across at her. 'Anyway, Harriet, I'm grateful to you for coming, but I think perhaps I'll take over now, if you don't mind. I'm sure Julie will let you know how things are and so on. Please don't feel you have to stay. I'm here now and I'll take her home when she's finished.'

'Of course. Could you tell her to give me a ring? I don't want her to think I just went, if you know what I mean?'

'Don't worry, I'll explain what happened, I promise.'

'Thanks.' Harriet got up and gathered her handbag and coat from beside her on the sofa. 'I'll see you soon then.'

'Yes, OK. Bye, Harriet.'

Harriet walked towards the door, but paused and turned back just before she reached it. 'Michael, it's difficult to say this in the way I really want to, but — well, I hope so very much that things work out.'

'Yes, thank you, Harriet, I'm sure you do.'

'No, I really mean it. I shall be thinking of you both over the next couple of weeks. You really do deserve so much for it to be a success. Then I know her moods would go too, you see. It's so much muddled up with this baby thing and—'

'Yes, I know. I do see what you're trying to say, Harriet, and I'm very grateful. I know everything's going to be fine, and don't worry about today. I'm getting used to it.'

He smiled up at Harriet, who smiled back at him and turned to go.

It seemed only minutes later that Juliet walked into the waiting room. She had a set, tense look to her face, which, still bare of make-up, looked hard and pale in the cold daylight from the window. She glanced at Michael as she crossed to collect her coat from where she had draped it over the arm of the sofa, seemingly unsurprised at his presence.

'Shall we go?' she asked, as she stood in the doorway, looking across at him.

'Yes, OK. How are you? How many?'

'Both. Two. I'm fine. Let's go.'

Michael was grateful that the waiting room was empty of witnesses to the bleak little scene. Unable to summon up the energy to pretend an optimism he didn't feel, but equally weary of recriminations and arguments, he kept silent as he rose from the chair and the two of them made their way into the hall. After running the usual gauntlet of eternally cheerful photographs and smiling receptionists, it was a relief to emerge into the cold greyness outside and to walk along the noncommittal, damp pavements towards the car.

'Did you find a meter?' asked Juliet, not turning to

look at him but gazing straight ahead of her as they walked.

'Yes. Well, no — a Pay and Display. It's not far.'

They walked on in silence for a few moments, then Juliet suddenly stopped. 'Michael — I'm not going to let anything go wrong this time. You do know that, don't you?'

Ignoring her oddly threatening tone, Michael assumed his usual placatory one. 'Of course. I'm sure it won't. I'm sure we're on the way now.' But he had stopped too, and taking Juliet's shoulders in his hands, he gently turned her towards him. 'I'll look after you, Jules, you know that. Don't worry — I'll take care of you. You must let me in, darling, that's all. I can't help if you freeze me out like this, and it's not fair.'

He moved aside slightly as a crocodile of school-children, wearing grey overcoats and blue velvet berets, rounded the corner and came briskly towards them. He watched the giggling, chattering girls as they passed, gloved hands clasping them firmly together in pairs, diagonally slung satchels flapping against their hips as they walked. Michael found himself smiling at them and glanced back at Juliet, expecting her, too, to be aware of the small tide of youth flowing past them with such inexorable cheerfulness. But she was still staring ahead, her gaze fixed somewhere just over Michael's shoulder, her thoughts clearly far from their surroundings.

'It wasn't Anthony who put them back,' she said, 'do you think that matters?'

'What?' said Michael, 'Anthony Northfield, you mean?'

'Yes.'

'No, of course it doesn't matter.'

The stream of little girls had passed them now, and Michael took Juliet's arm and began to walk slowly along the street again. 'I don't know why you've got such a thing about him; they're all equally good. Who was it this time?'

'I can't remember what he's called, but he was very kind about it all.'

'Well, there you are then. It doesn't make any difference who does it – Professor Hewlett explained that, didn't he? He did tell us that it would depend on who was around so that the procedures were done at the perfect moment, do you remember?'

'Yes, I know. Still, it's odd isn't it?'

They had reached the car now, and Michael leant down and unlocked the driver's door with his key. The other door locks popped up as he did so.

'Why didn't you use the thing?' Juliet asked, as she stooped to get in the front passenger seat.

'It's not working at all now,' said Michael. 'What's odd?'

'Well, you know, that it wasn't Anthony.'

'Why?'

~

'Michael.

'Michael.

'Michael.'

The soft, repetitive whisper broke into his dream, and Michael opened his eyes and looked unseeingly into a purple darkness, trying to make sense of where he was. He felt the usual twinges of anonymous dread gathering in his belly and maturing into fully fledged knowledge and awareness as he slowly awoke, but this time the edge was taken off them by a small and puzzling intrusion of warmth and hope. As he struggled to identify this alien feeling, the whisper came again out of the darkness, and at the same time his brain began to translate the signals his eyes had been struggling to convey to it, and he made out the silhouette of a head, leaning over him, very close. He managed to raise himself up on to one elbow, and suddenly knew exactly where he was.

'Anna? Anna, what is it? Is something wrong? Do you want to talk?'

She didn't answer, but gently lifted the sheet and blankets and slipped her small, thin body under them and next to his on the sofa. Michael moved to make room for her, turning his hips sideways and pressing himself hard against the back of the sofa, his tee-shirt and shorts twisting as the material clung to the coarse fabric of the upholstery. 'Are you all right?' he whispered. His right arm was under Anna's back, where it had been pinned as she lay down next to him; the other he balanced awkwardly along the side of his left hip.

'Yes, I'm OK,' she whispered back, 'I'm sorry to wake you.'

'Don't be silly.'

As she turned her body a little towards him, Michael realised with a pleasurable start that, from below the short sleeve of his shirt, the skin of his arm under Anna's back met soft, warm flesh. For a few seconds they both lay still, their breathing almost in step, then Michael whispered again, almost touching her hair with his lips as he turned his head.

'Don't worry, Anna. Do you know, I've still got a feeling he's fine. I really have.'

He felt a small shaking on his arm, like the vibration from a purring kitten, and lifted his head to try and see her face in the darkness, but only the outline of her head was dimly visible against the light background of the carpet.

'Anna? Are you crying?'

For a moment she didn't answer, then a small voice came out of the darkness, 'Yes. I don't think I'll ever see him again. I don't think I can bear it.'

'Oh, my dear. My dear.' He lifted his left hand and brought it gently to where he guessed her eyes must be. The wetness of her cheek came as a shock; she must have been crying for some time, alone in her bed, before she had come creeping to wake him in the darkness. He smoothed the dampness from her face and into her hair, feeling the wet patch where the tears had already gathered over her temple. He reached down and lifted a corner of the sheet and patted it gently over her face and the side of her head.

'Thanks,' she said quietly. 'Sorry, I just can't help it.'

'You don't have to explain — you told me that, remember? I'm the one person you really don't have to explain or apologise to, Anna. You cry if you want to.'

Michael's arm was resting on top of the sheet now, removed from the warmth of her body by the layer of thin, blue fabric. Beneath his forearm he could feel, very faintly, the beating of her heart. Anna pulled her hand out from under the clothes and took Michael's, clasping it with a ferocity that took him by surprise.

For a further few minutes they lay in silence, taking comfort in the closeness of their bodies and of their thoughts, then, slowly, Anna drew Michael's hand up towards her face and, very gently, took one of his fingers into her mouth and sucked the tip of it, like a baby sucking at a teat. Michael held his breath and wondered at the violent sensations of desire that washed over him. As Anna took his finger from her mouth she gave a tiny groan and, still grasping his hand in hers, used them both to push the sheet down and away from them to gather in folds over their legs. The whiteness of her body was visible even in the dim light, and Michael took in all at once her nakedness and the small blur of darkness between her legs. Their hands were resting on her belly, then Michael gently disengaged his from hers and brought it up towards her breast. He laid it gently over the warm roundness, feeling the hardness of the nipple pressing against his palm and the beating of her heart, strongly now, against his thumb. He stroked the soft skin, surprised and excited by the full, generous roundness of the breast against her slim chest. His fingers played gently with the nipple, exploring the puckered flesh as he circled it, then very gently he slid his hand down to beneath her arm and lifted the weight of the breast up and towards him, bending his head as he did so, pushing the upright nipple towards his open mouth. He sucked at her as she had at his finger, with quiet, tender concentration, while she moved against him and turned her body towards him. Still lapping gently at her breast, he stroked his hand down the side of her waist and over her hip, then softly moved it to between her legs.

Anna sighed, but there was a catch in her breath that caused Michael to raise his head and look up at her silhouetted features. 'Oh God, Anna,' he whispered, 'you're crying again. Do you want me to stop?'

'No, no don't. Yes, I'm crying, but don't stop. For God's sake, don't stop.'

Michael kept his hand gently exploring the wetness between her legs, then bent his head again to kiss her neck. She arched her head back and he moved his mouth up to beneath her chin, kissing and licking so softly that his lips barely touched the white skin. Anna lowered her head back down again and breathed on to his face, as he tried to see her eyes in the low light. They touched lips to lips, mouths open and breathing into each other, sweeping skin against skin in tiny movements from side to side, until he felt the hard tip of her tongue push between his teeth and he opened his mouth and pushed his own tongue against hers, twisting and sucking them together. She was snuffling and whimpering in the effort to keep her mouth on his, then suddenly pulled her head away from him with a gasp. 'I can't breathe!' she laughed in a whisper.

'It's all that crying,' Michael smiled back into the darkness. 'No more, now, Anna. Stop crying and concentrate.'

He slipped a finger firmly up inside her and she gasped again in pleasure.

'You're lovely,' he murmured. 'I'm here, Anna. Feel me. I'm here.'

After a few moments he moved his hand to her thighs and roughly pushed her legs wide apart, so that one slipped over the side of the sofa. As he lifted his body carefully on to hers she bent the other leg and wrapped it over his back, and he felt, when he pushed into her, a jolt of exhilaration, as, with a thrust born of the strength of despair, she raised her hips up to meet his.

'Now,' he whispered as they moved together, 'just forget.'

She was moaning and grunting as he pushed harder into her, trying to speak but the words getting lost in the effort of squeezing every ounce of physical sensation out of the moment.

'Forget,' he whispered as she gripped his shoulders tightly with the ends of her fingers and began to thrash about under his relentless rhythm, 'just for a tiny fraction of time, I'm – going – to – make – you – *forget*.'

'Andy, how do you feel about bow ties?'

'Mmmm?'

'What do they do for you?'

'On you do you mean?'

'Yes. And no. Generally as well. I just thought maybe I should be getting a bit more the Great Man-ish if you know what I mean. A bit more style in the old bedside manner.'

Anthony was studying himself in the bathroom mirror as he called to Andrea, who was sprawled on the bed next door reading *Hello!*. 'I remember when I was a student being very impressed with our prof's ties. He wore a different one every day, and I don't remember them ever coming round again, although I suppose they must have. Grateful patients used to shower him with them. What do you think? Charmingly eccentric or irritatingly young fogey?'

'They're a bit, um, what's his name, aren't they? You know. Used to be on Question Time. Ages ago.'

'Oh, Robin Day you mean? Yes, maybe you're right.' Anthony removed the bow tie that he had mentally superimposed on his reflection. He thought for a moment. 'Braces aren't right are they?'

'No. Definitely not! I think you look great as you are. Your packaging as the serious and talented young doctor is spot on as far as I'm concerned. And I should know, remember.'

'Well, yes, exactly. That's why I asked you, my darling. I'm well aware of your brilliance at selling the product. It's only, I just feel a bit — how shall I put it — *bland*.'

Andrea looked up from studying some fascinating pictures of the beautiful Viennese home of a rather odd-looking bejewelled Austrian aristocrat and took a long look at him as he walked into the bedroom. 'No, I don't think so. Perhaps a more exciting shirt occasionally.'

'How do you mean?'

'I don't know. Pink or something.'

'Mmm. Do you mean colour or make?'

'What?'

'Pink the colour or do you mean a Thomas Pink shirt?'

'Oh. I meant colour. But both, preferably.' Andrea lay back on the pillows and scratched her midriff absent-mindedly. 'You're far too good-looking as it is, if you ask me. Which reminds me; how's your old lady fan doing? Still besotted?'

'You surely can't be referring to one of my patients. Show a little more respect please. The lady of whom I assume you speak is into a second cycle. I didn't implant her as I wasn't in theatre that day. So I have no idea of exactly how she is, but she must be coming up for her blood test some time pretty soon.' Anthony was assuming an indifference he didn't feel. The thought of Juliet still stirred an unease deep inside him, and made him especially nervous in the context of Andrea. 'I haven't heard any talk about her starting again or anything, so I assume she hasn't had a bleed. I'll find out how she's doing today if you like. Check her exact timing for you. Satisfied?'

'Mmm. Is she pretty?'

Anthony squatted down by the side of the bed and leant his folded arms on the duvet. 'Darling, you're not serious when you talk like this are you? Not even a tiny bit? You do know, don't you, that I'm crazy about you and never think about looking at another woman. And I'm only teasing when I tell you about adoring patients. I have absolutely no desire to flirt with them. Quite apart from the fact that it might be a bit irritating to be struck off at this early stage of my glittering career. Darling?'

'Yes, yes, yes of course. I know. But watch it anyway.'

Was Anthony imagining the small hint of threat behind the bantering tone?

'MICHAEL!'

This time a scream, not a whisper. The urgency in Juliet's voice was frightening, and Michael woke with a start. He was sitting in front of the gas log fire, his head leaning at an awkward angle against the wing of the armchair, his jaw slack and open, using the excuse of a cancelled afternoon appointment as an opportunity to come home and doze off after lunch. He closed his mouth quickly, feeling the dry sour taste as he moved his tongue around and tried to answer. A dry squeak came out, and he cleared his throat as he began to move his limbs, which had stiffened uncomfortably during his nap. 'What? What is it?'

Juliet came into the room in a blur of intense, frantic energy. Michael was aware of her scarf brushing his face as she dived towards him, almost knocking him back into the chair from the semi-erect position he had reached, before she squatted in front of him, her raincoat billowing into folds on the floor around her, her face tensed, her eyes at once utterly focused on his and yet at the same time looking somewhere beyond or behind him – as if she were living in two dimensions at the same moment, both equally vivid and real: one existing in the immediacy of the present and the other in the timeless distance of some other plane.

He sat back down into the chair and looked at her. 'Christ, Julie, you scared me. What's —'

'MICHAEL, MICHAEL —'

'Julie, for God's sake calm down! Don't shout at me. Just tell me, just tell me what it is.'

She suddenly laughed, her eyes still staring at him, but their intensity softened a little by the way the skin crinkled up around them. Michael held his breath and looked into her face as she paused, her hair framed by a coloured halo of out-of-focus lights on the small Christmas tree behind her; then she leant towards him as her laugh quietened into a beaming, confident smile.

'Michael, don't look so afraid, darling. We've done it, we've done it!'

A shock of understanding hit him like a blow in the stomach. He sat bolt upright in the chair and gripped her hard round the shoulders. 'Do you – oh Julie, do you mean —?'

'Wait, darling, wait a second. I've been saying this to you in my head all the way back from the clinic. Don't spoil it. Don't say anything yet. I want to be the one to say it first; there'll never be another time when I can say this for the very first time in my life. I've got to do this. I want to be able to remember this moment for ever, the time when I said it out loud for the first time. And it's true – oh God almighty it's *true*. I can't believe it. I just can't believe it! Yes, darling, yes – don't look so upset. Smile at me, Michael, smile at me, darling, please—'

And he did. Michael smiled so broadly he thought his cheeks would split. He too laughed out loud, and reached forward to hold his wife gently in his arms, to fold her still scarfed and raincoated body closely to him. They stayed wrapped together without speaking for a few seconds, her breathing fast and loud in his ear, his mind already jangling with echoing repetitions of the as-yet-unspoken phrase hanging between them.

As her body calmed and her breathing slowed, Michael moved his arms tenderly from her back and once more on to her shoulders. He pulled back a little to look at her, and for another moment they stared at each other in a kind of fascinated awe, not smiling now but quietly serious.

'Well?' he said at last, almost whispering. 'Well, darling? What do you have to tell me?'

She couldn't help the smile that blossomed again at her mouth. It spread to her eyes, lifting her cheeks and pulling her face up into a picture of youthful happiness, radiant in its expression of her uncontainable inner joy. She leant forward to whisper in his ear, and he felt her breath against his skin before she spoke.

'I'm pregnant.
'I'm pregnant.
'Oh Michael – I'm pregnant.'

Chapter Fifteen

'The big problem, of course, is when to tell the grandmother.'

'Oh God yes, of course, your mother. But she doesn't approve does she?'

Juliet gave Harriet a wry look across the kitchen table, which was strewn with used cups, half-empty cereal bowls and assorted toys. 'I wouldn't bet on it. I think we'll find that once it's a *fait accompli*, in spite of it all being horribly "unnatural" and me being a terrible wife and so on, she'll rather enjoy the doting granny act.'

'Well, surely, you don't want to tell her yet, do you? It's very early days, you know.'

Harriet absent-mindedly picked up a one-legged plastic Power Ranger from in front of her and threw it across the room into a wicker toy basket in the corner. 'In fact I'm thrilled you've even told *me*. Oh, Jules, it's such wonderful, wonderful news, isn't it?'

'Yes,' beamed Juliet, 'yes it certainly is.'

'How do you feel?'

'Fantastic. Absolutely fantastic. And sort of confident

– I can't explain it, it's funny. I just know it's all OK this time.' She paused and looked out of the window for a moment. 'I wonder what it is, Hat. What sex I mean. I don't have any feeling about that at all. I wonder what I've got growing inside me.'

Harriet stared at her for a moment, then suddenly leapt up from the table and dashed towards the door. 'Hang on – I've got the very thing! How extraordinary – I can never find anything I want in this God-awful flat, but I saw exactly what we need just yesterday when I was digging out the Christmas decorations. That's amazing,' she continued as she left the room and shouted from the bedroom, 'it must be an omen. I haven't seen it for years, and then, just the day before we – hang on, where is it now – I know I saw it in – here we are. Brilliant – I knew it.'

Harriet bustled back into the kitchen holding a piece of cord with a small shiny object attached to it, which, as she brought it nearer, Juliet could see was what appeared to be a curtain ring. 'Oh, don't be so ridiculous, Hattie,' she laughed, 'don't tell me you're going to go divining or whatever they call it.'

'You can laugh,' answered Harriet, 'but I may tell you that my grandmother correctly forecast the sex of at least a dozen babies with this little piece of gadgetry.'

'I'd hardly call it "gadgetry". An old curtain ring on a bit of string.'

'It's not a curtain ring. It's her wedding ring. And this bit of *string*, as you call it, has unfailingly produced the right result over and over again. Even with my little darlings.'

'Was she divorced, then? Or widowed, or what?'

'What do you mean?'

'Well, why wasn't she wearing the ring?'

'She was. When she was here to wear it, I mean. She used to take it off and tie it on to this very piece of cord whenever she wanted to tell the sex of a baby.'

'Before it was born, presumably. Otherwise she could have just had a look.'

'You can mock all you like, but it works.'

'Does it find water too? Or oil, or anything really useful?'

'That's enough – you're very skittish today; I can't think what's come over you, apart from pregnancy of course. There'll be tears before bedtime, you mark my words. Now shut up and lie down on the sofa and I'll tell you which brand of human being you're unwisely planning to bring into the world.'

Juliet got up from the table and smilingly lay down on the battered sofa in the corner of the kitchen. She felt more like a young girl than a woman halfway through her thirties; a little light-headed, almost giggly.

'This is ridiculous. I'll be able to have a scan pretty soon and —'

'Oh, this is far better than a scan. Nothing is as early, or as reliable, as Granny's patent diagnostic ring.'

'I see.'

Juliet lay still while Harriet gently placed a hand over her abdomen and felt down towards her crutch. In her other hand she held the cord by its end and lifted it into a position directly over where she guessed Juliet's womb to be discreetly hidden under the layers of fat, skin and clothing, letting the ring hover half an inch or so above the material of Juliet's skirt.

'Does it work through clothes, then?'

'Oh yes, I don't think Granny would have been able to use it otherwise. Naked human flesh would have been far too much for her to take.'

Juliet watched, fascinated, as the ring began, very slowly, to circle clockwise.

'Oh you're doing that yourself,' she laughed.

'No, I'm not. I'm not, honestly. Look, my hand isn't moving at all, is it? It's not me, it's the ring.'

'Oh sure. Very likely. My father knew an obstetrician who used to predict the sex of babies. He'd tell the mother quite definitely whether she was having a boy or girl, then if it turned out not to be what he'd said, he'd show her a notebook. Next to her name would be written the sex of her baby – correctly this time, of course. "Look," he'd say, "I knew it was a boy. I just had a feeling you wanted a girl and I needed to keep you happy during the pregnancy, so I told you a little white lie. But, as you can see, I knew what it really was, and I knew you wouldn't mind by the time he was born."'

'And if by chance he was right first time, presumably the notebook never made an appearance?'

'Of course not.'

'Yes, well, that's very clever. But this really does work.'

'So?'

'It's a boy.'

'Where's the notebook?'

'No notebook. This is definitely and unequivocally a little chap.'

Anna woke first. Daylight, coloured and diffused by the red curtains, was filling the room, and she realised with a puzzled, almost guilty awareness, that this was the first time she had woken to find the sun already up since Harry's disappearance. She had lived through every moment of the other dawns, watching through eyes sore and raw from crying and lack of sleep, as the light had inched its slow, inexorable way into the room, signalling the end of a night of helpless longing and the beginning of another day; a day that would either be filled again with empty despair or one that would bring news of the only reason left to live.

Now on this morning she felt different. She had woken with the usual lurch of terror, but deep within herself she knew there was an almost imperceptible change; so slight as to be too subtle to search for mentally lest it escape altogether, but strong enough to exist unquestionably. She was aware without opening her eyes of Michael's arm still thrown across her body, of the warmth of his thigh touching hers. She listened to his steady breathing. Each intake of breath verged on becoming a snore as it was drawn in through his nose, fluttered round the back of his throat, then turned to a sigh, gently moving the hair of Anna's cropped black fringe, as it escaped again through his mouth, which was pressing heavily on her forehead. It was comforting to bask in the regular rhythm of it; to be alone and uninterrupted in her thoughts and yet physically to be not alone; to be clasped firmly by another body, which was as yet too deeply asleep to be aware of her existence in this new day.

She kept very still so as not to wake him, too relieved to have the edge taken off her permanent state of misery by this human contact to want to change anything. Her left ear rested against his breastbone, and she could feel as well as hear the shuddering little spasms of his heart as it formed a background to his breathing, quickening the pattern of its beating a little every time Michael breathed in, then slowing again as she felt the faint draught of exhaled air across her forehead. Her world became bounded by this rhythm of sound and feeling. The pulse of her own body also sounded in her ear as she listened, mingling with his heartbeat and stepping in and out of time with it as the two beats kept pace for a few seconds and then diverged, her quicker beat passing his like a runner lapping his rival, only to rejoin him again to beat in unison once more.

Michael moaned in his sleep, then, as he attempted to turn and found himself constricted by the small body beside him, his breathing changed, and he lay very still for a few seconds as if suspended in mid-movement. He suddenly opened his eyes and stared straight into Anna's.

For a moment or two he was silent, then he frowned a little and whispered to her, the smell of his breath sharp and sour on her face.

'How extraordinary. How can it be possible?'

She whispered back, 'What is it, Michael? Are you all right?'

'I wasn't sure it could be true. I didn't want to open my eyes in case I'd imagined all this. How can I feel such joy in the middle of this nightmare? Anna, when I woke just now and felt you next to me — I don't know how to tell you this — just for a moment I didn't think of *them*. I thought only about us.'

She gave a faint, wry smile. 'I didn't,' she said.

'No, of course not. But I'm not going to apologise for this, Anna.' He tucked the sheet up round them both with one arm, then held it tightly round her. 'I'm here for you now, I'm not leaving you alone until we've found him.' He looked down at her and smiled. 'You are completely beautiful, you know. Whatever happens from now on, I know I've found something that I shall never forget. Perhaps only two people so desperate could feel this. I understand what you were trying to tell me now. Nothing matters; nothing is right or wrong.' He kissed her gently on the forehead then rested his head back on the arm of the sofa, filled with a strange and not unpleasant confusion of emotions.

'Michael, I can't —'

'It's all right. Don't say anything. It's all right. We're here together, and just for now let's hang on to that and not try and make any sense out of it. Don't move

– let me hold you like this for a few more moments.'

As they lay clasped together, Michael looked around the small room. The opening buds of a small bunch of daffodils on the windowsill, brought in by WPC Susan Calvert in a kindly attempt to bring a little of the March sunshine into the wintry unhappiness of the room, made a splash of yellow against the curtains. The threadbare armchair, lace-covered coffee table and unwelcoming plastic-seated chairs were becoming quite familiar to him, and even the uncomfortable sofa on which he was lying had come to acquire a friendly intimacy. Now it held even greater significance, and he knew red Dralon would never look quite the same again. His head still lay propped up on one arm of the sofa, his right eye an inch or so from the mass of blood-red fabric, and he found himself marvelling at the intricacy of the thousand woven tufts of shiny nylon. 'It's really rather magnificent,' he muttered to himself.

'What's that?'

'Nothing. It's just that you've made me take a whole new look at your sofa. It's amazing.'

'Oh sure,' sighed Anna. 'I'm going to get up now – can you move your arm?'

He watched her as she walked towards the bedroom. The back view of her thin, pale body bathed in the warm, red light stirred such a strong protective instinct in him that it almost hurt.

'Anna?'

'Yes?'

As she turned, he took in quickly with a tiny electric

216

shock of desire the sight of what he had up to now only known by touch: her full breasts, flat stomach and long, slim legs.

'Come here a moment – just for a second.'

She moved back towards him, utterly unshy in her nakedness, and squatted down beside the now awe-inspiring sofa as he raised himself on one elbow and looked at her. Very slowly and gently he bent his head towards her and kissed her on the lips, so softly and carefully that it made her feel like crying again. 'I'll look after you,' he whispered, 'whatever happens, I'll look after you, I promise.'

'Have they given you a date yet?' asked Mrs Palmer, as she swerved to avoid a startled young man in jeans and anorak on the zebra crossing.

'Oh Mummy – for heaven's sake, do be careful. Yes, September the fourth.' She could hardly keep from smiling as she said it.

'So you'll be at your biggest by late summer. Nothing too heavy then, and of course you get surprisingly hot when you're carrying. Do get a move on!' She hooted impatiently at the car in front.

'Mummy, he's turning right, don't—'

'We'll go straight up to the first floor, and ask Mrs Wallis to help us. I know it's early days, but we might as well make a start so there's one less thing for you to worry about when you start to get sick and then tired and heavy.' (Great, thought Juliet, thanks, Mother.)

'Now, let's see; any sign of a meter? Oh look – are they coming or going?'

She stopped suddenly and peered out of the window. Juliet was aware of a red car behind them slamming on the brakes. Being driven by her mother meant having to be utterly thick-skinned about the reactions of other drivers at the best of times. But the fact that it was the height of the Christmas shopping rush meant those reactions were all that bit nearer to breaking point. Juliet had once mentioned something about lane discipline, to be greeted with incomprehension: Mrs Palmer's driving was more of the weaving, drifting style, making her way in chatty unawareness of her effect on other motorists, whom Juliet could see in the wing mirrors gesticulating as they desperately dodged to avoid collision.

They sat out the hooting and shouts until the meter was free, then, after some inventive reversing, left the car at an interesting angle in the parking bay. As they walked purposefully into Harrods, Juliet found herself idly wondering if it had been a mistake after all to tell her mother of the pregnancy. She had held out for two weeks, but a nagging instinct left over from childhood had made the secret burn inside her with such pervasive guilt, that she finally decided the downside of revealing it and enduring her mother's interference was more bearable than the tension of keeping it to herself. Just as she had foreseen, her mother's reaction was practical and positive, the reservations about the method by which the pregnancy had been procured apparently forgotten or superseded by the importance of doing everything in the right way from now on. Already instructions were flying about birth announcements ('Only *The Times*, whatever anyone else tells you.'); the place of birth ('Obviously Queen Charlotte's.'); the layette; the christening; and all the other hundred and one things that must be seen to be put in motion correctly. Juliet was quite happy to let her mother take charge in this way; and Michael was his usual easy-going self about such things — as long as the mother-to-be was happy he would go along with whatever arrangements she thought best — and Juliet herself was in a state of such unreal emotional bliss that she felt as if she floated above such practicalities, protected from the sharp edges of decision-making by the cocooned wrapping of silky happiness in which she was enveloped.

'I'm mostly going to live in casual things, you know, Mummy. Tracksuits, jeans and things. It's really not worth buying anything too special.'

Her mother frowned and stopped walking for a moment. 'But darling,' she turned and looked at her, 'I'd really like to buy you something. Something pretty.'

For just a split second they looked straight into each other's eyes, and a flash of understanding passed between them.

'Yes, well, one outfit would be good, wouldn't it?' said Juliet. 'Thanks.'

They made their way through the throng of Christmas shoppers towards the packed lift and then up to the first floor, where after an uneventful crossing of a vista of coats, suits and dresses, they finally ran aground at one of the cash desks. A small woman in her sixties dressed in a navy blue suit over a neat white blouse looked up and removed a pair of glasses from her nose at their approach, letting them hang round her neck from a gilt chain, smiling in recognition as she disentangled a section of the spectacle chain from where it was caught over one ear in her hair. Juliet's mother greeted her with the friendly familiarity tinged with superiority that befitted the relationship. 'Ah, dear Mrs Wallis – you are still here. How lovely to see you again. This is my daughter – I don't think you've —'

'No, I haven't, madam. How do you do? How lovely to meet you. Your mother and I have known each other for many years.'

'Hello,' beamed Juliet back to her.

'I want to buy my daughter a maternity outfit. She naturally wants to buy herself mostly casual clothes, but I do think it would be good for her to have one smart outfit to mark such an important event.'

'I'm afraid I can't help you with that, Mrs Palmer – that's up on the fourth floor. But how very exciting for you. Is it the first?'

'Yes, yes it is,' answered Juliet, enjoying the warm rush of pleasure that she always felt at any discussion of her condition.

'And you're to be a granny, then, Mrs Palmer? It's such a thrill, I can tell you. Nothing like it – my three are my pride and joy.'

'Yes, I'm sure they are. How delightful.'

Juliet smiled to herself at her mother's quick dispatch of Mrs Wallis's grandchildren; naturally they were not of a class to discuss in the same breath as her own. A quick glance and patronising approval of a photograph or two, perhaps, but any implication that they were in some way directly comparable to the future Palmer grandchild and that it gave them something in common to chat about on equal terms had to be nipped in the bud immediately.

They said their polite goodbyes and headed back to the lift. When it stopped and opened briefly on the third floor, Juliet caught a glimpse of a sea of grand pianos, the white teeth of their keys smiling in the open-jawed lids of walnut, oak and polished black. She longed to run into the middle of them, to stretch out a hand to touch them. What a waste, she thought: how they look as if they want someone to play them, to fill the hall with music.

They left the lift on the fourth floor to be greeted by the exciting notice, 'Children's World'. Mrs Palmer spotted an assistant and strode off towards her through racks of smocked dresses, corduroy dungarees and little blue blazers. 'Could you tell me where the maternity clothes are, please?' she asked loudly.

'Yes, certainly, madam, they're just along the —'

'Oh Juliet, do look! Isn't that charming?'

'— just along the aisle there, and then left at the bottom.'

She was holding one of the tiny blazers by its sleeve.

'Oh darling, isn't that just sweet. Shall I buy it, do you think?'

'Mummy, don't be so silly,' laughed Juliet, 'that's for a three- or four-year-old. Give me a chance. Anyway, it might need to be a pink party frock instead.'

'Yes, it might, mightn't it?' She peered at the label hanging from the sleeve end, before letting it go. 'Good heavens — a hundred and four pounds.'

They walked on past clothes that were getting smaller and smaller, until by the time they reached the end of the aisle, Juliet's stomach was clenched in a confusing mixture of joy and anxiety as she looked at the rows of tiny white cardigans and blue romper suits hanging from display stands topped with a mixture of fluffy bunnies, pink and blue rattles and Christmas tinsel. She could only just stop herself from wrenching the miniature clothes from their hangers and burying her nose in them.

'This way, darling,' called her mother. 'I can see them. Over here.'

The maternity department wasn't large, and at a glance Juliet could see that they weren't the sort of clothes she pictured herself in at all, but she decided to make the effort to find something to please her mother.

'Don't pick anything tight, will you, Juliet? It looks simply frightful when things cling round the bump.'

'I think the bump looks marvellous. I certainly don't want to hide it, not at all. Did you see the *Vanity Fair* cover with Demi Moore?'

'What, dear?'

'Oh, never mind. Yes, I'm sure you're right.'

After a few minutes searching among the voluminous skirts and dresses, trying to avoid her mother's eye when she could sense her pulling something she knew she wouldn't like from one of the racks, Juliet managed to pick out two dresses that were simple enough to be useful and a saleswoman showed them into a small changing room while she went to collect them in her size.

As they were waiting, Juliet studied her mother, who had taken a compact from her bag and was powdering her nose, still chatting as she did so. Her normally immaculately coiffed hair was wispily disarrayed and Juliet noticed how the pinky powder was gathering unevenly in clogged patches on the papery dry skin and collecting in a thickened layer round the hairline, like debris left at a high-tide mark. Her red lipstick, worn away where the moist lips clashed repeatedly as she talked, still clung around the rim of her mouth — shooting away from it in little lines, like the rays of a sun drawn by a child, as the colour followed the creases etched into its outline. Mrs Palmer had never quite penetrated the mysteries of eye make-up, but a gesture at blue shadow was smudged across the upper lids, gathering in similar style to the lipstick in the deeply engraved creases, giving the unnerving appearance of the shiny skin being scored by sharp blue lines as she looked down or blinked. For the first time in her life, Juliet felt sorry for her. The delight at her pregnancy had provided her with a shield against the guarded tension she normally felt in her mother's presence, and she now saw her objectively as the insecure, elderly relic of a bygone era that she had become; quite at sea in the high technology world around her. Only in her small flat or in places like this was she comfortingly insulated from reality by a safe domain of polite shop assistants, quiet music, immigrants tolerated solely as cheery bus conductors or incommunicative workmen, and gin and tonics before dinner.

Mrs Palmer took a lipstick from her bag, popped off the lid and tilted her head back to get a clear view in the small mirror of her compact. She opened her mouth and stretched her lips over her teeth, still talking like a ventriloquist in a stream of consonant-less chatter, a gluey string of mucus wobbling between the yellowing rows as her jaws moved in the effort. Watching, Juliet was suddenly engulfed in a tide of nausea that swept up from the pit of her stomach and threatened to erupt at her throat. 'Oh my God!' she gasped, and only just managed to stop herself from falling off the chair with a hand on the mirror as she retched loudly and bent double.

'Darling!' cried her mother. 'Are you all right?'

'Yes, yes I think so,' panted Juliet, 'hang on a sec. Phoo! That was nasty. Sorry, Mummy, I thought I was going to throw up all over you for a moment.'

'Put your head between your knees.'

'No, Mummy, I'm OK now. I'm better.'

'Juliet, I do wish you wouldn't be so stubborn. You really must allow that other people do sometimes know what's best for you. Now, put your head between your knees. Did you have anything to eat this morning?'

'No, I didn't feel like it.'

'Well, there you are then. That's really stupid, isn't it. What do you expect? You must eat a little something in the mornings, I told you —'

'Mummy, stop it please.'

'—or you're bound to feel like this. You know how you've always been about eating and —'

'Mummy, stop it. Stop it!'

'—and you can't just think about yourself all the time now, like you usually do. You've got someone else to consider. Eat little and often.'

'*Stop it!*'

'A cup of tea with sugar in it in the morn —'

'STOP IT! SHUT UP FOR A MOMENT. Just shut up. *Please.*'

Juliet looked up to see an embarrassed assistant hovering round the entrance to the cubicle, a bundle of dresses balanced on one arm. 'I'm sorry, I'm afraid we'll have to call off the fitting after all,' she said quietly. 'I have a telephone call to make.'

She reached down to the floor for her handbag and lifted her coat off the back of the chair as she got up. She made her way out of the cubicle and walked quickly away from the two women across the crowded floor of the shop towards the lift.

Chapter Sixteen

The telephone rang in Michael's office just as he was finishing off a consultation with a claimant. Two weeks on, Michael continued to see the world in such benign terms from the rosy heights of his newly acquired 'father-to-be' status that he was considering accepting the dubious evidence of Mr Bartleet's latest claim, much against the advice of the assessors which lay in a green file on the desk in front of him. But something in the tone of voice of the caller changed his mood in a moment.

'Mr Evans?'

'Yes?'

'It's Anthony Northfield here. Dr Northfield from the clinic. I've just had a call from your wife, and I wonder if you could spare a moment to pop in?'

'Is she all right? Is the baby all —'

'Everything's fine. It's nothing like that. I'd just like a quick word, that's all. Nothing to worry about. Sorry to bother you at work, but I wanted to be sure of catching you.'

'Of course. Look, I could come over now if you—'

'No, no, there's really no need for that.'

'Shall I come over after I finish? Do you want to see both of us? About six-thirty? Will you still be there then?'

'Yes, that's fine. But, perhaps just a quiet word with you alone at this stage, if that's all right. There's no need to drag Mrs Evans over here.'

Disturbed, despite the doctor's reassurance, Michael agreed, put the phone down and looked back at Mr Bartleet, who had become increasingly unhappy during the telephone conversation.

One glance at Michael and the other man sensed, correctly, that his chances of a successful claim had diminished as rapidly as had the smile from his broker's face. Struggling against the thudding crash of plummeting hopes within him, he bravely tried to resurrect the atmosphere of bonhomie and good will that had existed only moments earlier. 'Well, now, Mr Evans. The ceiling. I'm delighted that you understand about my wife's problem with the tap; I think you were saying that you saw no reason why—'

'I'm sorry, Mr Bartleet. I have to agree with the assessment. I can find no merit in your claim whatsoever.'

As soon as he had dispatched his last client at six-twenty that evening, Michael made his way to the clinic, having resisted the temptation to telephone Juliet first, sensing instinctively that he should wait to talk to Dr Northfield before contacting her. He spent most of the car journey going over the possible reasons that could have necessitated the visit, trying to ignore the images of dead and deformed babies that insisted on taunting him, dancing and floating in front of him against the background of the rain-spattered windscreen. Instead he attempted to conjure up a positive cause for the sudden meeting – twins, perhaps? There had, after all, been *two* embryos implanted, and he remembered only too well the excitement he had felt when Professor Hewlett had warned them about the risk of multiple pregnancy initially. But surely Juliet would have been asked along too, if it were news of that kind? Or would they rather Michael broke it to her, afraid that the shock, although a welcome one, might upset her in her delicate condition?

He reached the clinic without coming up with a satisfactory answer and, after finding a space on a single yellow line just outside, climbed quickly up the front steps and ran the gauntlet of the cheery Happy Eater photographs before reaching a disappointingly empty front desk.

'Hello?' he called optimistically into the empty space, 'Hello? Anyone around?'

'Oh I'm so sorry, Mr Evans,' said a smiling and slightly breathless receptionist as she emerged from a door behind the desk, 'I was just putting the kettle on in the back. You've come to see Dr Northfield, haven't you? Do take a seat in the waiting room a moment and I'll tell him you're here.'

'Thank you.'

Michael recognised the girl from previous visits and

was comforted by her unassuming and friendly ordinariness. As she bent her head to reach for the telephone, the sight of her glossy blonde hair scooped behind one ear evoked a pang of something akin to nostalgia, which he quickly realised was because she reminded him of Juliet, which in turn reminded him of the worrying uncertainty of the reason for his being there.

'Come on, stop being so bloody foolish,' he admonished himself as he moved towards the waiting room, 'there's nothing to worry about. He said so.'

'Oh, Mr Evans?'

Michael felt pleased that she continued to remember his name so effortlessly and use it in such a familiar way. Since the last depressing trip to the clinic he had forgotten how welcoming the place could feel. 'Yes?'

'Dr Northfield is ready for you. Do make your way up – you know where to go, don't you?'

Her smile seemed so genuine, her encouragement so reassuring, that Michael basked in it for a split second before turning to the stairs. He'd forgotten how good it felt to be treated as part of the operation, a key player, an instigator and a beneficiary, and he felt suddenly in control. He was the father. He was needed to discuss some implications of his wife's pregnancy. No doubt this happened all the time.

But nothing could have prepared him for what was to come.

Harriet's front door bell rang at six-forty just as she was pouring herself a drink. Having vainly searched the fridge for some tonic, she was tossing up whether to go for vodka and Ribena or vodka and Tizer. The Ribena just tipped the balance and she added a glutinous quarter inch of it into the clear liquid in her glass before walking over to the receiver on the wall and lifting it with a hand still sticky from the bottle.

'Hello? Oh damn!'

'Hat? It's me. It's Jules. What's the matter?'

'Oh hi. No, nothing, it's all right, I've just covered the phone with Ribena – come up. What on earth are you doing here?' She pressed the buzzer and then opened the front door of the flat and stood waiting at the top of the stairs.

'Hi, kiddo. How're you feeling? Don't rush up the stairs now,' she called down to Juliet, 'I don't want any emergencies, you know. Come in. Do you want a drink? Carrot juice or milk or whatever?'

'Yes, OK, thanks. Did I hear you mention Ribena?'

They walked into the flat and Harriet closed the front door behind them.

'Sure, you'll get to know it very well over the next twelve years or so, I can tell you, so you might as well start now.'

Juliet smiled. 'Thanks.'

'Come in the kitchen, it's the only place that's free of all the kids' Christmas stuff. We're making our own paper chains this year, and I'm deeply regretting it already. Blue Peter has a lot to answer for. You wait.

You look wonderful, by the way. How was shopping with Mama? And where's Michael? Sitting at home waiting for his supper or slaving away at the office?'

'Oh, he's at home by now, I expect. I just felt like a buffer again, if you know what I mean. A bit of a neutral gap between mother and husband. And I had a call to make.'

'Do you want to use the phone?'

'No, I've done it thanks. No, I mean I had to stop shopping to make a call and then I didn't feel like going straight home. I had to think about it all a bit. Oh, thanks.'

Harriet handed her a mugful of purple liquid and sat opposite her, both in their usual places at the kitchen table. 'Everything all right?'

'Yes, fine. Why?'

'Oh, I don't know. You just seem a bit brittle, that's all. You've been so jolly lately, I don't like to see this little flicker of the old tense Jules.'

'Jolly! I'd hardly describe myself as *jolly* at the best of times,' laughed Juliet. 'No. I'm OK. I've just got rather an extraordinary situation to deal with and I'm not quite sure I know the best way to handle it.'

'What, being pregnant, do you mean?'

'No, no, not that. That's all wonderful. I don't really want to talk about it at the moment, if that's all right.'

'Sure.'

Harriet watched her as she sipped her Ribena. There was something about her friend she couldn't quite put her finger on. The contentment was still there and there were even hints of the radiance of the glorious second stage of pregnancy stealing prematurely into her face, but something else hovered there as well. It was almost as if the success of having finally achieved her goal was manifesting itself in a brittle superiority; a feeling of indulgent triumph that was distancing her – just fractionally – from Harriet.

'Don't go smug on me, Jules, will you?'

'What?'

'You're not the only person in the world to get pregnant, you know. And don't look so affronted, it doesn't suit you. You should be glad you've got me to say these things to you. I'm the only one who can and it's because I know you so well and feel I've been through all the problems with you.'

'What on earth are you talking about?'

'Look, you've been through so much to get it that I'm bloody well going to make sure this pregnancy and birth is as good as we can possibly make it, and my godchild is going to be the most perfect baby that ever was. Apart from my own two magnificent specimens, of course, who somehow, God knows how, have managed to grow up as just about the most attractive, most charming children I know. In spite of the influence of that bastard their father. Oops! Sorry – as you were – strike out that last phrase, please.

'All I mean is you're not to cut yourself off from poor old me just because you're feeling frightfully clever at the moment. Getting pregnant is one of the easiest things in the world, old girl. Just because it wasn't like that for you doesn't give you the right to feel self-satisfied or unduly proud of yourself. Happy, *yes*. Glowing, *definitely*. But smug and superior, *no*. At least not while I'm around.'

Juliet was staring at her, the faint hint of knowing smugness in her eyes in no way diminished by this speech. She sighed slightly, then leant on her elbows and rested her chin on her folded hands.

'I can't decide. Whether or not to tell you,' she said.

As Michael walked into Anthony Northfield's office on the second floor of the clinic, the young doctor rose and walked round the desk to shake hands and to usher Michael into one of two upright chairs in front of it, taking the other himself. Michael looked hard at Anthony's face, seeking an immediate clue as to the reason for the visit, but finding only the friendly but inscrutable smile of the concerned professional. Aware peripherally of the framed abstract prints on the cream walls, the neat black laptop open on the bare white desk, the sleek stainless steel light fittings and minimal furnishings, Michael felt out of place, sensing the stream-lined efficiency of an office in the City, but missing the rôle he would normally take in such surroundings. If this had been a meeting about insurance, pensions or premiums he would have found the atmosphere helpful and positive, but to be here in his capacity as a patient – or, more exactly, husband of a patient – made him feel very vulnerable. His total dependence on this building and its inhabitants for the future happiness of himself and Juliet placed him on the defensive, and he realised how much more comfortable he had been in the old-fashioned surroundings of Professor Hewlett's room next door, where the large mahogany desk and faded, comfortable armchairs had reassured rather than confronted.

'Is she all right?' he asked as he sat down.

'Yes, Mr Evans,' answered Anthony, sounding relieved that the conversation had been opened. 'Yes, as I said, she's fine. I think what we have is more of an emotional problem. Your wife, as you know, has been through a lengthy ordeal – the years of not getting pregnant were very taxing for her – I am sure it has been difficult for you both. Professor Hewlett and indeed all of us here have explained to you, the process of IVF in itself can be extremely debilitating and we quite often see some rather distressing effects on temperament.'

Michael was beginning to relax. He had become so used to Juliet's moods over the years, and particularly over recent months, that it hadn't until now struck him that, to outsiders, they could be really quite startling. It was suddenly quite clear to him that she had been rude, difficult or obstructive with some of the doctors or nurses, or even just more emotionally demanding than their usual patients. He geared himself up to start explaining how little these moods really meant and how apologetic Juliet would be once she realised the trouble or distress she had been causing.

But Anthony went on. 'There is something I believe I ought to bring to your attention. It isn't easy for me to discuss this with you, but I feel now that I must. I'm afraid your wife appears to have convinced herself of an emotional — or perhaps I should say of a romantic — attachment that has no basis in reality.'

Michael had read of hairs creeping on the backs of necks but he had never before knowingly experienced the phenomenon in the way he did now. It felt as if each individual hair was slowly lifting itself from its horizontal position to stand to frozen attention in the moment's silence that fell between the two men.

'I'm sorry, I don't quite understand . . .' he began.

Anthony cleared his throat. He knew he wasn't handling this as well as he had wanted to; when he had rehearsed it in his mind earlier, the projected scene of the confrontation had been brisker, shorter and far easier than the reality in which he now found himself. Insecurity was making him hesitant and tentative. Why was he finding this so difficult? As he had told himself over and over again during the afternoon, this wasn't his first experience of emotional problems with patients, but for some reason this time it felt threatening, serious and almost sinister. He tried to assume a confidence he didn't feel as he continued.

'This is not really that unusual, Mr Evans, and normally I might not have said anything. But the fact is your wife has developed an attachment to a very strong degree indeed. And I want to make absolutely sure there's no room for any possible misunderstanding.'

How stupidly he had put that. There might never have been any possibility of 'misunderstanding' if he hadn't planted the idea of it in this man's head.

'I still don't quite see.'

'Mrs Evans is suffering from a mild delusion, no doubt induced by the traumatic effects of her emotional tension over a long period of time.'

'Yes?' Michael was beginning to feel irritated by the purposefully cryptic nature of the doctor's conversation.

'Well, to be blunt, Mr Evans, your wife is convinced that I have an emotional attachment to her.'

'Really? Well that's not too serious is it? I expect she just wants to feel that—'

'No, sorry, I'm still not making myself clear . . . She telephoned me this afternoon — I have to say I've been aware of something like this brewing for a while, but I didn't realise just how far it had gone. It is very clear to me now that she is extremely confused. The fantasies she talked of indicate that she is under a severe misapprehension. It puts me in a rather awkward position, but I felt it important to have a chat with you. Your wife is utterly convinced that I have been communicating messages to her for several weeks and that there is some sort of relationship between us. As you can see, I had to bring this out in the open before you heard it from her yourself, and came to any unfortunate conclusions.'

Anthony was almost smiling, covering the turbulence that was churning inside with an assumed nonchalance.

You smug bastard, thought Michael. *You smug, conceited, self-satisfied bastard. All you're worried about is yourself. That's what all this is about. Juliet said something stupid on the phone, you've got the wrong end of the stick and now you're frightened you've said something that she'll repeat to me and you'll get into trouble.*

'Don't worry, Dr Northfield, I understand completely,' he said calmly. *But, he thought, I would just like to know whether you feel perhaps you've in some way contributed to the situation. Whether maybe you've been flirting with my wife, for instance? Whether your bedside manner got just that little bit too intimate? Whether one of the procedures became a little too enjoyable?* A mental picture of Northfield in his blue coat with his arm between Juliet's naked, straddled legs suddenly flashed into his mind, and Michael almost gasped.

'I would like to assure you, Mr Evans, that I have never at any stage said or done anything that could possibly justify your wife feeling that I have anything other than a purely professional interest in her.' Anthony half wondered why the hell he had just said that, when there was no suggestion of anything of the kind, but he fixed the smile back on his face and ploughed on: 'I do stress again, Mr Evans, that this is not uncommon. But you'll obviously appreciate that I think it much better that I should not take part in any further treatment or discussion with her, should it be necessary. If all goes well, there shouldn't —'

'What did she say to you?'

'When?'

'On the telephone, you said she called you this afternoon.'

'She said something to the effect that she thought that —'

'No – exactly. I want to know *exactly* what she said.'

Anthony sighed and looked down at his hands, which were clasped together in his lap. The smile had faded and he looked serious and weary. Michael almost felt sorry for him.

'She said she received all the messages I was sending her and that it was time I stopped pretending. That she knew how I felt about her from the way I looked at her and the things I said, and that she felt the same way. That she was ready to recognise my love for her publicly. She was going to come round straightaway and talk about our future together.'

After a short pause Anthony lifted his head and looked straight into Michael's eyes for a moment, then he took a deep breath and said, almost gently, 'And a lot more along the same lines. I just couldn't seem to reach her rationally at all. I wouldn't have mentioned this to you if I thought it would just go away, Mr Evans. As you can imagine, I'd obviously rather not have had to bring it up at all.'

Michael could feel how red his face had become, flushed with a mixture of anger and humiliation, and with the effort of combating the infuriating desire to cry. The only person with whom he could consider discussing such a personal and embarrassing problem was the one that was the cause of it, and he suddenly felt completely alone. His contact with his parents over the years since his move to London had been intermittent and almost formal in its politely restrained warmth – a matter of telephone calls, occasional Christmas visits and factual, newsy letters – and there was no one else he could turn to in a moment such as this.

'So why *are* you telling me?' he asked gruffly.

Anthony answered immediately. 'I think you should consider taking her to see a psychiatrist. It's generally far better to tackle such things before they become entrenched, and I know a professional will be able to —'

'Are you sure that's really necessary? After all, she's obviously in a very emotional condition and . . .'

Anthony looked serious, and, for once, a little older than his years. 'Yes, I'm sure, Mr Evans. I'm completely sure. I'll give you the name of someone, and I do ask you to make an appointment as soon as possible. I think this is a matter of some urgency.'

Chapter Seventeen

Juliet had slipped into a semi-comatose feverish slumber; the still, cold form of the small baby lying silently beside her. The occasional car passed by the house, outlining the two human forms with an edging of thin bright white from the light of its headlamps which reflected intermittently off the ceiling of the darkened room. To the casual eye, ignoring the squalor and detritus of the filthy surroundings, they could have been a quietly sleeping mother and child; a peaceful twosome in loving unconsciousness simply needing the passage of night and the dawning of a new day to bring them to happy awareness and the normality of everyday life. The emptiness of their bellies, the chill of their skin, the loneliness of their hearts: all would have been invisible to the onlooker, all hidden beneath the appearance of calm and restorative sleep.

Even the dreaming had stopped. Juliet's mind had subsided into deeper patterns than those that permitted the swirling thoughts and images of the hallucinations of sleep; and in a natural and unconscious attempt at self-preservation, Harry's exhausted, hungry and thirsty body had switched off every function except those necessary for breathing and moving the blood around his tiny body.

The rustling continued – or did it? The almost imperceptibly tiny movements of Juliet's head against the material of her collar that had caused it still went on. But without her own ear awake to hear it and to magnify it into disproportionate audibility, did it still exist? Or had it disappeared along with the sensibility of the human instrument that had helped to produce it?

'You see, Hat, something rather wonderful has happened, and I'm just trying to sort out my thoughts before I decide how to tackle it. There's a young doctor at the clinic who fancies me —'

'Oh yes? Some young smoothie, I'll bet. Well, go on. I'm all ears. Has he propositioned you or what? Is there going to be a thrilling scandal? Come on, give me the juicy gossip.'

But Juliet didn't laugh at this in the way that Harriet had expected her to do. She still looked oddly removed, as if she were listening to her friend's chatter with one ear, but keeping most of her attention turned inward, to some secret knowingness that gave her the only well-qualified interpretation of all that surrounded her. The look on her face reminded Harriet of a friend who had found Jesus at the age of forty-one, and with whom all rational and constructive conversation had subsequently had to be abandoned in the face of the terrifying, all-embracing certainty of her own opinions – which had swept aside the possibility of there being any other view. Or of other girlfriends who had 'gone into counselling' and who had, under enthusiastic instruction, contemplated their own navels to such an extent that everything they saw, read or heard thereafter was similarly viewed through a small redundant aperture. As soon as Harriet heard speak of people 'finding their own space', 'feeling good about themselves' or 'becoming at peace in their own bodies', she would run a mile, knowing that invariably such 'inner journeys' would end in disaster and that she, who had plenty of 'baggage' of her own to contend with, would be left to pick up the pieces. On first acquaintance she had spotted in Lauren, the usurper of her husband's affections, the varnish of therapy-speak, and it drove her wild to see how her ex-husband, with whom she had laughed so many times at such things, was taken in by it. She had nearly hit him when he told her on one occasion that Lauren nourished his 'inner child', which, by implication, Harriet had been ignoring. Trying to explain that she had been a little busy nurturing the two outer children with their demands of food, washing and general dogsbodying had been useless, and evoked the same slightly pitying look of patient understanding that was now infecting Juliet.

'Hey, Jules, don't take me seriously. I'm only joking! What's going on with you?'

'He loves me, Harriet.'

Her friend hadn't called her 'Harriet' ever since she could remember, and the formality of it was chilling.

'Well, great. Good for you. It's always nice to have someone after you. But he hasn't said this has he? I'm sure they're not allowed to, you know. Doctor-patient relationship and all that — he could be struck off. Jules?'

'No, you don't understand. He really loves me, desperately. And I love him. It's the most important thing in my life now. It's extraordinary. I knew it some time ago, you see, but now it's time to do something about it. I'm going to have to leave Michael, of course, and then I'll be free for Anthony. It's all terribly special.'

She wore a gentle, serene smile, and it was this, more than what she had been saying, that suddenly brought home to Harriet the fact that Juliet was serious. 'Jules, what is this? Look at me — this is weird. What about the baby? I can't believe you're really telling me this. This should be the most wonderful time of your life; you're having the baby you've always wanted; Michael adores you and is as thrilled about the baby as you are; and now you're coming out with all this rubbish. Whatever this stupid doctor has said to you, you must forget it, right now.'

'Oh Harriet, you just don't begin to understand,' smiled Juliet. 'There isn't a choice in this — there isn't a decision to be made about forgetting it, not forgetting it. He's been making moves ever since I first went to the clinic, and he doesn't want to wait any longer. I have to be with him. You see I can't be complete until I am. Don't look so worried, it's just something beyond your experience, that's all.'

'Don't see him any more. Jules — I mean it. This is

very important. You must *not* see this guy any more. You don't need to go back to the clinic now, just keep checking in with your midwife until it's time for the delivery. Keep well away. Are you listening to me? I don't know what the hell's going on in your head, but this craziness could really screw things up for you.'

Juliet laughed and put her hand on Harriet's. 'No, no, no—'

'Juliet,' Harriet went on, 'just one thing I beg you; don't tell anyone else about this. I expect your emotions are completely messed up at the moment. All the hormone treatment and stuff they've been giving you — just think what you were always like before your periods — you were hell on earth — well, this is just an extension of that, I reckon. A sort of antenatal fever. You do know you're talking complete crap, don't you? But some people aren't going to understand all this, you could get yourself into big trouble, you know. Now, Juliet, I want you to tell me, seriously, has this guy said anything to you? Anything at all?'

'He looks at me,' smiled Juliet.

Ah, thought Harriet, there's the rub.

'So this is entirely something you've decided for yourself, is it? Even if there's a grain of truth in it, you've exaggerated it, my dear, I can tell you that for nothing. This guy has been mildly chatting you up and you've got it all out of perspective.' Harriet knew she was talking too fast, but she felt a desperate urge to get through to her friend, to penetrate the viscous barrier of self-deception that she could now see was covering Juliet

245

like an invisible caul. 'You've invented all this; you must be able to see that, surely. I don't know why, but obviously something has tipped you over the edge, old girl, and your neurons have got a bit crossed or whatever. Jules, look at me — where have you gone? What's happening?'

'How foolish I am,' said Juliet. 'Of course I should have realised you wouldn't understand. How could someone who's been abandoned by her husband possibly appreciate how I can be so very much loved by this beautiful man? I sympathise with your jealousy, Harriet, but there's no need to treat me as if I were as stupid as you are.' And with that she stood up from the kitchen table and calmly made her way out of the flat.

In an elegant conference room in the Intercontinental Hotel eighteen children dressed as chickens were standing in a line awaiting the press. Each of them held a large card with one letter boldly inscribed on it in red, spelling out along the line from left to right: 'CENTRE FARM CHICKENS'. Andrea stood well back from the line and eyed it through narrowed, critical eyes. The words bobbed uncomfortably up and down with the varied heights of the letter bearers, and Andrea conferred with her assistant, Jennifer. 'It's not too good, is it? It'd look much better if the letters were all on the same level. Couldn't you get them all the same height?'

'You said get kids between four and twelve so I did.

I thought you wanted a good range. I could easily have ordered them by height, if you'd said.'

'Shit. Never mind. I think they'd look better in order of height then, don't you? D'you think the words should go up from the left or down? Which is more positive?'

'Well, *chicken* is our operative word, isn't it? So maybe that should be highest. On the other hand the client might feel the brand name shouldn't be any lower than the product. How about high each end and lowest in the middle?'

'Try it. But quickly.'

Jennifer clapped her hands and in the best authoritative tone she could muster shouted at the children. 'OK, everyone, we want you to make a new line. Shortest in the middle and bigger each end, so you sort of dip in the middle. OK?'

Jennifer wasn't used to dealing with anyone under eighteen. The bemused children made a game effort to shuffle themselves about into the required new order, but it was quickly apparent that the milling throng was incapable of finding its own redesigned format, and Andrea impatiently stepped forward and began to manhandle them into position, briskly exchanging their letters in an attempt to keep the order intact. This proved to be easier said than done, as no sooner had she placed two or three of them together in ascending footage, than one of the younger ones would inevitably start wandering about and confusing the measurements, until Andrea was horrified to find that she had left herself with no discernible line – and no readable words – at all, and that if she didn't sort something out pretty quickly, the press would be greeted by a sea of aimlessly wandering chickens. She decided to abandon the swooping arrangement and concentrate on a simpler pattern of highest on the left, reading in descending order to the right.

'Tallest over here,' she barked, wishing she could pinion each child to the floor as she moved them, 'and give it the "C".'

She had six positioned in a reasonably ordered line and was just moving the seventh into position, when out of the corner of her eye, she saw a fluffy wing shoot up in the air from the 'E' standing second in line.

'Can you keep still a moment, please,' she called over to it, 'it's really hard to get this organised and have a good look at it if you keep fiddling about.'

But the wing stayed in the air, and some muffled words came from its owner.

'Oh, for goodness sake,' Andrea muttered irritably, 'what is it? I can't hear what you're saying.' She moved across to the number two, who was tightly gripping an 'E' with one wing and still holding the other in the air.

'Please, Miss,' said a small voice from within the white feathers, 'I need the toilet.'

'Jennifer!' shouted Andrea. 'Please take this child to the Ladies. I thought you'd done all that?'

'I did,' countered Jennifer, moving briskly forward in her smart navy suit, brown bob swinging, to collect the child, 'but you did say to make sure they all had plenty to drink so we didn't get any problems like last time, and I think some of them have drunk masses of orange squash. I knew this would happen. Now, listen children,' she raised her voice as she turned to confront the other chickens, 'are there any more of you who want to go to the loo, because it's now or never, and we haven't got much time.'

Six more wings shot in the air, and Jennifer hurriedly escorted the feathered troupe out of the conference room, while Andrea tried to arrange the remnants into order.

The lavatories proved to be up two flights of stairs. Jennifer's competence at dismantling just enough chicken costume to allow for their use was strained to its limit, and when two of the inhabitants proved to be boys, she almost despaired. She managed to persuade a grudging male attendant in the cloakroom next door to cope with them, then returned to the female flock awaiting her in the Ladies. By the time she had undressed and dressed each one and then indulged their insistence on washing their hands slowly and carefully with soap from a reluctant dispenser, and drying them under the single electric blow drier, nearly twenty minutes had passed.

She returned to the ground floor to find the press already there, holding glasses of wine in one hand and briefing packs in the other, looking rather disinterestedly at a haphazard line of ruffled chickens bearing the mysterious words: 'CTR FAM CKENS.'

'Oh no,' she heard one of her party of birds say in

dismay from out of a yellow felt beak, 'they've started already. We've missed it!'

One of the others began to cry. Jennifer squatted down beside the whimpering bundle of polyester feathers and whispered at it that if it would just stop crying and be a good little chicken it could have a bag of sweeties at the end of the afternoon. As she stood up again, pleased at the apparent success of this simple strategy, she saw a smartly dressed blonde woman walking across the deep pile red carpet towards her.

'Oh hello,' Jennifer greeted her, 'have you come for Centre Farm? Do help yourself to a press pack from the table. We'll be starting the presentation very soon now.'

'Are you Andrea?' the woman asked, smiling at her.

'No, I'm Jennifer. Andrea's just over there – in the blue suit. I'm sure she'll be happy to see you. You are from . . . ?'

'It doesn't matter. I'll wait until she's free. Thank you.'

'And then just as I was about to start the video presentation this ghastly woman came up to me and calmly told me you and she were in love and going to set up house together. Not exactly what I was hoping to hear at the first promotion for an extremely important client, I can tell you. I had to hand the whole thing over to Jennifer – who, as you know, has about as much talent for presentation as a gnat – and take the bloody woman out into the corridor. I'd be grateful if you could keep your screwballs away from me in future. That is, if she is a screwball; I have to say I'm not at all sure. She was horribly convincing.'

Andrea hadn't even bothered to remove her coat, but had accosted Anthony as soon as she entered the house, bearing down on him with a breathless and furious account of her extraordinary encounter with Juliet.

Anthony looked shocked, and grasped her hand in his as he answered. 'Oh Christ, Andy. This is a nightmare! I had hoped I'd scotched this one. I did tell you about this woman, didn't I? You do remember that I told you about her? I knew she was a bit odd, but I must say I hadn't foreseen anything like this. She phoned me up yesterday and was rattling on about the weirdest things.'

'She phoned you up? What for?'

'Well, this. For all of this. For what she told you.' He put down the *Evening Standard* he had been reading and sat forward in his armchair.

'Why didn't you tell me?'

'There wasn't any point. You know I have plenty of traumatised patients and they —'

'Yes, maybe, but you don't have plenty of patients with whom you're madly in love and going to live with and going to fuck – or already have fucked, perhaps? Yes, of course, silly me, why am I assuming this is all fantasy? You have, haven't you? You have fucked her. Good, was it?'

'Oh Andy, for God's sake, shut up. Don't be pathetic. I'm very sorry she ruined your presentation but she's obviously sick and you really can't blame me for it.'

'Why not? You obviously encouraged her or she wouldn't be thinking this way in the first place.'

'Bollocks. I'm not enjoying this, you know. This is all a complete and utter fantasy.'

'How did she know about me then? How did she know where to find me?'

'For God's sake – I must have talked about you, I don't know, when I was in theatre or something. Probably told her about your work. It would have been easy for her to — look, Andy, we've had this before, haven't we, and laughed about it? This one is just a bit more over the top, that's all. I've even had to tell her husband.'

'You've what?'

'Well, I had to. She was telling me all sorts of crazy things, Andy, and nothing I could do would put her off. It was really strange. Everything I said just sort of bounced off her, and she just listened to me in that calm way, as you said, and then went on spouting all her nonsense. I had to tell him – supposing she'd gone home and repeat—Well in fact I know she was going to – I know she was going to repeat all this to him and then what sort of trouble do you think I'd have been in? The woman needs treatment.'

'God, this is so humiliating. You've been discussing her infatuation or obsession or whatever completely behind my back. Ugh! It's so revolting, it makes me creep. This affects me too, you know. She's dangerous. You should have told me.'

Anthony suddenly felt frightened. Not only had he had to put up with a ridiculous scene on the telephone from a woman he was finding it increasingly difficult not to hate, but he'd also had to cope with a jealous husband followed by a disbelieving and accusing girl-friend. It was all unnerving him considerably, *and* he had a horrible feeling that Andrea was loving every minute of it; using her knowledge of his need for her to make him beg, plead, cling. How was it that she always man-aged to get the upper hand in this sort of situation? He was the one being chased by another woman; it should make him feel desirable, sought after. He tried to muster the manly forcefulness he needed, but heard himself whining instead of sounding masterful.

'OK, that's it. Think what you like. This is a time when I could really do with your support, you know, but if you want to make a fight out of it, go ahead.'

Just then the telephone rang. Andrea was relieved to have an excuse to move, not knowing otherwise how to extricate herself from a scene she'd had no intention of making when she'd thought everything through on her way home from the hotel. She had imagined herself as the patient, understanding companion, sophisticated enough to treat the ludicrous allegations of the blonde with the contempt they deserved. Bitter unreasoning jealousy and anger had overwhelmed her during the conversation with Anthony and taken her completely by surprise. But, once started, she knew this emotional reaction gave her an intriguing power. For now she had got full juice out of it, so the phone had rung at the perfect moment to avoid weakening and ending up with a soppy scene of forgiveness on the sofa. There was a long way to go before she would be ready for that. As she walked over to take the call, she decided to pull herself together and use a cool approach for the next phase.

'Hello?'

'Oh, hello, Andrea, are you still there? This is Juliet. Can I speak to Anthony please?'

Andrea threw the receiver down on the table. It skidded across the white shiny surface, slid off the edge and hung dangling from its curly cord. 'It's your lover,' she spat at Anthony, 'go fuck yourself.'

Michael and Anna were walking through the grey landscape that surrounded her flat. With her was the pager that the police had given her to ensure she could always be reached in the event of there being any news, and she reached into her pocket, pulled it out and checked for the third time that it was on.

'OK?' said Michael, putting an arm round her shoulders and giving a little squeeze.

'Yes, OK. It's on. I can't help feeling nervous, though. I always think they'll forget I've got it and try to phone and I won't be there, and then what would they do?'

'Of course they know you've got it. That's exactly why they gave it to you. We won't stay out long, I promise. I just want to get you out of that flat for a few minutes, that's all. We'll walk twice around the building and then go back, OK?'

'Yes. Yes, all right.'

Michael looked at the colourless stretches of deserted and filthy concrete that surrounded them. The only sign of life was a group of three boys of about twelve who were leaning on the pillars in the shadowed space underneath the block of flats, watching Michael and Anna silently and belligerently. Michael thought idly of asking them why they weren't at school, but quickly judged better of it. Anna had told him of the gangs of youths that tended to roam the buildings, children as young as ten or eleven among them, dealing in drugs or indulging in petty crime, frightening the elderly people into barricading themselves in their homes, and making the lives of the other inhabitants as they came and went a miserable gauntlet-run. He looked at the boys, imagining, as he so often did when he watched children, that one of them was his son. What chance would such a son have, starting from here? What possible reason could Michael give to persuade him to go to school, when every probability was that, even in the unlikely event of his leaving with any decent qualifications, the chances of employment were minimal? What sort of life had they led up to now, these boys, to produce the expressions of jaded, cynical unhappiness that he saw etched into their faces? He remembered sitting in his comfortable armchair at home and reading in his comfortable middle-class newspaper of children of four or five, part of the growing so-called underclass, who had lived the whole of their short lives left alone for hours at a time in a world of TV and video. When handed a book, they would turn it over in puzzlement, literally not knowing what it was for or how it worked. Michael thought of the times his father had tried to get him interested in books that he himself had enjoyed as a child: books like *Emil and the Detectives* or *The Wind in the Willows*. Michael had scoffed at him and damned them, with all the authority of his eight or nine years, as boring and old-fashioned. It was only recently that such moments had started to come back to him, filling him with a sweet sad nostalgia and a desperate wish to be able to go back, to climb on his father's knee and read about the adventures of Ratty and Mole or Emil, and to see the smile on his father's face. How much he had taken for granted. These children would never be given the chance to be so dismissive; they were virtually unteachable, and would grow up to become as unhappy and inadequate parents as theirs had been before them.

'What a mess,' said Michael aloud, and Anna turned her head to look up at him, then looked across herself at the three youths.

'What them? Oh they're all right. Leave them alone.'

'No, I didn't mean that – I just felt sorry for them, that's all.'

'There's no need to do that; don't be so patronising – they're tougher than you or me put together. Don't give us your pity, Michael – we don't want it and it's no help.'

Chapter Eighteen

'Juliet, you've got to listen to me. I'm trying to be understanding, I really am, but you're pushing me too far. You must never, ever contact Anthony Northfield again — ever. Not even once. We can still make things work, but you've got to stop this craziness right now.'

'Michael, you don't understand — it's not a question of my stopping anything — it's all gone much too far for that. Anthony and I have denied our love for far too long as it is and —'

'Shut up! Just shut up!' Michael lunged towards her in the small hallway and grasped her hard by the shoulders. 'You've got my son inside you, you bloody woman! Our son's inside you! You don't have these kind of choices, understand? I've indulged your selfishness too much; you're not going to do this to me, Juliet, I won't let you. You're staying here until the baby is born and then you can do what you like, I don't care. But you're not taking my son away — do you hear?'

'I'd hardly call it *your son*, Michael, would you? If it is a son, that is — I love the way your pathetic male ego can't imagine it being anything else. It's not as if you were ever really very good at that kind of thing is it? We may have used your sperm, but if you want to get technical about it, I must say I think Anthony has every right to claim just as much parenthood as you. How do you think I'd have ever got pregnant without him? Ever thought of that?'

'What the hell are you talking about, you stupid, silly woman? *Listen*. Just listen to me quietly for a moment.' Michael let go of her and his arms fell to his sides as he leant back against the wall. He took a deep breath, and began again, slowly and calmly: 'I want you to think back over the way things happened and where we are now.

'I am your husband. You couldn't get pregnant. We went to see Professor Hewlett because we needed help. It took a long time and you went through a lot of emotional trauma — as they said you would. You did eventually get pregnant — much to our delight, as you may remember — and everything was going well. Now you've dreamt up this absurd infatuation with this unpleasant young doctor and you're letting it all get out of hand. You've got everything twisted because you've been upset and—'

'Oh really, Michael, don't be so childish. You don't have to go through this history business, you know. I'm not mad. I haven't forgotten anything — I'm quite well aware of what's been going on. It's just that I've also been aware of Anthony's love, which is something I tried to keep from you as long as I could. I thought I could just leave here and things would sort themselves out. But it hasn't been quite that easy. I'm sorry, darling – I really am. It's not something we can change, though, you see. It's just the way it is and I have to go to him.'

There was something in the gently patient, even sympathetic, way she was explaining this to him which finally convinced Michael that Juliet really believed, completely and wholeheartedly, everything she was saying. He reluctantly admitted to himself that Anthony Northfield was right and that he could no longer deal with this on his own.

'Juliet, come into the sitting room for a moment. I'm not going to try to persuade you out of anything you feel you need to do, I promise you that. But please just come and sit down with me for a while.'

'Certainly.'

They moved into the small, warm sitting room, where – it seemed to Michael – such a short time ago Juliet had brought him the news of her pregnancy. He had felt a little surge of pleasure each time he had entered the room since the happy day she had sat at his feet and told him: even the armchair had seemed to glow with satisfaction at the privileged position it had taken in the momentous moment when he had discovered the presence of his future child. But even then, he now realised, this viper had been coiled inside her; she had known of it, nurtured it even, and said nothing. Through his enlightened eyes the room looked sad, empty and defeated, and the Christmas tree seemed to mock him with its false promise of happiness. As he gently took Juliet's coat off her shoulders and slid it down her arms, he felt a pang of terror at the sight of the deceptively flat belly that had, up until the last few days, brought him such proud excitement.

'Sit down, Julie. Please.'

'All right – but you're not going to change my mind, you know. You can't make me. I can go where I want. That's the law.'

It was all he could do to restrain himself from shaking the madness out of her, but he closed his eyes for a moment and clenched his fists in an effort to control himself before sitting down opposite her.

'Just please do one thing for me. Will you go and see someone about all this with me? Talk to someone objective who won't ask you to do anything you don't want to, but who may be able to advise us how to cope with it? Please, Juliet, it's the least you can do for me.'

'Do you mean a psychiatrist? You still think I'm imagining all this, don't you?'

'No – well, yes, actually I do, but don't let's start all that again – that's not my point. Just let's go and see a professional who can try to explain it.'

The coldness in her eyes was frightening him, but, much to his surprise she suddenly smiled at him, and said cheerfully: 'Yes. Yes, all right, if you like.'

Anthony arrived at his Maida Vale home late that evening. He left the car in a residents' parking bay and walked towards his front door; cold, tired and a little depressed. The polish had been stripped off his life by the Evans incident: the long-dreaded crack in the thin exterior of his confidence had appeared, and he sensed it widening to reveal the inadequacy he had always known was hiding beneath. They would find him out – they were already finding him out. He knew that this woman's obsession threatened to peel away the success he had worked so hard to achieve; and it was all his fault. If he could only handle this with the cool, removed professionalism that he knew it deserved, there need be no problem: he had done nothing wrong, only his own lack of nerve made it so menacing. He felt once again like the clumsy son and big brother who, however hard he tried, never quite kept up with the triumphs of the rest of his family; triumphs they acquired so easily and with so little effort compared to his hours of struggle.

The husband had talked to Hewlett, and however supportive the professor had been in the two discussions he'd had with Anthony since, he knew it had irritated the old boy and had slightly, albeit irrationally, diminished the younger doctor's standing in his boss's eyes. Image was all important to the clinic; Hewlett never shunned publicity, and revelled in the news items he was occasionally asked to take part in, whether of the positive 'Miracle baby for hopeless couple' type or of the 'Shock horror – woman to bear twins at 50' variety. In every case he was only too happy to trot along to the television studios or to give telephone quotes on anything related to the easily exploitable sensationalist aspects of IVF. Occasionally he had sent Anthony along in his stead, particularly when charm was called for to help to put across to the general public such delicate matters as multiple pregnancy and selective embryo destruction. Any tarnish on the character of one of his staff – even if totally undeserved – would be bad for image and therefore for business. The whole situation left Anthony feeling very disturbed.

He dug a hand into his pocket and searched around for his door key, his breath steaming in the cold, dark air, his briefcase heavy in the other hand. He heard his own impatient grunting in the silence of the quiet street, and sniffed as the cold began to make his nose run. Suddenly, without any warning or hint of movement from within, the front door was thrown wide open a few inches from his face and for a fraction of a second his mind refused to interpret the confusing signals it was receiving from the sight of the person confronting him.

'Hello, darling, I've been waiting for you. Come in.'

The automatic urge to get in out of the cold was strong enough to overcome the initial resistance Anthony felt to moving any closer to the radiantly smiling figure of Juliet Evans, who was standing in the doorway with one hand still holding the open front door, and with the other reaching out to usher him in.

'Jesus Christ,' he muttered as he pushed past her, squeezing himself against the opposite wall so as to avoid touching any part of her. 'How the hell did you get in? Where's Andrea? What the hell are you doing in my house? Don't shut the front door! I'm afraid I shall have to ask you to leave immediately. Could you go, please?'

But it was too late. Juliet had closed the door and had turned to face him, a triumphant, determined look on her face. She moved towards him and he backed away down the short corridor, but then, as he reached the entrance to the sitting room, he stood still and held his arm across the doorway, blocking any chance of her going in. She too had stopped, and stood patiently waiting to see what he would do next. Her hair looked recently brushed and hung in a shining waterfall around her face, and she was fully, and beautifully made-up, lips a scarlet focus for Anthony's reluctant gaze. She wore a belted raincoat of some fluid, fine material that was pulled in tightly, emphasising the slimness of her waist and the rounded femininity of her breasts and hips. The promise of early pregnancy gave her a voluptuous ripeness and she looked – even in his angry, bewildered state, Anthony registered the fact automatically – beautiful.

'Andrea let me in. She didn't seem very pleased,' she laughed. 'Now she's gone out. Perhaps you should give me a key, darling? When is she leaving?'

The telephone rang in the sitting room behind him. As Anthony turned to move into the room he shouted over his shoulder at her, knowing as he did so that he was handling it badly, that he was overreacting: 'Please get out of my house, Mrs Evans. If you don't leave immediately I shall call the police——Hello?'

He looked away from her and frowned as he listened

to the voice on the other end of the telephone, then looked up at her again as he went on, 'Yes it is . . ., Yes, yes she's here now. Come and fetch her please or —'

As he spoke, Juliet walked into the room and across to where he was standing by the small telephone table. 'What is it?' she asked. 'What do they want?'

Anthony ignored her and turned his back, speaking again into the receiver. 'Well, I don't know. I'm not sure I can . . . all right. All right, if I can.'

He turned round again to look back at her, and a jolt of horror flashed through him, making his groin shrivel and cramp and reaching his head in an explosion of red shock. Juliet had undone her coat and was slipping it off her shoulders and Anthony took in, at one horrified glance, the large, swollen breasts, white belly and dark, dark triangle at its base. The mixture of panic and repelled excitement that jarred through him made him catch his breath.

'Oh no!' he gasped. 'Get out! Put your coat on and get out!' He shouted down into the receiver: 'Your bloody wife's standing here with nothing on! You'd better do something about this, I'm telling you, or I'm calling the police.' *What am I doing?* he thought. *I've got to calm down. I can handle this.*

He slammed the receiver down and turned to the undressed woman, who was standing quietly next to him, seemingly unaffected by his enraged state.

'Come on, darling,' she murmured, holding her arms out towards him, 'come on, my love — don't make trouble. I know everything, I told you. And don't call me Mrs Evans, you silly boy. You don't have to——'

Anthony picked up the coat from the floor and pulled it roughly around her shoulders, attempting to cover as much flesh as possible without touching her skin with his hands, and at the same time marching her, unresisting, towards the front door. 'I'll take you home,' he muttered. 'I'll put you in my car and take you home.'

'Whatever you say, darling. There's no hurry. Whatever you say.'

The green painted front door was covered in brass plates like an old soldier's chest with ribbons; the dilapidated, well-worn building displaying its colours in the impressive number of 'FRCP's it had accumulated over recent years. Once inside, the presence of the medical establishment was far less obvious. If the fertility clinic a couple of streets away hid its identity behind jolly staff photographs and informal furnishings, this masqueraded as the town house of a respectable nineteenth-century family. Dark, mahogany bookcases lined the large ground-floor waiting room; a vast gloomily coloured Persian rug was on the floor, a dusty chandelier hung from the intricately patterned ceiling. The receptionist, too, seemed as if she had been left over from some other era: the long skirt, cardigan and grey perm all looked as if they were covered in a fine layer of dust, and as she raised her spectacles to her eyes, the lenses appeared dull and cloudy. Michael thought she must have been preserved in her entirety in a damp chest somewhere, to be raised intermittently from her suspended state by the ringing of the bell, in order to greet the patients with her unsmiling, fusty melancholy.

'God, just imagine if you were suffering from depression or something,' he whispered to Juliet as they sat together side by side on uncomfortable straight-backed chairs at the enormous polished wooden table in the empty waiting room, 'I should think she'd finish you off completely.'

Juliet smiled in the polite, detached way she had adopted over the last couple of days since agreeing to make the pilgrimage to the psychiatrist, and Michael sighed. He still found himself talking to her in the old way; half expecting her to shake her head and laughingly tell him she had been pretending and that everything she had said about Anthony Northfield was a stupid practical joke.

He leant forward and picked up a copy of *Country Life* from a dog-eared pile in front of him, and was unsur-prised to find it a year and a half out of date. After a few half-hearted flips of the pages, he flung it on the table and leant back in his chair, forcing it to rock back on its turned wooden legs. 'Not that it would have made much difference, even if it had been bang up to date, of course,' he said out loud, aware that he might as well have been talking to himself, but ploughing on in a relentless disregard for the indifference of his wife beside him, trying to lift the oppressive atmosphere by at least a gesture at normal chatter. 'I suppose pictures of debs coming out or going in or whatever they do nowadays are pretty much interchangeable. Pity I caught sight of the year really, or I'm sure I'd have been perfectly happy. This is when you miss *Punch* of course. You never realised how much you depended on all those unfunny jokes to cheer you up in waiting rooms until they weren't there. Somehow old *Tatlers* and *Horse and Hound* just don't bring one quite the same lightness of spirit, if you know what I mean.'

The perm appeared around the door and informed them that 'Professor Field is ready for you' in a tentative whisper. Michael thought how perfectly the voice suited the personality, and as they followed her down the passage towards the back of the building, he imagined how shocking it would have been if she had popped her head round the door and come out with a loud, resonantly jolly, 'Hello there! He'll see you now, you two; he'll soon cheer you up – come along, please!'

They reached the smallest lift he had ever seen, which had been fitted into what was obviously originally the well of the back stairs, and the perm heaved the heavy, double, old-fashioned iron gates back and ushered them inside, murmuring something Michael couldn't quite hear as she did so. 'Sorry?' he said as she heaved them shut again.

'Please press Two,' she repeated and retreated down the corridor again to disappear into her cubbyhole off the hall.

On Floor Two, Michael pulled back the gates with difficulty, admiring retrospectively the perm's hidden strength, and deciding all her energy must have been channelled into lift work leaving none for vocal projection. On the landing a black-coated, striped-trousered figure was waiting for them, who, to Michael's relief, greeted them loudly and warmly.

'Not the largest lift in the world, is it? I have to ask any patients I suspect may be claustrophobic to use the stairs I'm afraid,' he cheerfully remarked.

Michael and Juliet smiled politely and followed the professor's grey head into his consulting room, which was only marginally less dreary than the ground floor, but which was lightened considerably by the personality of the inhabitant.

'Now do please sit down,' he said, gesturing to two chairs in front of a desk by the window. He sat opposite them behind the leather surface, still smiling in benign, fond-uncle style at the two of them. Michael thought how remarkably he fitted the traditional image of the kindly but eccentric professor: the bald head, fringed with eminently grey tufts above his ears, sported obligatory half glasses over which peered what would have been described in a children's story as 'twinkling blue eyes'.

He painstakingly took a full history from them both, during which Michael was relieved to find Juliet's account emerged calmly and factually. It was only when she began to describe the recent 'love affair' that he began to squirm, and it took all his restraint not to shout out in fury at the insulting and humiliating drivel she came out with. Perhaps sensing Michael's discomfiture, Professor Field asked to see Juliet alone, explaining that he was in no way implying that she had secrets from her husband, but that it was important to hear her account without any embarrassment she might feel at his presence in the room.

'Then I would like to see you alone, Mr Evans,' he said. 'It would be a help to me to talk to you privately, for exactly the same reasons.'

'Yes, of course,' said Michael, rising from the chair, 'shall I wait downstairs, or —'

'No, let me show you.' Professor Field got up and walked over to the door, then opened it for Michael and gestured to a door further along the corridor. 'Do wait in there,' he smiled at him, 'we won't be long.'

The receptionist grinned at Anthony as he strode into the clinic. 'Hello, lover,' she said, 'another pile of letters awaits you and this came for you this morning.' She lifted a large basket of red roses from behind the desk, and grunted as she passed it across to him.

'Oh Christ,' he sighed, 'not more! And don't laugh about it, Laura. It's not funny. Give me the letters, please, I'd like to get rid of all this before Prof sees them.'

She handed him a pile of six or seven envelopes, all addressed in the same hand, and he shifted the flowers over on to one arm and reached out to take them. She smiled again as she whispered, 'Cheer up – once she has the baby her hormones will be sorted out and she'll forget all about you.'

'Thanks a lot,' he answered as he carried the

unwanted offerings towards the stairs, 'only eight
months to go. If Andy rings, no mention of the flowers,
OK? Or the letters.'

'No, of course not. Sorry, Anthony, we're not really
laughing about it. It'll all blow over, you'll see.'

'I believe your wife is suffering from what we call de
Clérambault's syndrome: a *psychose passionelle*. I'm sure
your French is —'

'Yes.'

Professor Field looked at Michael over the top of
his glasses, the eyes serious and concerned, the twinkle
nowhere to be seen now and even their colour appearing
less blue and more grey than before.

'It's not as uncommon as you might think,' he went
on, 'but it is comparatively rare to see it in such an
extreme form. It differs from what you might call a
more straightforward erotic paranoid delusion, although
there are obviously many similarities. The de Clérambault patient – generally a woman – will typically delude
herself that a man, with whom she may have had little
or virtually no contact, is in love with her. The *victim* –
if you'll forgive the word – may well be a public figure
in politics, on the screen, stage or television; or it's often
a priest or —' he paused, just for a fraction of a second,
'—a doctor.' He was speaking quietly but firmly, the
authority in his voice reassuring but at the same time
frightening because of the weight which it gave to the
discussion.

Any secret fantasy remaining within Michael that this was some sort of bad dream or joke was now shattered.

'This is a very difficult time for you, and I take this very seriously indeed. Having had this first consultation with Juliet, I consider that her present state of nervousness and insecurity is not unconnected with her early anorexia, which she says you know about.' He took off his glasses and placed them gently down on the desk, then rubbed his face with one hand, before placing it down on the blotter in front of him and studying its splayed fingers as he spoke. 'People suffering from this type of psychosis have these feelings very strongly, as, of course, you are only too well aware. She feels valueless without her delusional love; the rejection of her advances will merely be interpreted by her as paradoxical and as a communication of hidden emotions. In other words she will simply believe that all the time he really loves her. It may confuse her, but not change her view.'

'Oh my God,' Michael said quietly. He put his hand to his forehead and looked down at his lap. 'What has – why has she got it?'

'I could give you all kinds of instant theories about background, personality, the trauma of fertility treatment, but I would be far more honest if I said to you that we don't really know. There is no one cause that I can pinpoint at this stage, although her childhood history would tend towards emotional disorders in adulthood. The important thing is where we go from here. I hope and believe that treatment will be successful, but I must warn you that in my opinion it is going to take some time, and I'm afraid you are going to have to be extremely patient.'

'Yes, I see.'

'Let me tell you that I am convinced nothing you could have done would have prevented this. I am anxious to reassure you on that score.'

'I understand. Thank you.'

'I intend to begin a regimen of treatment as soon as possible. It will, of course, owing to the pregnancy, necessarily exclude some of the pharmaceutical approaches I might normally consider using. However, there still remain plenty which have been tested as safe in such circumstances. I'd also like to admit her to hospital.'

'Oh no, I don't think she can. I don't —'

'Why do you feel that would be a problem?'

'Because she just won't. She can't bear hospitals; we've already had talks about trying to have the baby at home because she's so terrified.'

'All right, Mr Evans. At this stage I'll rely on your feelings. You, after all, are the person who is closest to her and knows most about her. I'm a great believer in listening to the partner in these situations. We need to keep her as stable as possible: that is the priority now. I shall arrange for her to have outpatient treatment. It's extremely important for her that you are patient and tolerant; her actions at present derive from an illness and are not a reflection on you or how she feels about you. You must keep this in mind.'

'I see. Thank you very much.'

Chapter Nineteen

Juliet began daily visits to Wimpole Street, and to Michael's relief accepted the routine without protest or any apparent reluctance. He learnt not to broach the subject of Anthony, as any mention of him produced such a disheartening response that he thought it best to keep their lives in a state of suspended reality, floating above the emotional horror lurking beneath the surface. Christmas had come and gone without being celebrated in the Evans' household, and Michael had been glad to see the back of it, relieved when the moment came for him to throw out the brightly decorated tree. Its wilted, dried-up branches, still bearing the superficial trappings of joyous festivity, had seemed to taunt him and he relished its destruction. On Professor Field's advice, Juliet had given up her job, eliciting an agonising call from the estate agents to Michael, sympathising with him on the imminent divorce and reassuring him that, as a valuable member of the team, Mrs Evans would be welcome back on the staff whenever their domestic problems were sorted out.

At first Michael too took time off and stayed at home, but as the days went by and Juliet appeared calm and resigned to the regime of treatment, he began to spend a few hours at the office each day, in an attempt to restore a small amount of normality to their lives, and knowing that, once all this was over, hanging on to his job would be seen to have been essential. In spite of her apparently settled acceptance of the new routine, there was always a sharp corner of anxiety in him when he returned from the office as to whether he would find Juliet at home or an empty house – the latter occasions provoking an hour or two of terrified waiting for the telephone or door bell to ring with news of humiliation and embarrassment. But always she came back without comment or explanation, daring Michael with her silence to question her. He never did, restraining himself to a brief noncommittal greeting for fear of hearing that she had been sitting outside the Weymouth Street clinic in her car all afternoon, or following Anthony home.

After a couple of weeks of relative calm, Michael began to feel almost hopeful, seeing in Juliet the occasional hint of her old self, and one evening he decided to risk buying her a bunch of flowers, a little gesture that in the days before Anthony – an emotional universe away – had been a frequent and appreciated part of their married life.

It was nearly seven-thirty by the time he got home, holding the rustling bunch of wrapped chrysanthemums under one briefcase-carrying arm while he let himself in with the other hand. As soon as he opened the door he knew something was very wrong. There was a strange sound coming from upstairs, something disturbingly familiar, but which he hadn't heard for a long time, and it was the matter of a second or two until he registered it as a woman crying. Not just crying: a kind of moaning, desperate sobbing that made Michael shudder with the misery of it. He dropped his case and the pathetically inadequate flowers and rushed up to the bedroom, where the distraught figure of Juliet was sitting on the edge of the bed, her head in her hands, and her shoulders heaving.

'Julie, Julie, darling, whatever is it?'

He squatted down next to the bed and put his arm around her. She looked up at him and he almost flinched at the sight of her red, swollen face, the open mouth pulled down into an ugly curl, tears mixing with mucus and saliva in a sticky sheen over the bloated features. She was gulping and taking involuntary, juddering breaths that jerked her head to and fro in little nods in an effort to control the weeping and, although she tried to answer him, Michael could make no sense of what she said. He dreaded hearing what he was sure was coming: some imagined slight from Anthony that had thwarted her obsession. But he persevered, forced by the strength of her obvious grief into continuing his questioning, yet feeling himself drawn irresistibly towards his own humiliation.

'What? What, darling?' he persisted. 'What is it? What are you trying to tell me? What's the matter?'

Juliet drew in her breath in a huge, sighing, sob that

pulled the tendons of her neck into sharp, ugly relief, then let it out in an involuntary series of choking gasps as she spoke: 'H-h-he-he's-g-goh-goh-gone.'

'What do you mean *he's gone?*'

'N-n-ot th-ere,' she gasped, 'not – there – any – more.'

In spite of himself, Michael recognised a tiny spark of something like relief flash deep inside him for a split second; a subconscious awareness for the first time of the possibility of the disappearance of his unwilling rival. 'Where? Where has he gone?'

'WHAT?' She turned and shouted at him with such force and fury that he drew back instinctively. '*Where has he gone?* How can you ask that? How can you be so cruel? How do I know where he's gone? He's not gone *anywhere* – he's just not there. Not any more.'

'Juliet, please, you're not making any sense. Just tell me as calmly as you can what's happened, and I'll try to help you.'

But she turned and threw her head back down into her hands again and cried with such pitiable intensity that Michael simply put his arm around her shoulders once more and pulled her gently on to his chest, stroking her matted hair with his hand. They sat together for a few moments not saying anything, while her shaking body slowly calmed and the doleful noise of her weeping lessened.

Michael continued to stroke her head gently, but at the same time gradually became aware that quite apart from the obvious distress of the woman in his arms, something else was worrying at him, gnawing uncomfortably at the back of his mind. He forced himself to examine it, to face what it was that was bothering him. As he did so, a slowly dawning but insistent thought of such unhappiness confronted him that he tried, too late, to turn away from it and put his thoughts elsewhere. Fear travelled up through his body like a cold wave, clutching at the organs in its path, leaving them chilled, until the full terror reached his brain and made him wince with pain.

He pushed Juliet a little away from him and looked at her. 'Julie, who's gone?' he said quietly, curling inwardly with the dread of what was to come, praying with every nerve in his body that he was wrong, and that this was a truth he didn't have to face.

'What?' she whimpered. 'What do you mean, *who*? The baby of course. My baby.'

He dropped his arm from around her and threw his head back, screaming inside with unbearable despair but letting it out only in a tortured whisper: 'Oh dear God, no, please, no.'

'I'm empty, Michael. I had life inside me and now it's not there any more.' She had stopped shuddering now, but her voice still quivered with misery as she went on. 'The heartbeat – I heard it; they played it to me – now it's gone. He's gone. The life, it was growing there, it was part of me, it was inside me, and now there's nothing. I just don't understand – it was there and now it's over. Just a lump of meat, Michael, he was just a lump of red jelly – it's – oh God, what am I going to do? Red jelly sliding down my leg – I can't stand it. Put it back – I want it back – don't take it away from me, I can't stand it – my baby! I want my baby back! God, please, please, I'll never hurt anyone ever again, please, please, God, let me have my baby back.'

'Oh darling, my poor darling.' Michael suddenly hugged her to him, as tightly as he could, the strength of his sorrow flooding his body and making him squeeze her closer.

'I want my baby, Michael, I want my baby, oh please,' she murmured through her crying, 'oh please, please.'

He couldn't help it; as he sat with his head resting on hers and his arms still tight around her, he broke into desperate, uncontrollable sobs, hoarse and jarring in the small room.

In the cold dark room in Streatham, somewhere deep at the back of her mind the woman lying half comatose on the floor had come to a momentous decision. Perhaps for the first time in weeks, she saw the situation with a clarity and truth that made it unavoidable. Anthony wasn't coming. Now that she could see it, understand it, it was so obvious that she couldn't think why she hadn't known it before. The shock of realisation brought her suddenly to full consciousness, and with a flicker of strength born of her innate practicality and sense of purpose, which she could see now had been so cruelly misrouted for so long, she reached into the bag lying next to her for the bottle of Chlorpromazine. In spite

of the childproof top, she opened it easily with a click
that echoed in the silence, and as she began to cram
the tiny pills into her mouth, turned her head to look
across at the little body lying beside her.

'Poor baby,' she whispered, 'poor baby. Where's your
mummy? I'm so sorry.'

The shock of losing the baby seemed to jolt Juliet back
into a state of rationality that appeared to Michael
to be well on the way to being that of her normal
self. She continued to visit Professor Field and to take
the prescribed anti-psychotic Chlorpromazine, but
Michael liked to assume that the sessions were now
more concerned with the very real loss of her precious
baby than with the fantasised love of the young
doctor.

He grieved for the loss of his child more than he
could ever have foreseen and, although to all outward
appearances their lives settled into a more comfortable
and stable regularity, the sense of something missing, of
somebody missing, hung over them both in an unacknowledged cloud of depression. They spoke of it little,
each unwilling to voice their extreme unhappiness for
fear of seeing it reflected in the other, which would give
it even greater reality.

A week after the loss of the baby Michael telephoned
Mrs Palmer, surprising himself by the depth of his sympathy for her, realising that he hadn't known until he
heard it in her voice, just how much the potential

grandchild had meant to her. He also jotted a note to Harriet, anxious that in the event of her contacting Juliet, she should be forewarned.

Juliet continued to stay away from work, spending most of the time when she wasn't visiting Professor Field lying on her bed watching television, or pottering quietly around the house. Michael secretly dared to hope that Anthony might be out of their lives for good, but there were still occasions when she left the house for several hours without explanation, leaving him cringing with imaginings.

'I do love you, you know,' he said to her on her return from one such outing. 'I'm not going to ask where you've been, but I hope you know that I'm here, just as I ever was. I can't forget the baby, and I don't want to, but I believe we can be just as we were before if we're both patient and just show a little more kindness to each other. And if we perhaps try to talk about things a little more.'

They were standing in the hallway where he had waited for her as he heard her key in the lock. She slowly took off her raincoat and the scarf from around her neck and folded them neatly over her arm as she turned to look at him.

'Do you think we can start again?' she asked quietly.

'Yes, that's just what I'm saying. I think we can. I think —'

'No, I don't mean that. I mean, do you think we can try again? Try the IVF again?'

As Michael involuntarily looked quickly away to hide

his reaction from her, he saw himself reflected in the hall mirror on the opposite wall. The face that looked back at him — as was always the case when he caught sight of himself unexpectedly — was older and more weary than the image he unconsciously carried around with him from day to day. But its expression of sheer surprise, tinged with a hint of what could be either panic or hope, gave it a naivety that softened the hard lines and produced a look of almost comic childishness.

He smiled at his reflection for a moment, then rubbed his hand over his face as he walked into the sitting room. Juliet draped her coat and scarf over the bottom of the bannisters and followed him.

'Are you serious, Julie?' he said very quietly, with his back to her. 'Don't say this if you're not, please. I don't think I could go through it all again without— I couldn't bear it.'

'Of course I'm serious.'

He lowered himself into the armchair and blew out an exhausted breath as he leant back. Juliet sat on the floor at his feet and leant her crossed arms on his knees, resting her forehead on them so that he could see nothing but the top of her head. The parting in the blonde hair looked pink and naked and vulnerable, and he gently traced along it with his forefinger in silence, not wanting to say anything that might destroy the fragile sense of closeness that neither of them had experienced for so long.

'I think it's too soon to do anything just yet,' he whispered eventually, 'but when you're ready, and fit again, and it's the right time, then yes, let's try again. But Julie,' the serious tone of voice made her look up at him, 'you are not to go back to the clinic. Not to that clinic. Nor anywhere near that man again. I don't know what your feelings are —' Juliet began to answer but he continued in a voice that was loud enough to stop her, '—and I don't want to know. So if we do try again, it's going to have to be somewhere else; someone else. Do you understand?'

'I'll have to go and talk to them.'

'What do you mean?'

'Well, I'll have to get my notes – see Professor Hewlett – tell them what's happening. I can't just log on, or whatever you call it, somewhere else. I'm going to have to go back there and sort things out. You know.'

'*No.*'

'What?'

'I don't trust you – no, I don't mean that. I mean, I can't trust your illness or whatever it is that changed you. There has to be a way of getting your notes and finding a new clinic to go to. There's one at the Hammersmith Hospital isn't there? They talked about it, do you remember?'

'Mmm.'

'It's too soon now, in any case. When it's time, we'll find a way, don't worry. Just do it the way I want, Julie, or everything is hopeless.'

'Could you make sure you slice it *extremely* thinly? And can you cut off the fat before you put it in the thing? It's far too fatty.'

Mrs Palmer liked to buy the food for her entertaining in Selfridges Food Hall. She would never have dreamt of buying anything else there – clothes and household goods were invariably purchased on account at Harrods or in one of the smarter Sloane Street boutiques – but she had got into the habit of food shopping in the large Oxford Street store ever since she had popped in after a visit to her optician's in Wigmore Street many years before and, being a woman of habit, had continued to patronise them whenever she needed something not available in her small local grocer's.

The girl serving her was not fazed in the least by Mrs Palmer's imperious commands. 'I can't cut the fat off. I have to slice it just as it is,' she said. She returned her customer's beady glare without embarrassment, holding the large Italian ham in one hand, awaiting further instruction.

'Good heavens, girl, I can't serve my guests all that fat! Cut it off. Cut a piece off the top there before you slice it,' dictated Mrs Palmer, leaning over the counter and gesturing with a gloved hand at the outside of the ham as she spoke. The girl moved back a little to avoid any contact between the black leather of the glove and the white shiny outside of the ham, which was looking dangerously likely.

'And don't you think it looks a bit dry and dark?

Look, that other one's much fresher. Give me slices off that one.'

The glove pointed at a second ham behind the counter, wrapped securely in polythene.

'I'm sorry, madam, I can't open a new one,' answered the girl, standing guarding her ham steadfastly.

'Why not? Where's Mr Albert?'

'He's not here today.'

Mrs Palmer sighed loudly and shook her head in resigned irritation. 'Well you'd better give me slices off that then. But I want a reduction – there's far too much fat. And throw away the first couple of slices – they'll be too dry.'

As the girl turned towards the slicing machine, Mrs Palmer thought she saw just the slightest toss of the white-hatted head, and was mulling over how interesting it was that all the new fancy white coats and hygiene regulations in the world couldn't produce good service like you used to get in the old days, when a voice called her name and she turned to see Harriet Aynsley, accompanied by two young children, walking towards her from the bakery section.

'Hello, Mrs Palmer! It's Harriet. Juliet's friend. How are you?'

'Yes, Harriet. I'm very well thank you. How are you? It's good to see you. And this is?'

'This is Jessica, and this is Adam. You remember Juliet's mother, kids, don't you? Mrs Palmer?'

The children mumbled some inaudible greetings to which Mrs Palmer gave an equally noncommittal reply.

She registered Harriet's creased coat and the children's rumpled socks and unkempt hair, and was reminded how she had always been wary of the close friendship between this woman and her daughter. Even when the girls were at school she had considered Harriet an unsuitable companion, but had not wished to goad Juliet into a stronger friendship by showing outright opposition; at the same time making it quite clear that she didn't really approve. Once the girls had emerged into adulthood, she had been disappointed to find the closeness continuing, and had often wondered if she should have been firmer in her initial guidance.

'I was so sorry to hear about the baby,' said Harriet, as Adam entwined himself round her legs and hooted like an owl at his sister.

'Yes, it was very tragic, wasn't it. Look, don't you think that ham is frightfully dark and fatty-looking? Do you think I should make them open the other one? I have people for dinner tomorrow. I don't often serve it but —'

'No, I think it looks fine.' Harriet was peering over at the slicer, where paper-thin leaves of prosciutto were being gently laid one by one on to strips of waxed paper. 'I think it's meant to be like that. It looks good. Are you going to put melon with it?'

The girl slicing the meat sent a little inward message of thanks to the newcomer, and carried on slicing.

'Oh, that's an awfully good idea. Yes, that's what they do, don't they? Yes, perhaps I will.'

Harriet unexpectedly found this reply very touching.

The old lady, in the fur coat that must have been the height of fashion when first acquired but which was now not only dated, but also politically incorrect, suddenly looked so vulnerable that it caught Harriet unawares and made her stop short and see Mrs Palmer in a new light. How difficult it must be to keep up with the changing world, where you could be condemned for living the way you had been brought up, where the right thing to do in one generation could become outrageously wrong and insensitive in the next. Harriet thought of her own mother, who had spent so many years learning to stop talking about black people and to call them 'coloured', only to be told that yet again she was using the wrong word, and that much of her language was incorrect and offensive. Giving dinner parties in the forties and fifties must have been so easy for women like this — limited menus bought and cooked by a marvellous 'little woman'; dining table laid out in the accepted and unchanging way it had been for years; guests predictable and comforting. In a world of supermarkets, foreign food and self-catering, how did Cynthia Palmer cope?

'Look, would you like a coffee? I'm simply gasping for one. And if I don't give the children a drink and take them to the loo soon they're going to drive me potty.'

Mrs Palmer looked at Harriet with a flicker of gratitude that she quickly disguised behind her usual expression of natural superiority. 'What a lovely idea. Yes, why not? Let's go and have a coffee.'

286

As Michael and Anna walked through the front door of her flat the phone was ringing. Out of the blue, he had such an extraordinary flash of foreknowledge that it made him shout out loud. He had been here before. He knew what was going to happen, and he saw himself going through the motions a split second before it did happen, as if following a preordained script of irresistible portent.

'Go – go, Anna, quickly, answer it. They've found something. I know it.'

He watched her as she listened intently to the speaker on the other end of the line, trying to pick up from her staring eyes and frowning expression confirmation of what he still felt sure was coming.

'Yes,' she was saying, 'right, yes, I see. Oh God – do you – OK. He's here ... Wait, let me put him on ... No, I want you to speak to him.'

Suddenly she jerked the receiver towards him. 'Michael, you talk to them, please.... I can't handle this.'

'What is it?'

She just shook her head and pushed the telephone even closer to his face. As he took over, he felt a surge of such enormous joy that he almost burst out laughing. Where did it come from, this feeling of thrilling expectation? What right had he to feel something wonderful was about to happen? It was dangerous, he knew that at the same time that he let himself wallow in it. And he smiled into the phone with a mixture of delight and terrifying anticipation. 'Yes? Michael Evans here.'

'Mr Evans. We have a very strong lead as to the whereabouts of your wife and the child. I thought it only right to tell you. I have a unit on its way there now and—'

'Where? Where are they? I'm coming too. Now.'

'I'm not sure that's such a good idea, Mr Evans. Forgive me – but we don't quite know what we'll find and—'

'I know that, man, for God's sake. I'm not stupid. Just tell me where they are.'

After Michael put the phone down he looked over at Anna. She was staring at him with a look of such terror that he almost wept. He moved towards her quickly and wrapped his arms round her, whispering in her ear. 'I'm going to find them. I'm going now. Do you want to come?'

'No, I can't do it. I can't, Michael. You go. Go on – quickly. I'm all right. Tell them to fetch me. Leave me here and go. Please. I want you to.'

Chapter Twenty

Mrs Palmer watched the two children drinking their Cokes at the next table and could feel their teeth disintegrating with every sip. She was tempted to question Harriet on just how often they were given this kind of coloured, sugary drink, and to ask what was wrong with a glass of water or milk for heaven's sake. But she held back, remembering how she had offended an old friend recently by attempting to give advice on the upbringing of her granddaughter. Children nowadays appeared to be allowed to do exactly as they wished – if she had her way these two would be neatly dressed and sitting upright on their chairs with an apple or biscuit in front of them, instead of lolling about with their elbows all over the table eating chocolate bars. But far be it from her to interfere; it had been made clear to her more than once by those of Harriet's generation that her advice was not always welcome. She also hesitated to enquire too closely into Harriet's wellbeing: she even checked herself from opening with her usual gambit of asking after the family's health, as she had a dim memory of Juliet telling her that Harriet was separated from her husband. The ease with which couples appeared to split up, realign and then split again was another modern phenomenon she found inexplicable and threatening, and not a subject to be brought up without fear of controversy, as once a discussion was opened she found it hard to contain her views, which were definite and uncompromising. In her day one stuck it out; not only for the sake of the children, but also, in truth, because it was the thing to do. And although few of her contemporaries had been what one could call 'happily married', it would never have occurred to them that this was a reason to separate. In smart circles, which were the only ones Mrs Palmer had inhabited in her younger days, divorced couples were whispered about behind their backs and considered thrillingly shocking. The matter-of-fact way in which such things were discussed today still amazed her, although there was a part of her that envied the openness of it. She sometimes felt she had years of bottled-up unhappiness stored inside her that would welcome the chance to unburden itself to a willing ear.

'How is Juliet?' asked Harriet, stirring a chocolate-sprinkled cappuccino. 'I haven't heard from her for some time — I know she was going through a difficult patch even before the miscarriage. Is she coping OK?'

'Well, yes, thank you, Harriet. She's fine. She's a very practical person, as you know, and she's had the benefit of a good background and family. I'm quite sure she'll handle this perfectly well. I lost one before I had Juliet, you know. It happens all the time — there's an awful lot of fuss made, and now you have all this counselling nonsense and so on, but you just have to pull yourself together and keep going, don't you?'

'Of course.'

There was an odd silence. Why did Harriet feel the old lady was trying to tell her something more? She seemed unsettled, and was frowning down at her coffee as if trying to decide something. Suddenly she lifted her head and looked directly at Harriet. 'I have no idea,' she said briskly.

'Sorry?'

'I really have no idea how she is. In fact I suspect you've probably seen her more recently than I have. I'm afraid she doesn't talk to me at the moment. I don't understand it. Michael told me about the baby — about losing it I mean. That was good of him. I've tried to ring her a few times but there's always an excuse. She's resting or — oh, I don't know. She doesn't want to speak to me. That's it really.'

Harriet watched the old lady's face as she spoke. Her cheek moved in soft limp quivers like old velvet around her mouth, where the unevenly applied lipstick followed a smudged, indefinite outline and mingled with drops of milky coffee in the corners. Heavy pink make-up failed to hide the large brown freckles of age that were scattered beneath it, and a dusting of powder was visibly trapped in the fine hairs that covered her upper lip and chin. The cruelty of the harsh light slanting across from the window made Harriet shift in her seat in an attempt to shade her companion's face from it with her own body.

'Well, she's been through a terrible time, hasn't she? Not just recently, I mean, but for a couple of years now. It's not surprising that —'

'That's very generous of you, Harriet, but I'm afraid there's more to it than that.' Mrs Palmer paused and looked out of the window for a moment. 'I think I failed her, you see. I tried to do my very best for her, but I think something went terribly wrong. Oh dear, I am sorry — do forgive me. How very embarrassing.'

'No, no it's not,' said Harriet. 'Not at all. It's good to talk about things sometimes. Look — I've got children. I know how impossible it is — the whole business. I used to read every article going; how you should stimulate them and all that stuff. But once you . . .' She broke off to glance across at Jessica and Adam, but they appeared too engrossed in their comics to be interested. 'Once you have them, you realise it's about all you can do just to get them through life without some ghastly accident. I always pictured myself as Mother Earth — you know, loose home-made sweaters and a ribbon in my hair. Babies on both arms. Wooden toys and word cards, no sweets, wholemeal home-baked bread — all that business. But when Jessica was born and I brought her back from the hospital, I had my work cut out to get her fed and changed and stop her crying. Just getting myself dressed in the morning was a triumph. They don't warn you, do they? Not properly. What it's really like, I mean.'

'Well, I had help of course. We all did in those days. And it seemed much simpler then, I don't know why. Nanny would put Juliet in her pram in the garden and she'd sleep most of the time. No, I mean later. When she was a young girl. That's when things got difficult for me. I just wanted her to be pretty, you see. I so much wanted her to be *pretty*, and I was only trying to guide her. It's easy to put on weight when you're young – and I've always had to struggle with mine. I thought I'd make it better for her. But now she tells me I was to blame for her problems – you know, the—'

'Yes, yes, I remember. I knew at school she was getting too thin.'

'Anyway, I regret it now. It's always so easy when you look back. And now she's not even speaking to me. We had a funny sort of incident in Harrods just before Christmas, when I was trying to help her with her maternity clothes, and since then I haven't heard a word. Michael's always very sweet when I ring; he makes excuses for her. She's in the bath or she's shopping or cooking. But she never rings back. I know. I know what's going on.'

'She's been very distant with me too. You mustn't blame yourself, Mrs Palmer, you really mustn't. I'm sure she'll be her old self soon. Just give it a bit of time. Is she trying again, do you know? Has Michael told you?'

'Do you think it's too late?'

'How do you mean? For her to get pregnant again? Oh, no I'm sure—'

'No, I mean, do you think it's too late for me?'

293

Mrs Palmer leant forward, and Harriet breathed in her sickly sweet perfume mingled with the smell of coffee on her breath.

'I want to make it up to her, somehow. Oh, goodness! What's come over me? I don't usually talk like this, Harriet. What must you think . . .'

'It's all right. Really. Go on.'

'I think I could be closer to her. She's all I've got — oh dear, that sounds like something from a book doesn't it? But she really is. Since her father died. I do love her so very much. I always have. But I'm not very good at showing it. The trouble is we didn't really show emotion much in my day; that may sound like a cliché but it's absolutely true. I was encouraged not to, in fact. Do you think it *is* too late?'

'No. No, I don't. I'm sure it isn't.'

The children looked up in fascination at the old lady sitting with their mother. She was crying.

'Andy! Andy, darling!'

Andrea carried on reading *Marie Claire*. She was lying on the bed with the magazine on her lap and a glass of white wine in one hand, feeling rather pleased with herself. She had continued to enjoy Anthony's discomfiture over the Evans affair and, having now convinced herself that he was entirely innocent, she was using the situation to her advantage and alternately forgiving and chastising him as the mood took her. The contrast of warmth and hostility was wearing him down, and she was pleasantly aware how the hot and cold of her emotional response to him was bringing him slowly but surely ever more under her control. Like playing a fish she reeled him in and let him out while all the time bringing him imperceptibly closer, sensing that his exhaustion was near.

He burst into the bedroom. 'Why didn't you answer me?'

'Oh sorry,' she said. 'I was thinking that's all. What is it?'

'Good news. I really think the bloody woman's out of our lives, darling. I don't know what's happened, but Hewlett's definitely being more like his old self with me. And the *Lancet* is publishing my paper — I told you they would.'

'Good.'

She looked down at the article about liposuction on the open page in front of her and wondered if it could be an answer to the bulges that were beginning to appear, worryingly, at the tops of her thighs.

'Andy?'

'Yup.'

'I do love you, darling.'

She left a wonderfully enigmatic pause while she considered how to play it this time.

'Do sit down, Mr Evans.'

Professor Hewlett gestured him towards the chair in front of his desk. It suddenly felt to Michael as though it were only a matter of days since he had sat in that same upright oak chair, listening with barely allowed hope to the possibilities that the doctor had outlined for successful treatment. So much had happened since, and he could feel in Professor Hewlett's attitude a reflection of the difficult situation that had meanwhile affected them both. There was a note here that he hadn't felt before, of something new that had passed between them that couldn't be ignored, and which would continue to reverberate.

'What can I do for you? How are you both?'

There was a coldness in the tone of the question that surprised him. Michael was only too aware of the embarrassment and difficulty that Juliet's short-lived obsession had brought about at the clinic, but he had assumed that, of all people, the professor would be well used to dealing with hysterical patients and therefore the last person to bear a grudge about such problems.

'We're all right. Thank you. But I wanted to ask your advice. My wife doesn't know I've come here, but before we take things any further I thought I should have a word with you about the right way to proceed.'

'By all means, Mr Evans. I'll help if I can, of course. Fire away.'

Michael felt as if he were back at school in the headmaster's study. The quiet in the room was broken only by the ticking of a clock, which he registered as a sound very rare in the days of quartz and batteries. It was at the same time reassuring and a little frightening. The professor peered at Michael in a way that made him look more judgemental than avuncular, and his black coat, crisp white shirt and silvery grey tie made the visitor feel awkwardly shabby.

'My wife is extremely anxious to try again.'

There was a pause, and the professor frowned at him, as if not understanding.

'To try again for a baby, I mean. Now, obviously I realise that there are —'

'I'm sorry, Mr Evans. I don't understand. Are you talking about the resumption of any kind of IVF programme?'

'Yes I am.'

There was another, longer pause, and Michael began to feel extremely uneasy, as if he had suggested something so extraordinary that it was at best hard to comprehend, and at worst shockingly inappropriate.

'I'd have thought you would realise that it's completely out of the question. I am surprised that you would —'

'No, no, quite. I do, of course, realise that owing to my wife's mental condition there has been the most unfortunate embarrassment caused to the clinic. I am not suggesting that she should return here. Naturally. I wouldn't wish that myself, as I'm sure you can imagine. I just thought you might be able to recommend an alternative clinic or hospital perhaps, where she could receive treatment. I thought you could send them her notes and so on. I do feel she is over her —'

'I am sorry, Mr Evans. I am surprised you should ask me this. I cannot possibly consider recommending Mrs

Evans to another IVF programme. I would have thought that was obvious.'

'Well,' blustered Michael, feeling more and more uncomfortable by the moment, 'I have to say I am a little confused. I knew you wouldn't want her back here, but such a blanket refusal to consider her interests seems a rather odd attitude to take.'

'What attitude would you expect me to take? Under the circumstances?'

'I suppose I imagined that you must have quite a few patients who show these sort of – what do you call them – emotional upsets. It didn't finally do any harm, did it? I'm sure if the pregnancy had continued she would have returned to normal and it would all have been forgotten. The tragedy of the mis —'

Professor Hewlett leant forward so suddenly that Michael stopped in mid-sentence.

The doctor was frowning now, and looking puzzled, as if he had misheard and was trying to decipher what the man in front of him had been trying to say. An expression of astonished comprehension suddenly came over his face, and he sat back a little and blew out his breath.

'Mr Evans. I am so dreadfully sorry. I fear I have been under a grave misapprehension. I thought you knew.'

'Knew what?' Michael felt a terrible sensation of something unspeakable fluttering deep inside him, stealing slowly upwards through his unwilling body.

'She told us you had made the decision together. Perhaps I was foolish to trust her. It's so easy to see these things with hindsight, of course. I'm so sorry.'

'What? Knew *what*?'

'Your wife came to me and asked for a termination.'

It took a second for Michael to take in what the professor had said. Realisation hit him like a blow to the stomach, and the implications reached into his heart and hurt so much he felt he would cry out with the pain of it. 'I don't understand. I . . .'

His speech petered out as it became clear to both of them that he understood only too well. His son, his beloved son. Not accident, not fate. His baby's death planned, intended, invited — welcomed.

'She came to us and asked us to terminate her pregnancy. She said that you and she had talked it over on many occasions and that you both felt you were not after all ready for her to bear a child. As you can imagine, this caused not a little distress among my staff. The statistics of successful pregnancy in IVF are still a great deal lower than I would wish, and the enormous time and effort involved — not to say the financial burden on yourselves — result in the emotional investment by everyone concerned being very high. I think I can say that this is the first time in my years here that I have ever had such a request. I found it personally very upsetting.'

Michael was still too shocked to speak. He sat back in his chair, feeling sick and frightened, not wanting to hear any more but at the same time desperate to know the details, still hoping against all logic that there might have been some mistake, that they were talking about the wrong woman, or that he had misunderstood.

Professor Hewlett went on: 'I had a very long talk with her. I tried everything I could to dissuade her, but she was adamant. I found her mental state to be apparently quite stable, and also telephoned her psychiatrist, whom of course you know – Professor Field. I could not, naturally, without her permission let him know why I was consulting him; but he assured me that, although she was still under treatment, she was in a perfectly fit state to make rational decisions about matters other than the specific delusion. I advised her that we could not consider taking such a step at the clinic, and that I thought it best if she made such arrangements elsewhere. I didn't see her again, but understood from one of my staff that she had indeed found someone to carry out the procedure for her. I have to say we were all very sad indeed to hear of it. I have so many desperate women here, Mr Evans, so many unbearably sad stories of longing and regret. I'm sure you can understand how I feel. I can't possibly recommend to any clinic or hospital that they enrol your wife on their IVF programme. I could not in all conscience advise them that she might not have a similar change of heart again. But I am more sorry than I can say to hear that you were unaware of the nature of the loss of your wife's pregnancy.'

Michael's anger rose within him until he felt he would choke.

The pills made their way slowly down Juliet's gullet but, meeting the dry resistance of its lining, began to stick to its sides and form a plug of semi-dissolved chemicals halfway down its length. As this backlog was joined by yet more pills from above, as Juliet crammed more and more of them into her mouth, her stomach joined in the revolt against the onslaught on her body and began to heave in an attempt to repel the unwanted invaders. The plug was squeezed upwards by the intense force of the cramping muscles around it, but at the same time the efficiency of its movement caused her stomach to throw its contents upwards. This wasn't much, after the semi-starvation of the last few days, but enough mucus, stomach juices and phlegm became mixed with the upwardly mobile pills to form a slurry of vomit which was ejected into her mouth.

Her conscious attempt at ending her life had so far been unsuccessful, and would have continued to be so; paradoxically it was the instinctive urge to preserve it that led to her fulfilling her wish. As the foul-smelling liquid rushed up into her mouth her body made an automatic and desperate attempt to breathe in, and instead of the oxygen they craved, her lungs inhaled the unwanted and rejected contents of her stomach. Perhaps somewhere deep inside her a message was sent from nerve to nerve, like the last wishes of a dying patient — *not strive officiously to keep alive*. Certainly her struggle to breathe was short-lived and insufficient, and it wasn't long before her brain became starved of oxygen and began to shut down. As she made her way down the black tunnel towards the bright light created by its death throes, it was Michael she cried out to in her heart and his dead baby that she hoped to find as she made her way towards it.

~

'Juliet! Juliet!'

He found her in the kitchen, making herself a cup of tea. Seeing her turn to look at him in surprise as he shouted her name, he found himself wondering again if there had been some terrible mistake. Could this woman, calmly dipping a teabag into a mug, really have planned to kill their child? This woman who had striven with him for so long and against such odds to achieve the pregnancy they both so much longed for? All through the horrific weeks of her obsession with Anthony Northfield he had still been able to see the old Juliet lurking somewhere beneath the changes that had come over her, but knowing now the level of the deception she had been practising almost took his breath away. All the years of loving her and knowing her, being irritated by her and laughing with her, seemed to be completely nullified. The person who could do this to him – without any apparent degree of guilt or conscience – was not the woman he had thought he'd known. It was all he could do to stop himself grabbing her and shaking the complacency out of her.

'Why didn't you tell me?'

'What?'

'Why didn't you tell me you had an abortion?'

'I never said I didn't. You just assumed I'd had a miscarriage and it seemed simpler to leave it that way.'

'But you were so upset; you were — you remember — you were so horribly upset. How could you have—'

'Yes, well I *was* upset. It's not a very pleasant thing to go through you know, and I knew when I'd done it that I'd made a mistake.'

'Then WHY? For God's sake, WHY? How could you, Julie? How could you do it? After everything — I don't understand. I thought you wanted our child as much as I did.'

'Anthony didn't want the baby.'

There was a terrible silence.

'But I was wrong you see. I realised that as soon as I'd done it. It wasn't the baby that was the problem; I misunderstood. It was *you*. That's why I need to get pregnant again, before it's too late.'

Michael knew he should feel sorry for her, he knew he should try to be understanding; that she was ill; that she couldn't help herself. But at that moment he felt something for this woman that he would never have believed possible; with all his heart and soul he hated her.

He looked at her coldly, then spoke quietly: 'They won't consider you for fertility treatment, you know. After what you've done. They won't even think about it. You may have wrecked my life, and finished my son's, but they won't let you do it again.'

After a few seconds Juliet slowly put down her mug, walked out of the kitchen and, after picking up her handbag from the hall table and her raincoat from the chair next to it, she calmly made her way out of the house, shutting the front door firmly behind her.

Michael would not see her alive again.

An ambulance and two police cars were waiting outside the house in Streatham as Michael arrived. A policeman ushered him up the steps and into the shabby room on the first floor where, although it appeared to be full of people, his eye was drawn immediately to the figure lying on the floor. Two men in green overalls were squatting on one side of it, and a tall man in a raincoat stood opposite them. They were talking in hushed voices as he entered the room but, on seeing him, they stopped immediately and the tall man came towards him.

'Mr Evans. I'm very sorry. I'm afraid it's very bad news, sir.'

'Yes . . . yes I can see.'

How did he know straightaway that she was dead? He'd always heard that people just looked as though they were sleeping; but Juliet didn't. As he knelt down beside her, he knew she had gone – not just that she had died, but that she had literally gone, that her essence, or whatever part of her it was that made her 'Juliet', wasn't there any more. Michael had never had any sense of religion, had never entertained the possibility of a benign God as anything more than a fairy story left over from the Dark Ages – to him it had always seemed obvious that on all the evidence He must be either utterly power-less or completely indifferent to the horror and suffering of the world that He had created. So the idea of prayer had always been laughable, but, as he gathered Juliet's limp body in his arms and cradled her head on his lap, he found himself silently screaming against something or somebody at the cruelty of it all. He rested his head on her forehead and cried quietly to himself.

The detective put a hand gently on his back and attempted a sympathetic pat. As Michael raised his head to look up at him, he became aware of some frantic activity going on to one side of him. A further group of green-coated paramedics was gathered around something else on the floor.

'Is that . . . ?'

'They're doing what they can. I'm afraid the baby's very poorly.'

'But still alive?'

'Yes, sir. Just, I gather. Just still alive.'

Michael held Juliet's body even tighter. He buried his head down into her hair and, clenching his teeth with the pain of it all, whispered into her cold, unhearing ear at the God he knew wasn't there. 'Dear God, let the baby live. She only wanted to be a mother, you bastard. She wasn't a bad woman. Please, dear Lord, don't let another tiny life be wasted; don't let her have killed it, she loved the baby. I know she must have loved the baby. Please, dear God, let the baby live.'

'I think we should let them take her away now, sir. Forgive me, Mr Evans, but I must ask you to move now, so we can let the —'

'No. Just a moment. Let me be for just a moment.'

Michael held his wife quietly, his head still buried in

her neck, then after a few moments he drew back and looked into her face.

'Don't worry, sir, you'll be able to see her again, if you so wish. To say your goodbyes in private.'

'Yes. Thank you.'

Michael laid her body back down on the floor very, very gently and then stood up and let the two men move to either side of her. They lifted Juliet carefully on to a canvas stretcher and carried her out of the room. He watched the little procession move into the shadows at the top of the staircase, then looked away from them and over towards where he knew the baby lay, surrounded by the squatting figures of the paramedics. As they moved to and fro, he caught glimpses of tubes, dials, rubber and steel.

Suddenly he saw a brief flash of something soft and human amidst the technology: a tiny, pale face, eyes closed, nose and mouth covered by the clear plastic of an oxygen mask. Michael was transfixed; in this room full of death a bitter struggle for life was taking place in the small limp body, and he willed it on with all his strength.

It seemed like hours as he waited, listening; the only sound that of concentrated effort and the occasional muffled comment from one of the men gathered around Harry on the floor.

A sudden movement by a paramedic made Michael start. He half rose into a kneeling position, his body tense, his senses alerted to what might come next.

'We have a heartbeat,' one of the men said quietly.

After a few seconds, a reply: 'OK, let's move him.'

The small group stood up and gently and slowly lifted between them the tiny little figure, still attached to tubes, wires and boxes. As they began to walk carefully towards the door, Michael leapt forward and gripped the detective by the forearm.

'Let me go with the baby,' he begged. 'Please let me go with him. Let me do this for her; I can't let him die. She didn't mean that to happen – I know she didn't.'

'I can't see why not, sir. But hurry.'

Michael sat in the ambulance watching little Harry's struggle for survival in almost unbearable tension. Still in shock from the discovery of his dead wife, he felt as if he would be unable to cope if the baby should die in front of him, and that he would implode in a black hole of human misery. It was as if somehow his presence, the projection of all his energy, thought and hope, was an essential part of Harry's life force: as if the focus of his will was holding the small being suspended above a chasm of darkness, and that if Michael lessened his concentration for even a second, Harry would fall.

By the time they reached the hospital he was exhausted. As the ambulance drew up outside the entrance one of the men put a hand on his shoulder sympathetically. 'It's all right, sir. He's going to be fine now. We've got him stable. Take it easy; you've had a severe shock. Just try to relax now.'

Michael followed the small stretcher out of the ambulance into the hospital and along the corridor towards Intensive Care. A sudden scream ahead stopped him short. As in slow motion, he saw the pale girl with the jet black hair running towards them, arms outstretched, mouth open.

'HARRY! OH MY HARRY! HE'S ALIVE! MY BABY'S ALIVE!'

Michael almost doubled up with the intense pain that he suddenly felt in his chest. As if he'd thrust a hand into boiling water and found it freezing, he was incapable of registering whether terrible joy or wonderful pain was filling his heart. He watched as Anna reached the stretcher and bent over Harry's foil-wrapped form, running alongside it to keep up with the fast walking of the men, her face lit up with so much relief, love and happiness that it made him want to shout out with the wonder of it. He stopped, still watching, spellbound, then bent over and slumped into one of the chairs that lined the corridor and put his head in his hands. A passing nurse stopped and came over to him, leaning down to put a hand on his arm.

'Are you all right? Can I help you?'

'I'm fine,' Michael gasped, leaning his head back against the wall, and trying to catch his breath. 'Yes, thank you, I'm fine.'

'You came in with the baby, didn't you? Shall I show you where they are?'

'No, no thanks. They just need each other for now. And I have to go. I have to go to my wife.'

'Oh I see. All right then.' The nurse looked a little confused, but smiled at him as she straightened up. 'If you're sure you're OK?'

'But nurse —'

'Yes?'

Michael stood up and looked at her, his face tear-stained and weary, but with the smallest glimmer of hope lighting his eyes. 'Could you give the young lady — the baby's mother — could you give her a message for me, please?'

'Yes, of course. What is it?'

'Could you tell her I'll come back for her? Tell her I send my love to her and Harry, and — please — tell her — I'll come back.'

The Question

Jane Asher

'The white-hot fury of a woman scorned ignites the pages of Jane Asher's clever and disturbing novel'   *Daily Mail*

It all starts with a chance remark on the telephone, just a casual conversation on a normal working day. But it leads Eleanor Hamilton to an appalling and deeply disturbing discovery: John, her husband of twenty years, has been leading a double life – a life of unbelievable duplicity and betrayal.

Jealousy, anger and confusion follow, all-consuming and shocking, driving Eleanor to extraordinary limits in her desire for revenge. Then fate intervenes in the shape of a terrible accident . . .

But out of tragedy grows an unexpected love affair, and at the same time John finds the tables turned against him as he awaits deliverance and Eleanor bides her time. The question is, whose prayers will be answered – and how?

'A perceptive and sometimes truly shocking novel'

Sunday Express

'Asher has a gift for suspense'   *The Sunday Times*

0 00 651045 0